THE

HERAPATH

PROPERTY

BY

J. S. FLETCHER

Publisher's Logo
NEW YORK

ALFRED · A · KNOPF

MCMXXII

Published October, 1921

Second Printing, May, 1922

PRINTED IN THE UNITED STATES OF AMERICA

CONTENTS

chapter

I   Jacob Herapath is Missing,................... 9

II   Is it Murder? 18

III   Barthorpe Takes Charge, ...27

IV   The Pressman,............. 36

V   The Glass and the Sandwich, ...45

VI   The Taxi-cab Driver, ...54

VII   Is There a Will? 64

VIII   The Second Witness, ...74

IX   Greek Against Greek, ...83

X   Mr. Benjamin Halfpenny,................... 91

XI   The Shadow, ...100

XII   For Ten Per Cent, ...109

XIII   Adjourned,.................... 118

XIV   The Scottish Verdict, ...127

XV   Young Brains, ...136

XVI   Nameless Fear, ...145

XVII   The Law, ...154

XVIII   The Rosewood Box, ...163

XIX   Weaving the Net, ...172

XX   The Diamond Ring, ...181

XXI   The Deserted Flat, ...190

XXII   Yea and Nay, ...199

XXIII   The Accusation, ...208

XXIV   Cold Steel, ...217

XXV   Professional Analysis, ...226

XXVI   The Remand Prison, ...235

XXVII The Last Cheque, 244

XXVIII The Hotel Ravenna,........... 253

XXIX   The Note in the Prayer-book, ...263

XXX   The White-haired Lady, ...273

XXXI   The Interrupted Dinner-party,.............. 283

XXXII The Yorkshire Proverb,........... 290

XXXIIIBurchill Fills the Stage, ...294

XXXIVDavidge's Trump Card, ...304
XXXV The Second Warrant,..............312

THE

HERAPATH

PROPERTY

CHAPTER I

jacob herapath is missing

This was the third week of Selwood's secretaryship to Jacob Herapath. Herapath was a well-known man in London. He was a Member of Parliament, the owner of a sort of model estate of up-to-date flats, and something of a crank about such matters as ventilation, sanitation, and lighting. He himself, a bachelor, lived in one of the best houses in Portman Square; when he engaged Selwood as his secretary he made him take a convenient set of rooms in Upper Seymour Street, close by. He also caused a telephone communication to be set up between his own house and Selwood's bedroom, so that he could summon his secretary at any hour of the night. Herapath occasionally had notions about things in the small hours, and he was one of those active, restless persons who, if they get a new idea, like to figure on it at once. All the same, during those three weeks he had not once troubled his secretary in this fashion. No call came to Selwood over that telephone until half-past seven one November morning, just as he was thinking of getting out of bed. And the voice which then greeted him was not Herapath's. It was a rather anxious, troubled voice, and it belonged to one Kitteridge, a middle-aged man, who was Herapath's butler.

In the act of summoning Selwood, Kitteridge was evidently interrupted by some person at his elbow; all that Selwood made out was that Kitteridge wanted him to go round at once. He dressed hurriedly, and ran off to Herapath's house; there in the hall, near the door of a room which Herapath used as a study and business room, he found Kitteridge talking to Mountain, Herapath's coachman, who, judging by the state of his attire, had also been called hurriedly from his bed.

"What is it, Kitteridge?" demanded Selwood. "Mr. Herapath ill?"

The butler shook his head and jerked his thumb towards the open door of the study.

"The fact is, we don't know where Mr. Herapath is, sir," he answered. "He hasn't slept in his bed, and he isn't in the house."

"Possibly he didn't come home last night," suggested Selwood. "He may have slept at his club, or at an hotel."

The butler and the coachman looked at each other—then the coachman, a little, sharp-eyed man who was meditatively chewing a bit of straw, opened his tightly-compressed lips.

"He did come home, sir," he said. "I drove him home—as usual. I saw him let himself into the house. One o'clock sharp, that was. Oh, yes, he came home!"

"He came home," repeated Kitteridge. "Look here, sir." He led the way into the study and pointed to a small table set by the side of Herapath's big business desk. "You see that tray, Mr. Selwood? That's always left out, there, on that table, for Mr. Herapath every night. A small decanter of whiskey, a syphon, a few sandwiches, a dry biscuit or two. Well, there you are, sir—he's had a drink out of that glass, he's had a mouthful or so of sandwiches. Oh, yes, he came home, but he's not at home now! Charlesworth—the valet, you know, sir—always goes into Mr. Herapath's room at a quarter past seven every morning; when he went in just now he found that Mr. Herapath wasn't there, and the bed hadn't been slept in. So—that's where things stand."

Selwood looked round the room. The curtains had not yet been drawn aside, and the electric light cast a cold glare on the various well-known objects and fittings. He glanced at the evidences of the supper tray; then at the blotting-pad on Herapath's desk; there he might have left a note for his butler or his secretary. But there was no note to be seen.

"Still, I don't see that there's anything to be alarmed about, Kitteridge," he said. "Mr. Herapath may have wanted to go somewhere by a very early morning train——"

"No, sir, excuse me, that won't do," broke in the butler. "I thought of that myself. But if he'd wanted to catch a night train, he'd have taken a travelling coat, and a rug, and a bag of some sort—he's taken nothing at all in that way. Besides, I've been in this house seven years, and I know his habits. If he'd wanted to go away by one of the very early morning trains he'd have kept me and Charlesworth up, making ready for him. No, sir! He came home, and went out again—must have done. And—it's uncommonly queer. Seven years I've been here, as I say, and he never did such a thing before."

Selwood turned to the coachman.

"You brought Mr. Herapath home at one o'clock?" he said. "Alone?"

"He was alone, sir," replied the coachman, who had been staring around him as if to seek some solution of the mystery. "I'll tell you all that happened—I was just beginning to tell Mr. Kitteridge here when you come in. I fetched Mr. Herapath from the House of Commons last night at a quarter past eleven—took him up in Palace Yard at the usual spot, just as the clock was striking. 'Mountain,' he says, 'I want you to drive round to the estate office—I want to call there.' So I drove there—that's in Kensington, as you know, sir. When he got out he says, 'Mountain,' he says, 'I shall be three-quarters of an hour or so here—wrap the mare up and walk her about,' he says. I did as he said, but he was more than three-quarters—it was like an hour. Then at last he came back to the brougham, just said one word, 'Home!' and I drove him here, and the clocks were striking one when he got out. He said 'Good night,' and I saw him walk up the steps and put his key in the latch as I drove off to our stables. And that's all I know about it."

Selwood turned to the butler.

"I suppose no one was up at that time?" he inquired.

"Nobody, sir," answered Kitteridge. "There never is. Mr. Herapath, as you've no doubt observed, is a bit strict in the matter of rules, and it's one of his rules that everybody in the house must be in bed by eleven-thirty. No one was ever to sit up for him on any occasion. That's why this supper-tray was always left ready. His usual time for coming in when he'd been at the House was twelve o'clock."

"Everybody in the house might be in bed," observed Selwood, "but not everybody might be asleep. Have you made any inquiry as to whether anybody heard Mr. Herapath moving about in the night, or leaving the house? Somebody may have heard the hall door opened and closed, you know."

"I'll make inquiry as to that, sir," responded Kitteridge, "but I've heard nothing of the sort so far, and all the servants are aware by now that Mr. Herapath isn't in the house. If anybody had heard anything——"

Before the butler could say more the study door opened and a girl came into the room. At sight of her Selwood spoke hurriedly to Kitteridge.

"Have you told Miss Wynne?" he whispered. "Does she know?"

"She may have heard from her maid, sir," replied Kitteridge in low tones. "Of course they're all talking of it. I was going to ask to see Miss Wynne as soon as she was dressed."

By that time the girl had advanced towards the three men, and Selwood stepped forward to meet her. He knew her as Herapath's niece, the daughter of a dead sister of whom Herapath had been very fond; he knew, too, that Herapath had brought her up from infancy and treated her as a daughter. She was at this time a young woman of twenty-one or two, a pretty, eminently likeable young woman, with signs of character and resource in eyes and lips, and Selwood had seen enough of her to feel sure that in any disturbing event she would keep her head. She spoke calmly enough as the secretary met her.

"What's all this, Mr. Selwood?" she asked. "I understand my uncle is not in the house. But there's nothing alarming in that, Kitteridge, is there? Mr. Herapath may have gone away during the night, you know."

"Kitteridge thinks that highly improbable," replied Selwood. "He says that Mr. Herapath had made no preparation for a sudden journey, has taken no travelling coat or rug, or luggage of any sort."

"Did he come in from the House?" she asked. "Perhaps not?"

Kitteridge pointed to the supper-tray and then indicated the coachman.

"He came in as usual, miss," he replied. "Or rather an hour later than usual. Mountain brought him home at one o'clock, and he saw him let himself in with his latch-key."

Peggie Wynne turned to the coachman.

"You're sure that he entered the house?" she asked.

"As sure as I could be, miss," replied Mountain. "He was putting his key in the door when I drove off."

"He must have come in," said Kitteridge, pointing to the tray. "He had something after he got in."

"Well, go and tell the servants not to talk, Kitteridge," said Peggie. "My uncle, no doubt, had reasons for going out again. Have you said anything to Mr. Tertius?"

"Mr. Tertius isn't down yet, miss," answered the butler.

He left the room, followed by the coachman, and Peggie turned to Selwood. "What do you think?" she asked, with a slight show of anxiety. "You don't know of any reason for this, do you?"

"None," replied Selwood. "And as to what I think, I don't know sufficient about Mr. Herapath's habits to be able to judge."

"He never did anything like this before," she remarked. "I know that he sometimes gets up in the middle of the night and comes down here, but I never knew him to go out. If he'd been setting off on a sudden journey he'd surely have let me know. Perhaps——"

She paused suddenly, seeing Selwood lift his eyes from the papers strewn about the desk to the door. She, too, turned in the same direction.

A man had come quietly into the room—a slightly-built, little man, grey-bearded, delicate-looking, whose eyes were obscured by a pair of dark-tinted spectacles. He moved gently and with an air of habitual shyness, and Selwood, who was naturally observant, saw that his lips and his hands were trembling slightly as he came towards them.

"Mr. Tertius," said Peggie, "do you know anything about Uncle Jacob? He came in during the night—one o'clock—and now he's disappeared. Did he say anything to you about going away early this morning?"

Mr. Tertius shook his head.

"No—no—nothing!" he answered. "Disappeared! Is it certain he came in?"

"Mountain saw him come in," she said. "Besides, he had a drink out of that glass, and he ate something from the tray—see!"

Mr. Tertius bent his spectacled eyes over the supper tray and remained looking at what he saw there for a while. Then he looked up, and at Selwood.

"Strange!" he remarked. "And yet, you know, he is a man who does things without saying a word to any one. Have you, now, thought of telephoning to the estate office? He may have gone there."

Peggie, who had dropped into the chair at Herapath's desk, immediately jumped up.

"Of course we must do that at once!" she exclaimed. "Come to the telephone, Mr. Selwood—we may hear something."

She and Selwood left the room together. When they had gone, Mr. Tertius once more bent over the supper tray. He picked up the empty glass, handling it delicately; he held it between himself and the electric light over the desk; he narrowly inspected it, inside and out. Then he turned his attention to the plate of sandwiches. One sandwich had been taken from the plate and bitten into—once. Mr. Tertius took up that sandwich with the tips of his delicately-shaped fingers. He held that, too, nearer the light. And having looked at it he hastily selected an envelope from the stationery cabinet on the desk, carefully placed the sandwich within it, and set off to his own rooms in the upper part of the house. As he passed through the hall he heard Selwood at the telephone, which was installed in a small apartment at the foot of the stairs—he was evidently already in communication with some one at the Herapath Estate Office.

Mr. Tertius went straight to his room, stayed there a couple of minutes, and went downstairs again. Selwood and Peggie Wynne were just coming away from the telephone; they looked up at him with faces grave with concern.

"We're wanted at the estate office," said Selwood. "The caretaker was just going to ring us up when I got through to him. Something is wrong—wrong with Mr. Herapath."

Table of Contents

CHAPTER II

is it murder?

It struck Selwood, afterwards, as a significant thing that it was neither he nor Mr. Tertius who took the first steps towards immediate action. Even as he spoke, Peggie was summoning the butler, and her orders were clear and precise.

"Kitteridge," she said quietly, "order Robson to bring the car round at once—as quickly as possible. In the meantime, send some coffee into the breakfast-room—breakfast itself must wait until we return. Make haste, Kitteridge."

Selwood turned on her with a doubtful look.

"You—you aren't going down there?" he asked.

"Of course I am!" she answered. "Do you think I should wait here—wondering what had happened? We will all go—come and have some coffee, both of you, while we wait for the car."

The two followed her into the breakfast-room and silently drank the coffee which she presently poured out for them. She, too, was silent, but when she had left the room to make ready for the drive Mr. Tertius turned to Selwood.

"You heard—what?" he asked.

"Nothing definite," answered Selwood. "All I heard was that Mr. Herapath was there, and there was something seriously wrong, and would we go down at once."

Mr. Tertius made no comment. He became thoughtful and abstracted, and remained so during the journey down to Kensington. Peggie, too, said nothing as they sped along; as for Selwood, he was wondering what had happened, and reflecting on this sudden stirring up of mystery. There was mystery within that car—in the person of Mr. Tertius. During his three weeks' knowledge of the Herapath household Selwood had constantly wondered who Mr. Tertius was, what his exact relationship was, what his position really was. He knew that he lived in Jacob Herapath's house, but in a sense he was not of the family. He seldom presented himself at Herapath's table, he was rarely seen about the house; Selwood remembered seeing him occasionally in Herapath's study or in Peggie Wynne's drawing-room. He had learnt sufficient to know that Mr. Tertius had rooms of his own in the house; two rooms in some upper region; one room on the ground-floor. Once Selwood had gained a peep into that ground-floor room, and had seen that it was filled with books, and that its table was crowded with papers, and he had formed the notion that Mr. Tertius was some book-worm or antiquary, to whom Jacob Herapath for some reason or other gave house-room. That he was no relation Selwood judged from the way in which he was always addressed by Herapath and by Peggie Wynne. To them as to all the servants he was Mr. Tertius—whether that was his surname or not, Selwood did not know.

There was nothing mysterious or doubtful about the great pile of buildings at which the automobile presently stopped. They were practical and concrete facts. Most people in London knew the famous Herapath Flats—they had aroused public interest from the time that their founder began building them.

Jacob Herapath, a speculator in real estate, had always cherished a notion of building a mass of high-class residential flats on the most modern lines. Nothing of the sort which he contemplated, he said, existed in London—when the opportunity came he would show the building world what could and should be done. The opportunity came when a parcel of land in Kensington fell into the market—Jacob Herapath made haste to purchase it, and he immediately began building on it. The result was a magnificent mass of buildings which possessed every advantage and convenience—to live in a Herapath flat was to live in luxury. Incidentally, no one could live in one who was not prepared to pay a rental of anything from five to fifteen hundred a year. The gross rental of the Herapath Flats was enormous—the net profits were enough to make even a wealthy man's mouth water. And Selwood, who already knew all this, wondered, as they drove away, where all this wealth would go if anything had really happened to its creator.

The entrance to the Herapath estate office was in an archway which led to one of the inner squares of the great buildings. When the car stopped at it, Selwood saw that there were police within the open doorway. One of them, an inspector, came forward, looking dubiously at Peggie Wynne. Selwood hastened out of the car and made for him.

"I'm Mr. Herapath's secretary—Mr. Selwood," he said, drawing the inspector out of earshot. "Is anything seriously wrong?—better tell me before Miss Wynne hears. He isn't—dead?"

The inspector gave him a warning look.

"That's it, sir," he answered in a low voice. "Found dead by the caretaker in his private office. And it's here—Mr. Selwood, it's either suicide or murder. That's flat!"

Selwood got his two companions inside the building and into a waiting-room. Peggie turned on him at once.

"I see you know," she said. "Tell me at once what it is. Don't be afraid, Mr. Selwood—I'm not likely to faint nor to go into hysterics. Neither is Mr. Tertius. Tell us—is it the worst?"

"Yes," said Selwood. "It is."

"He is dead?" she asked in a low voice. "You are sure? Dead?"

Selwood bent his head by way of answer; when he looked up again the girl had bent hers, but she quickly lifted it, and except that she had grown pale, she showed no outward sign of shock or emotion. As for Mr. Tertius, he, too, was calm—and it was he who first broke the silence.

"How was it?" he asked. "A seizure?"

Selwood hesitated. Then, seeing that he had to deal with two people who were obviously in full control of themselves, he decided to tell the truth.

"I'm afraid you must be prepared to hear some unpleasant news," he said, with a glance at the inspector, who just then quietly entered the room. "The police say it is either a case of suicide or of murder."

Peggie looked sharply from Selwood to the police official, and a sudden flush of colour flamed into her cheeks.

"Suicide?" she exclaimed. "Never! Murder? That may be. Tell me what you have found," she went on eagerly. "Don't keep things back!—don't you see I want to know?"

The inspector closed the door and came nearer to where the three were standing.

"Perhaps I'd better tell you what we do know," he said. "Our station was rung up by the caretaker here at five minutes past eight. He said Mr. Herapath had just been found lying on the floor of his private room, and they were sure something was wrong, and would we come round. I came myself with one of our plain-clothes men who happened to be in, and our surgeon followed us a few minutes later. We found Mr. Herapath lying across the hearthrug in his private room, quite dead. Close by——" He paused and looked dubiously at Peggie. "The details are not pleasant," he said meaningly. "Shall I omit them?"

"No!" answered Peggie with decision. "Please omit nothing. Tell us all."

"There was a revolver lying close by Mr. Herapath's right hand," continued the inspector. "One chamber had been discharged. Mr. Herapath had been shot through the right temple, evidently at close quarters. I should say—and our surgeon says—he had died instantly. And—I think that's all I need say just now."

Peggie, who had listened to this with unmoved countenance, involuntarily stepped towards the door.

"Let us go to him," she said. "I suppose he's still here?"

But there Selwood, just as involuntarily, asserted an uncontrollable instinct. He put himself between the door and the girl.

"No!" he said firmly, wondering at himself for his insistence. "Don't! There's no need for that—yet. You mustn't go. Mr. Tertius——"

"Better not just yet, miss," broke in the inspector. "The doctor is still here. Afterwards, perhaps. If you would wait here while these gentlemen go with me."

Peggie hesitated a moment; then she turned away and sat down.

"Very well," she said.

The inspector silently motioned the two men to follow him; with his hand on the door Selwood turned again to Peggie.

"You will stay here?" he said. "You won't follow us?"

"I shall stay here," she answered. "Stop a minute—there's one thing that should be thought of. My cousin Barthorpe——"

"Mr. Barthorpe Herapath has been sent for, miss—he'll be here presently," replied the inspector. "The caretaker's telephoned to him. Now gentlemen."

He led the way along a corridor to a room with which Selwood was familiar enough—an apartment of some size which Jacob Herapath used as a business office and kept sacred to himself and his secretary. When he was in it no one ever entered that room except at Herapath's bidding; now there were strangers in it who had come there unbidden, and Herapath lay in their midst, silent for ever. They had laid the lifeless body on a couch, and Selwood and Mr. Tertius bent over it for a moment before they turned to the other men in the room. The dead face was calm enough; there was no trace of sudden fear on it, no signs of surprise or anger or violent passion.

"If you'll look here, gentlemen," said the police-inspector, motioning them towards the broad hearthrug. "This is how things were—nothing had been touched when we arrived. He was lying from there to here—he'd evidently slipped down and sideways out of that chair, and had fallen across the rug. The revolver was lying a few inches from his right hand. Here it is."

He pulled open a drawer as he spoke and produced a revolver which he carefully handled as he showed it to Selwood and Mr. Tertius.

"Have either of you gentlemen ever seen that before?" he asked. "I mean—do you recognize it as having belonged to—him? You don't? Never seen it before, either of you? Well, of course he might have kept a revolver in his private desk or in his safe, and nobody would have known. We shall have to make an exhaustive search and see if we can find any cartridges or anything. However, that's what we found—and, as I said before, one chamber had been discharged. The doctor here says the revolver had been fired at close quarters."

Mr. Tertius, who had watched and listened with marked attention, turned to the police surgeon.

"The wound may have been self-inflicted?" he asked.

"From the position of the body, and of the revolver, there is strong presumption that it was," replied the doctor.

"Yet—it may not have been?" suggested Mr. Tertius, mildly.

The doctor shrugged his shoulders. It was easy to see what his own opinion was.

"It may not have been—as you say," he answered. "But if he was shot by some other person—murdered, that is—the murderer must have been standing either close at his side, or immediately behind him. Of this I am certain—he was sitting in that chair, at his desk, when the shot was fired."

"And—what would the immediate effect be?" asked Mr. Tertius.

"He would probably start violently, make as if to rise, drop forward against the desk and gradually—but quickly—subside to the floor in the position in which he was found," replied the doctor. "As he fell he would relinquish his grip on the revolver—it is invariably a tight grip in these cases—and it would fall—just where it was found."

"Still, there is nothing to disprove the theory that the revolver may have been placed—where it was found?" suggested Mr. Tertius.

"Oh, certainly it may have been placed there!" said the doctor, with another shrug of the shoulders. "A cool and calculating murderer may have placed it there, of course."

"Just so," agreed Mr. Tertius. He remained silently gazing at the hearthrug for a while; then he turned to the doctor again. "Now, how long do you think Mr. Herapath had been dead when you were called to the body?" he asked.

"Quite eight hours," answered the doctor promptly.

"Eight hours!" exclaimed Mr. Tertius. "And you first saw him at——"

"A quarter past eight," said the doctor. "I should say he died just about midnight."

"Midnight!" murmured Mr. Tertius. "Midnight? Then——"

Before he could say more, a policeman, stationed in the corridor outside, opened the door of the room, and glancing at his inspector, announced the arrival of Mr. Barthorpe Herapath.

Table of Contents

CHAPTER III

barthorpe takes charge

The man who strode into the room as the policeman threw the door open for him immediately made two distinct impressions on the inspector and the doctor, neither of whom had ever seen him before. The first was that he instantly conveyed a sense of alert coolness and self-possession; the second that, allowing for differences of age, he was singularly like the dead man who lay in their midst. Both were tall, well-made men; both were clean-shaven; both were much alike as to feature and appearance. Apart from the fact that Jacob Herapath was a man of sixty and grey-haired, and his nephew one of thirty to thirty-five and dark-haired, they were very much alike—the same mould of nose, mouth, and chin, the same strength of form. The doctor noted this resemblance particularly, and he involuntarily glanced from the living to the dead.

Barthorpe Herapath bent over his dead uncle for no more than a minute. His face was impassive, almost stern as he turned to the others. He nodded slightly to Mr. Tertius and to Selwood; then he gave his attention to the officials.

"Yes?" he said inquiringly and yet with a certain tone of command. "Now tell me all you know of this."

He stood listening silently, with concentrated attention, as the inspector put him in possession of the facts already known. He made no comment, asked no questions, until the inspector had finished; then he turned to Selwood, almost pointedly ignoring Mr. Tertius.

"What is known of this in Portman Square, Mr. Selwood?" he inquired. "Tell me, briefly."

Selwood, who had only met Barthorpe Herapath once or twice, and who had formed an instinctive and peculiar dislike to him, for which he could not account, accepted the invitation to be brief. In a few words he told exactly what had happened at Jacob Herapath's house.

"My cousin is here, then?" exclaimed Barthorpe.

"Miss Wynne is in the larger waiting-room down the corridor," replied Selwood.

"I will go to her in a minute," said Barthorpe. "Now, inspector, there are certain things to be done at once. There will, of course, have to be an inquest—your people must give immediate notice to the coroner. Then—the body—that must be properly attended to—that, too, you will see about. Before you go away yourself, I want you to join me in collecting all the evidence we can get on the spot. You have one of your detective staff here?—good. Now, have you searched—him?"

The inspector drew open a drawer in the front desk which occupied the centre of the room, and pointed to some articles which lay within.

"Everything that we found upon him is in there," he answered. "You see there is not much—watch and chain, pocket articles, a purse, some loose money, a pocket-book, a cigar-case—that's all. One matter I should have expected to find, we didn't find."

"What's that?" asked Barthorpe quickly.

"Keys," answered the inspector. "We found no keys on him—not even a latch-key. Yet he must have let himself in here, and I understand from the caretaker that he must have unlocked this door after he'd entered by the outer one."

Barthorpe made no immediate answer beyond a murmur of perplexity.

"Strange," he said after a pause, during which he bent over the open drawer. "However, that's one of the things to be gone into. Close that drawer, lock it up, and for the present keep the key yourself—you and I will examine the contents later. Now for these immediate inquiries. Mr. Selwood, will you please telephone at once to Portman Square and tell Kitteridge to send Mountain, the coachman, here—instantly. Tell Kitteridge to come with him. Inspector, will you see to this arrangement we spoke of, and also tell the caretaker that we shall want him presently? Now I will go to my cousin."

He strode off, still alert, composed, almost bustling in his demeanour, to the waiting-room in which they had left Peggie—a moment later, Selwood, following him down the corridor, saw him enter and close the door. And Selwood cursed himself for a fool for hating to think that these two should be closeted together, for disliking the notion that Barthorpe Herapath was Peggie Wynne's cousin—and now, probably, her guardian protector. For during those three weeks in which he had been Jacob Herapath's secretary, Selwood had seen a good deal of his employer's niece, and he was already well over the verge of falling in love with her, and was furious with himself for daring to think of a girl who was surely one of the richest heiresses in London. He was angry with himself, too, for disliking Barthorpe, for he was inclined to cultivate common-sense, and common-sense coldly reminded him that he did not know Barthorpe Herapath well enough to either like or dislike him.

Half an hour passed—affairs suggestive of the tragedy of the night went on in the Herapath Estate Office. Two women in the garb of professional nurses came quietly, and passed into the room where Herapath lay dead. A man arrayed in dismal black came after them, summoned by the police who were busy at the telephone as soon as Selwood had finished with it. Selwood himself, having summoned Kitteridge and Mountain, hung about, waiting. He heard the police talking in undertones of clues and theories, and of a coroner's inquest, and the like; now and then he looked curiously at Mr. Tertius, who had taken a seat in the hall and was apparently wrapped in meditation. And still Barthorpe Herapath remained closeted with Peggie Wynne.

A taxi drove up and deposited the butler and the coachman at the door. Selwood motioned them inside.

"Mr. Barthorpe Herapath wants both of you," he said curtly. "I suppose he will ask for you presently."

Kitteridge let out an anxious inquiry.

"The master, sir?" he exclaimed. "Is——"

"Good heavens!" muttered Selwood. "I—of course, you don't know. Mr. Herapath is dead."

The two servants started and stared at each other. Before either could speak Barthorpe Herapath suddenly emerged from the waiting-room and looked round the hall. He beckoned to the inspector, who was talking in low tones with the detective, at a little distance.

"Now, inspector," he said, "will you and your officer come in? And the caretaker—and you, Kitteridge, and you, Mountain. Mr. Selwood, will you come in, too?"

He stood at the door while those he had invited inside passed into the room where Peggie still sat. And as he stood there, and Selwood wound up the little procession, Mr. Tertius rose and also made as if to join the others. Barthorpe stopped him by intruding himself between him and the door.

"This is a private inquiry of my own, Mr. Tertius," he said, with a meaning look.

Selwood, turning in sheer surprise at this announcement, so pointed and so unmistakable, saw a faint tinge of colour mount to the elder man's usually pale cheeks. Mr. Tertius stopped sharply and looked at Barthorpe in genuine surprise.

"You do not wish me to enter—to be present?" he faltered.

"Frankly, I don't," said Barthorpe, with aggressive plainness. "There will be a public inquiry—I can't stop you from attending that."

Mr. Tertius drew back. He stood for a moment staring hard at Barthorpe; then, with a slight, scarcely perceptible bow, he turned away, crossed the hall, and went out of the front door. And Barthorpe Herapath laughed—a low, sneering laugh—and following the other men into the waiting-room, locked the door upon those assembled there. As if he and they were assembled on some cut-and-dried business matter, he waved them all to chairs, and himself dropped into one at the head of the table, close to that in which Peggie was sitting.

"Now, inspector," he began, "you and I must get what we may as well call first information about this matter. There will be a vast amount of special and particular investigation later on, but I want us, at the very outset, while facts are fresh in the mind, to get certain happenings clearly before us. And for this reason—I understand that the police-surgeon is of opinion that my uncle committed suicide. With all respect to him—I'm sorry he's gone before I could talk to him—that theory cannot be held for an instant! My cousin, Miss Wynne, and I knew our uncle far too well to believe that theory for a single moment, and we shall combat it by every means in our power when the inquest is held. No—my uncle was murdered! Now I want to know all I can get to know of his movements last night. And first I think we'll hear what the caretaker can tell us. Hancock," he continued, turning to an elderly man who looked like an ex-soldier, "I understand you found my uncle's body?"

The caretaker, obviously much upset by the affairs of the morning, pulled himself up to attention.

"I did, sir," he replied.

"What time was that?"

"Just eight o'clock, sir—that's my usual time for opening the office."

"Tell us exactly how you found him, Hancock."

"I opened the door of Mr. Herapath's private room, sir, to pull up the blinds and open the window. When I walked in I saw him lying across the hearth-rug. Then I noticed the—the revolver."

"And of course that gave you a turn. What did you do? Go into the room?"

"No, sir! I shut the door again, went straight to the telephone and rang up the police-station. Then I waited at the front door till the inspector there came along."

"Was the front door fastened as usual when you went to it at that time?"

"It was fastened as it always is, sir, by the latch. It was Mr. Herapath's particular orders that it never should be fastened any other way at night, because he sometimes came in at night, with his latch-key."

"Just so. Now these offices are quite apart and distinct from the rest of the building—mark that, inspector! There's no way out of them into the building, nor any way out of the building into them. In fact, the only entrance into these offices is by the front door. Isn't that so,

Hancock?"

"That's quite so, sir—only that one door."

"No area entrance or side-door?"

"None, sir—nothing but that."

"And the only tenants in here—these offices—at night are you and your wife, Hancock?"

"That's all, sir."

"Now, where are your rooms?"

"We've two rooms in the basement, sir—living-room and kitchen—and two rooms on the top floor—a bedroom and a bathroom."

"On the top-floor. How many floors are there?"

"Well, sir, there's the basement—then there's this—then there's two floors that's used by the clerks—then there's ours."

"That's to say there are two floors between your bedroom and this ground floor?"

"Yes, sir—two."

"Very well. Now, about last night. What time did you and your wife go to bed?"

"Eleven o'clock, sir—half an hour later than usual."

"You'd previously looked round, I suppose?"

"Been all round, sir—I always look into every room in the place last thing at night—thoroughly."

"Are you and your wife sound sleepers?"

"Yes, sir—both of us. Good sleepers."

"You heard no sound after you got to bed?"

"Nothing, sir—neither of us."

"No recollection of hearing a revolver shot?—not even as if it were a long way off?"

"No, sir—we never heard anything—nothing unusual, at any rate."

"You heard no sound of doors opening or being shut, nor of any conveyance coming to the door?"

"No, sir, nothing at all."

"Well, one or two more questions, Hancock. You didn't go into the room after first catching sight of the body? Just so—but you'd notice things, even in a hurried glance. Did you notice any sign of a struggle—overturned chair or anything?"

"No, sir. I did notice that Mr. Herapath's elbow chair, that he always sat in at his desk, was pushed back a bit, and was a bit on one side as it were. That was all."

"And the light—the electric light? Was that on?"

"No, sir."

"Then all you can tell us comes to this—that you never heard anything, and had no notion of what was happening, or had happened, until you came down in the morning?"

"Just so, sir. If I'd known what was going on, or had gone on, I should have been down at once."

Barthorpe nodded and turned to the coachman.

"Now, Mountain," he said. "We want to hear your story. Be careful about your facts—what you can tell us is probably of the utmost importance."

Table of Contents

CHAPTER IV

The coachman, thus admonished, unconsciously edged his chair a little nearer to the table at which Barthorpe Herapath sat, and looked anxiously at his interrogator. He was a little, shrewd-eyed fellow, and it seemed to Selwood, who had watched him carefully during the informal examination to which Barthorpe had subjected the caretaker, that he had begun to think deeply over some new presentiment of this mystery which was slowly shaping itself in his mind.

"I understand, Mountain, that you fetched Mr. Herapath from the House of Commons last night?" began Barthorpe. "You fetched him in the brougham, I believe?"

"Yes, sir," answered the coachman. "Mr. Herapath always had the brougham at night—and most times, too, sir. Never took kindly to the motor, sir."

"Where did you meet him, Mountain?"

"Usual place, sir—in Palace Yard—just outside the Hall."

"What time was that?"

"Quarter past eleven, exactly, sir—the clock was just chiming the quarter as he came out."

"Was Mr. Herapath alone when he came out?"

"No sir. He came out with another gentleman—a stranger to me, sir. The two of 'em stood talking a bit a yard or two away from the brougham."

"Did you hear anything they said?"

"Just a word or two from Mr. Herapath, sir, as him and the other gentleman parted."

"What were they?—tell us the words, as near as you can remember."

"Mr. Herapath said, 'Have it ready for me tomorrow, and I'll look in at your place about noon.' That's all, sir."

"What happened then?"

"The other gentleman went off across the Yard, sir, and Mr. Herapath came to the brougham, and told me to drive him to the estate office—here, sir."

"You drove him up to this door, I suppose?"

"No, sir. Mr. Herapath never was driven up to the door—he always got out of the brougham in the road outside and walked up the archway. He did that last night."

"From where you pulled up could you see if there was any light in these offices?"

"No, sir—I pulled up just short of the entrance to the archway."

"Did Mr. Herapath say anything to you when he got out?"

"Yes, sir. He said he should most likely be three-quarters of an hour here, and that I'd better put a rug over the mare and walk her about."

"Then I suppose he went up the archway. Now, did you see anybody about the entrance? Did you see any person waiting as if to meet him? Did he meet anybody?"

"I saw no one, sir. As soon as he'd gone up the archway I threw a rug over the mare and walked her round and round the square across the road."

"You heard and saw nothing of him until he came out again?"

"Nothing, sir."

"And how long was he away from you?"

"Nearer an hour than three-quarters, sir."

"Were you in full view of the entrance all that time?"

"No, sir, I wasn't. Some of the time I was—some of it I'd my back to it."

"You never saw any one enter the archway during the time Mr. Herapath was in the office?"

"No, sir."

"All the same, some one could have come here during that time without your seeing him?"

"Oh, yes, sir!"

"Well, at last Mr. Herapath came out. Where did he rejoin you?"

"In the middle of the road, sir—right opposite that statue in the Square gardens."

"Did he say anything particular then?"

"No, sir. He walked sharply across, opened the door, said 'Home' and jumped in."

"You didn't notice anything unusual about him?"

"Nothing, sir—unless it was that he hung his head down rather as he came across—same as if he was thinking hard, sir."

"You drove straight home to Portman Square, then. What time did you get there?"

"Exactly one o'clock, sir."

"You're certain about that time?"

"Certain, sir. It was just five minutes past one when I drove into our mews."

"Now, then, be careful about this, Mountain. I want to know exactly what happened when you drove up to the house. Tell us in your own way."

The coachman looked round amongst the listeners as if he were a little perplexed. "Why, sir," he answered, turning back to Barthorpe, "there was nothing happened! At least, I mean to say, there was nothing happened that didn't always happen on such occasions—Mr. Herapath got out of the brougham, shut the door, said 'Good night,' and went up the steps, taking his latch-key out of his pocket as he crossed the pavement, sir. That was all, sir."

"Did you actually see him enter the house?"

"No, sir," replied Mountain, with a decisive shake of the head. "I couldn't say that I did that. I saw him just putting the key in the latch as I drove off."

"And that's all you know?"

"That's all I know, sir—all."

Barthorpe, after a moment's hesitation, turned to the police-inspector.

"Is there anything that occurs to you?" he asked.

"One or two things occur to me," answered the inspector. "But I'm not going to ask any questions now. I suppose all you want at present is to get a rough notion of how things were last night?"

"Just so," assented Barthorpe. "A rough notion—that's it. Well, Kitteridge, it's your turn. Who found out that Mr. Herapath wasn't in the house this morning?"

"Charlesworth, sir—Mr. Herapath's valet," replied the butler. "He always called Mr. Herapath at a quarter past seven every morning. When he went into the bedroom this morning Mr. Herapath wasn't there, and the bed hadn't been slept in. Then Charlesworth came and told me, sir, and of course I went to the study at once, and then I saw that, wherever Mr. Herapath might be then, he certainly had been home."

"You judged that from—what?" asked Barthorpe.

"Well, sir, it's been the rule to leave a supper-tray out for Mr. Herapath. Not much, sir—whisky and soda, a sandwich or two, a dry biscuit. I saw that he'd had something, sir."

"Somebody else might have had it—eh?"

"Yes, sir, but then you see, I'd had Mountain fetched by that time, and he told me that he'd seen Mr. Herapath letting himself in at one o'clock. So of course I knew the master had been in."

Barthorpe hesitated, seemed to ponder matters for a moment, and then rose. "I don't think we need go into things any further just now," he said. "You, Kitteridge, and you, Mountain, can go home. Don't talk—that is, don't talk any more than is necessary. I suppose," he went on, turning to the inspector when the two servants and the caretaker had left the room. "I suppose you'll see to all the arrangements we spoke of?"

"They're being carried out already," answered the inspector. "Of course," he added, drawing closer to Barthorpe and speaking in lower tones, "when the body's been removed, you'll join me in making a thorough inspection of the room? We haven't done that yet, you know, and it should be done. Wouldn't it be best," he continued with a glance at Peggie and a further lowering of his voice, "if the young lady went back to Portman Square?"

"Just so, just so—I'll see to it," answered Barthorpe. "You go and keep people out of the way for a few minutes, and I'll get her off." He turned to his cousin when the two officers had left the room and motioned her to rise. "Now, Peggie," he said, "you must go home. I shall come along there myself in an hour or two—there are things to be done which you and I must do together. Mr. Selwood—will you take Miss Wynne out to the car? And then, please, come back to me—I want your assistance for a while."

Peggie walked out of the room and to the car without demur or comment. But as she was about to take her seat she turned to Selwood.

"Why didn't Mr. Tertius come into the room just now?" she demanded.

Selwood hesitated. Until then he had thought that Peggie had heard the brief exchange of words between Barthorpe and Mr. Tertius at the door.

"Didn't you hear what was said at the door when we were all coming in?" he asked suddenly, looking attentively at her.

"I heard my cousin and Mr. Tertius talking, but I couldn't catch what was said," she replied. "If you did, tell me—I want to know."

"Mr. Barthorpe Herapath refused to admit Mr. Tertius," said Selwood.

"Refused?" she exclaimed. "Refused?"

"Refused," repeated Selwood. "That's all I know."

Peggie sat down and gave him an enigmatic look.

"You, of course, will come back to the house when—when you've finished here?" she said.

"I don't know—I suppose—really, I don't know," answered Selwood. "You see, I—I, of course, don't know exactly where I am, now. I suppose I must take my orders from—your cousin."

Peggie gave him another look, more enigmatic than the other.

"That's nonsense!" she said sharply. "Of course, you'll come. Do whatever it is that Barthorpe wants just now, but come on to Portman Square as soon as you've done it—I want you. Go straight home, Robson," she went on, turning to the chauffeur.

Selwood turned slowly and unwillingly back to the office door as the car moved off. And as he set his foot on the first step a young man came running up the entry—not hurrying but running—and caught him up and hailed him.

"Mr. Selwood?" he said, pantingly. "You'll excuse me—you're Mr. Herapath's secretary, aren't you?—I've seen you with him. I'm Mr. Triffitt, of the *Argus*—I happened to call in at the police-station just now, and they told me of what had happened here, so I rushed along. Will you tell me all about it, Mr. Selwood?—it'll be a real scoop for me—I'll hustle down to the office with it at once, and we'll have a special out in no time. And whether you know it or not, that'll help the police. Give me the facts, Mr. Selwood!"

Selwood stared at the ardent collector of news; then he motioned him to follow, and led him into the hall to where Barthorpe Herapath was standing with the police-inspector.

"This is a newspaper man," he said laconically, looking at Barthorpe. "Mr. Triffitt, of the *Argus*. He wants the facts of this affair."

Barthorpe turned and looked the new-comer up and down. Triffitt, who had almost recovered his breath, pulled out a card and presented it with a bow. And Barthorpe suddenly seemed to form a conclusion.

"All right!" he said. "Mr. Selwood, you know all the facts. Take Mr. Triffitt into that room we've just left, and give him a résumé of them. And—listen! we can make use of the press. Mention two matters, which seem to me to be of importance. Tell of the man who came out of the House of Commons with my uncle last night—ask him if he'll come forward. And, as my uncle must have returned to this office after he'd been home, and as he certainly wouldn't walk here, ask for information as to who drove him down to Kensington from Portman Square. Don't tell this man too much—give him the bare outlines on how matters stand."

The reporter wrote at lightning speed while Selwood, who had some experience of condensation, gave him the news he wanted. Finding that he was getting a first-class story, Triffitt asked no questions and made no interruptions. But when Selwood was through with the account, he looked across the table with a queer glance of the eye.

"I say!" he said. "This is a strange case!"

"Why so strange?" asked Selwood.

"Why? Great Scott!—I reckon it's an uncommonly strange case," exclaimed Triffitt. "It's about a dead certainty that Herapath was in his own house at Portman Square at one o'clock, isn't it?"

"Well?" said Selwood.

"And yet according to the doctor who examined him at eight o'clock he'd been dead quite eight hours!" said Triffitt. "That means he died at twelve o'clock—an hour before he's supposed to have been at his house! Queer! But all the queerer, all the better—for me! Now I'm off—for the present. This'll be on the streets in an hour, Mr. Selwood. Nothing like the press, sir!"

Therewith he fled, and the secretary suddenly found himself confronting a new idea. If the doctor was right and Jacob Herapath had been shot dead at midnight, how on earth could he possibly have been in Portman Square at one o'clock, an hour later?

Table of Contents

CHAPTER V

the glass and the sandwich

Mr. Tertius, dismissed in such cavalier fashion by Barthorpe Herapath, walked out of the estate office with downcast head—a superficial observer might have said that he was thoroughly crestfallen and brow-beaten. But by the time he had reached the road outside, the two faint spots of colour which had flushed his cheeks when Barthorpe turned him away had vanished, and he was calm and collected enough when, seeing a disengaged taxi-cab passing by, he put up his hand and hailed it. The voice which bade the driver go to Portman Square was calm enough, too—Mr. Tertius had too much serious work immediately in prospect to allow himself to be disturbed by a rudeness.

He thought deeply about that work as the taxi-cab whirled him along; he was still thinking about it when he walked into the big house in Portman Square. In there everything was very quiet. The butler was away at Kensington; the other servants were busily discussing the mystery of their master in their own regions. No one was aware that Mr. Tertius had returned, for he let himself into the house with his own latch-key, and went straight into Herapath's study. There, if possible, everything was still quieter—the gloom of the dull November morning seemed to be doubly accentuated in the nooks and corners; there was a sense of solitude which was well in keeping with Mr. Tertius's knowledge of what had happened. He looked at the vacant chair in which he had so often seen Jacob Herapath sitting, hard at work, active, bustling, intent on getting all he could out of every minute of his working day, and he sighed deeply.

But in the moment of sighing Mr. Tertius reflected that there was no time for regret. It was a time—his time—for action; there was a thing to do which he wanted to do while he had the room to himself. Therefore he went to work, carefully and methodically. For a second or two he stood reflectively looking at the supper tray which still stood on the little table near the desk. With a light, delicate touch he picked up the glass which had been used and held it up to the light. He put it down again presently, went quietly out of the study to the dining-room across the hall, and returned at once with another glass precisely similar in make and pattern to the one which he had placed aside. Into that clear glass he poured some whisky, afterwards mixing with it some soda-water from the syphon—this mixture he poured away into the soil of a flower-pot which stood in the window. And that done he placed the second glass on the tray in the place where the first had stood, and picking up the first, in the same light, gingerly fashion, he went upstairs to his own rooms at the top of the house.

Five minutes later Mr. Tertius emerged from his rooms. He then carried in his hand a small, square bag, and he took great care to handle it very carefully as he went downstairs and into the square. At the corner of Orchard Street he got another taxi-cab and bade the driver go to Endsleigh Gardens. And during the drive he took the greatest pains to nurse the little bag on his knee, thereby preserving the equilibrium of the glass inside it.

Ringing the bell of one of the houses in Endsleigh Gardens, Mr. Tertius was presently confronted by a trim parlourmaid, whose smile was ample proof that the caller was well-known to her.

"Is the Professor in, Mary?" asked Mr. Tertius. "And if he is, is he engaged?"

The trim parlourmaid replied that the Professor was in, and that she hadn't heard that he was particularly engaged, and she immediately preceded the visitor up a flight or two of stairs to a door, which in addition to being thickly covered with green felt, was set in flanges of rubber—these precautions being taken, of course, to ensure silence in the apartment within. An electric bell was set in the door; a moment or two elapsed before any response was made to the parlourmaid's ring. Then the door automatically opened, the parlourmaid smiled at Mr. Tertius and retired; Mr. Tertius walked in; the door closed softly behind him.

The room in which the visitor found himself was a large and lofty one, lighted from the roof, from which it was also ventilated by a patent arrangement of electric fans. Everything that met the view betokened science, order, and method. The walls, destitute of picture or ornament, were of a smooth neutral tinted plaster; where they met the floor the corners were all carefully rounded off so that no dust could gather in cracks and crevices; the floor, too, was of smooth cement; there was no spot in which a speck of dust could settle in improper peace. A series of benches ran round the room, and gave harbourings to a collection of scientific instruments of strange appearance and shape; two large tables, one at either end of the room, were similarly equipped. And at a desk placed between them, and just then occupied in writing in a note-book, sat a large man, whose big muscular body was enveloped in a brown holland blouse or overall, fashioned something like a smock-frock of the old-fashioned rural labourer. He lifted a colossal, mop-like head and a huge hand as Mr. Tertius stepped across the threshold, and his spectacled eyes twinkled as their glance fell on the bag which the visitor carried so gingerly.

"Hullo, Tertius!" exclaimed the big man, in a deep, rich voice. "What have you got there? Specimens?"

Mr. Tertius looked round for a quite empty space on the adjacent bench, and at last seeing one, set his bag down upon it, and sighed with relief.

"My dear Cox-Raythwaite!" he said, mopping his forehead with a bandanna handkerchief which he drew from the tail of his coat. "I am thankful to have got these things here in—I devoutly trust!—safety. Specimens? Well, not exactly; though, to be sure, they may be specimens of—I don't quite know what villainy yet. Objects?—certainly! Perhaps, my dear Professor, you will come and look at them."

The Professor slowly lifted his six feet of muscle and sinew out of his chair, picked up a briar pipe which lay on his desk, puffed a great cloud of smoke out of it, and lounged weightily across the room to his visitor.

"Something alive?" he asked laconically. "Likely to bite?"

"Er—no!" replied Mr. Tertius. "No—they won't bite. The fact is," he went on, gingerly opening the bag, "this—er—this, or these are they."

Professor Cox-Raythwaite bent his massive head and shoulders over the little bag and peered narrowly into its obscurity. Then he started.

"Good Lord!" he exclaimed. "A glass tumbler! And—is it a sandwich? Why, what on earth——"

He made as if to pull the glass out of the bag, and Mr. Tertius hastily seized the great hand in an agony of apprehension.

"My dear Cox-Raythwaite!" he said. "Pray don't! Allow me—presently. When either of these objects is touched it must be in the most, quite the most, delicate fashion. Of course, I know you have a fairy-like gentleness of touch—but don't touch these things yet. Let me explain. Shall we—suppose we sit down. Give me—yes—give me one of your cigars."

The Professor, plainly mystified, silently pointed to a cigar box which stood on a corner of his desk, and took another look into the bag.

"A sandwich—and a glass!" he murmured reflectively. "Um! Well?" he continued, going back to his chair and dropping heavily into it. "And what's it all about, Tertius? Some mystery, eh?"

Mr. Tertius drew a whiff or two of fragrant Havana before he replied. Then he too dropped into a chair and pulled it close to his friend's desk.

"My dear Professor!" he said, in a low, thrilling voice, suggestive of vast importance, "I don't know whether the secret of one of the most astounding crimes of our day may not lie in that innocent-looking bag—or, rather, in its present contents. Fact! But I'll tell you—you must listen with your usual meticulous care for small details. The truth is—Jacob Herapath has, I am sure, been murdered!"

"Murdered!" exclaimed the Professor. "Herapath? Murder—eh? Now then, slow and steady, Tertius—leave out nothing!"

"Nothing!" repeated Mr. Tertius solemnly. "Nothing! You shall hear all. And this it is—point by point, from last night until—until the present moment. That is—so far as I know. There may have been developments—somewhere else. But this is what I know."

When Mr. Tertius had finished a detailed and thorough-going account of the recent startling discovery and subsequent proceedings, to all of which Professor Cox-Raythwaite listened in profound silence, he rose, and tip-toeing towards the bag, motioned his friend to follow him.

"Now, my dear sir," he said, whispering in his excitement as if he feared lest the very retorts and crucibles and pneumatic troughs should hear him, "Now, my dear sir, I wish you to see for yourself. First of all, the glass. I will take it out myself—I know exactly how I put it in. I take it out—thus! I place it on this vacant space—thus. Look for yourself, my dear fellow. What do you see?"

The Professor, watching Mr. Tertius's movements with undisguised interest, took off his spectacles, picked up a reading-glass, bent down and carefully examined the tumbler.

"Yes," he said, after a while, "yes, Tertius, I certainly see distinct thumb and finger-marks round the upper part of this glass. Oh, yes—no doubt of that!"

"Allow me to take one of your clean specimen slides," observed Mr. Tertius, picking up a square of highly polished glass. "There! I place this slide here and upon it I deposit this sandwich. Now, my dear Cox-Raythwaite, favour me by examining the sandwich even more closely than you did the glass—if necessary."

But the Professor shook his head. He clapped Mr. Tertius on the shoulder.

"Excellent!" he exclaimed. "Good! Pooh!—no need for care there. The thing's as plain as—as I am. Good, Tertius, good!"

"You see it?" said Mr. Tertius, delightedly.

"See it! Good Lord, why, who could help see it?" answered the Professor. "Needs no great amount of care or perception to see that, as I said. Of course, I see it. Glad you did, too!"

"But we must take the greatest care of it," urged Mr. Tertius. "The most particular care. That's why I came to you. Now, what can we do? How preserve this sandwich—just as it is?"

"Nothing easier," replied the Professor. "We'll soon fix that. We'll put it in such safety that it will still be a fresh thing if it remains untouched until London Bridge falls down from sheer decay."

He moved off to another part of the laboratory, and presently returned with two objects, one oblong and shallow, the other deep and square, which on being set down before Mr. Tertius proved to be glass boxes, wonderfully and delicately made, with removable lids that fitted into perfectly adjusted grooves.

"There, my dear fellow," he said. "Presently I will deposit the glass in that, and the sandwich in this. Then I shall adjust and seal the lids in such a fashion that no air can enter these little chambers. Then through those tiny orifices I shall extract whatever air is in them—to the most infinitesimal remnant of it. Then I shall seal those orifices—and there you are. Whoever wants to see that sandwich or that glass will find both a year hence—ten years hence—a century hence!—in precisely the same condition in which we now see them. And that reminds me," he continued, as he turned away to his desk and picked up his pipe, "that reminds me, Tertius—what are you going to do about these things being seen? They'll have to be seen, you know. Have you thought of the police—the detectives?"

"I have certainly thought of both," replied Mr. Tertius. "But—I think not yet, in either case. I think one had better await the result of the inquest. Something may come out, you know."

"Coroners and juries," observed the Professor oracularly, "are good at finding the obvious. Whether they get at the mysteries and the secrets——"

"Just so—just so!" said Mr. Tertius. "I quite apprehend you. All the same, I think we will see what is put before the coroner. Now, what point suggests itself to you, Cox-Raythwaite?"

"One in particular," answered the Professor. "Whatever medical evidence is called ought to show without reasonable doubt what time Herapath actually met his death."

"Quite so," said Mr. Tertius gravely. "If that's once established——"

"Then, of course, your own investigation, or suggestion, or theory about that sandwich will be vastly simplified," replied the Professor. "Meanwhile, you will no doubt take some means of observing—eh?"

"I shall use every means to observe," said Mr. Tertius with a significant smile, which was almost a wink. "Of that you may be—dead certain!"

Then he left Professor Cox-Raythwaite to hermetically seal up the glass and the sandwich, and quitting the house, walked slowly back to Portman Square. As he turned out of Oxford Street into Orchard Street the newsboys suddenly came rushing along with the *Argus* special.

Table of Contents

CHAPTER VI

the taxi-cab driver

Mr. Tertius bought a copy of the newspaper, and standing aside on the pavement, read with much interest and surprise the story which Triffitt's keen appetite for news and ready craftsmanship in writing had so quickly put together. Happening to glance up from the paper in the course of his reading, he observed that several other people were similarly employed. The truth was that Triffitt had headed his column: "Mysterious Death of Mr. Herapath, M.P. Is It Suicide or Murder?"—and as this also appeared in great staring letters on the contents bills which the newsboys were carrying about with them, and as Herapath had been well known in that district, there was a vast amount of interest aroused thereabouts by the news. Indeed, people were beginning to chatter on the sidewalks, and at the doors of the shops. And as Mr. Tertius turned away in the direction of Portman Square, he heard one excited bystander express a candid opinion.

"Suicide?" exclaimed this man, thrusting his paper into the hands of a companion. "Not much! Catch old Jacob Herapath at that game—he was a deuced deal too fond of life and money! Murder, sir—murder!—that's the ticket—murder!"

Mr. Tertius went slowly homeward, head bent and eyes moody. He let himself into the house; at the sound of his step in the hall Peggie Wynne looked out of the study. She retreated into it at sight of Mr. Tertius, and he followed her and closed the door. Looking narrowly at her, he saw that the girl had been shedding tears, and he laid his hand shyly yet sympathetically on her arm. "Yes," he said quietly, "I've been feeling like that ever since—since I heard about things. But I don't know—I suppose we shall feel it more when—when we realize it more, eh? Just now there's the other thing to think about, isn't there?"

Peggie mopped her eyes and looked at him. He was such a quiet, unobtrusive, inoffensive old gentleman that she wondered more than ever why Barthorpe had refused to admit him to the informal conference.

"What other thing?" she asked.

Mr. Tertius looked round the room—strangely empty now that Jacob Herapath's bustling and strenuous presence was no longer in it—and shook his head.

"There's one thought you mustn't permit yourself to harbour for a moment, my dear," he answered. "Don't even for a fraction of time allow yourself to think that my old friend took his own life! That's—impossible."

"I don't," said Peggie. "I never did think so. It is, as you say, impossible. I knew him too well to believe that. So, of course, it's——"

"Murder," assented Mr. Tertius. "Murder! I heard a man in the street voice the same opinion just now. Of course! It's the only opinion. Yet in the newspaper they're asking which it was. But I suppose the newspapers must be—sensational."

"You don't mean to say it's in the newspapers already?" exclaimed Peggie.

Mr. Tertius handed to her the *Argus* special, which he had carried crumpled up in his hand.

"Everybody's reading it out there in the streets," he said. "It's extraordinary, now, how these affairs seem to fascinate people. Yes—it's all there. That is, of course, as far as it's gone."

"How did the paper people come to know all this?" asked Peggie, glancing rapidly over Triffitt's leaded lines.

"I suppose they got it from the police," replied Mr. Tertius. "I don't know much about such matters, but I believe the police and the Press are in constant touch. Of course, it's well they should be—it attracts public notice. And in cases like this, public notice is an excellent thing. We shall have to hear—and find out—a good deal before we get at the truth in this case, my dear."

Peggie suddenly flung down the newspaper and looked inquiringly at the old man.

"Mr. Tertius," she said abruptly, "why wouldn't Barthorpe let you come into that room down there at the office this morning?"

Mr. Tertius did not answer this direct question at once. He walked away to the window and stood looking out into the square for a while. When at last he spoke his voice was singularly even and colourless. He might have been discussing a question on which it was impossible to feel any emotion.

"I really cannot positively say, my dear," he replied. "I have known, of course, for some time that Mr. Barthorpe Herapath is not well disposed towards me. I have observed a certain coldness, a contempt, on his part. I have been aware that he has resented my presence in this house. And I suppose he felt that as I am not a member of the family, I had no right to sit in council with him and with you."

"Not a member of the family!" exclaimed Peggie. "Why, you came here soon after I came—all those years ago!"

"I have dwelt under Jacob Herapath's roof, in this house, fifteen years," said Mr. Tertius, reflectively. "Fifteen years!—yes. Yes—Jacob and I were—good friends."

As he spoke the last word a tear trickled from beneath Mr. Tertius's spectacles and ran down into his beard, and Peggie, catching sight of it, impulsively jumped from her seat and kissed him affectionately.

"Never mind, Mr. Tertius!" she said, patting his shoulders. "You and I are friends, too, anyway. I don't like Barthorpe when he's like that—I hate that side of him. And anyhow, Barthorpe doesn't matter—to me. I don't suppose he matters to anything—except himself."

Mr. Tertius gravely shook his head.

"Mr. Barthorpe Herapath may matter a great deal, my dear," he remarked. "He is a very forceful person. I do not know what provision my poor friend may have made, but Barthorpe, you will remember, is his nephew, and, I believe, his only male relative. And in that case——"

Mr. Tertius was just then interrupted by the entrance of a footman who came in and looked inquiringly at Peggie.

"There's a taxi-cab driver at the door, miss," he announced. "He says he would like to speak to some one about the news in the paper about—about the master, miss."

Peggie looked at Mr. Tertius. And Mr. Tertius quickly made a sign to the footman.

"Bring the man in at once," he commanded. And, as if to lose no time, he followed the footman into the hall, and at once returned, conducting a young man who carried a copy of the *Argus* in his hand. "Yes?" he said, closing the door behind them and motioning the man to a seat. "You wish to tell us something! This lady is Miss Wynne—Mr. Herapath's niece. You can tell us anything you think of importance. Do you know anything, then?"

The taxi-cab driver lifted the *Argus*.

"This here newspaper, sir," he answered. "I've just been reading of it—about Mr. Herapath, sir."

"Yes," said Mr. Tertius gently. "Yes?"

"Well, sir—strikes me as how I drove him, sir, this morning," answered the driver. "Gentleman of his appearance, anyway, sir—that's a fact!"

Mr. Tertius glanced at Peggie, who was intently watching the caller.

"Ah!" he said, turning again to the driver, "you think you drove either Mr. Herapath or a gentleman of his appearance this morning. You did not know Mr. Herapath by sight, then?"

"No, sir. I've only just come into this part—came for the first time yesterday. But I'm as certain——"

"Just tell us all about it," said Mr. Tertius, interrupting him. "Tell us in your own way. Everything, you know."

"Ain't so much to tell, sir," responded the driver. "All the same, soon's I'd seen this piece in the paper just now I said to myself, 'I'd best go round to Portman Square and tell what I do know,' I says. And it's like this, sir—I come on this part yesterday—last night it was. My taxi belongs to a man as keeps half a dozen, and he put me on to night work, this end of Oxford Street. Well, it 'ud be just about a quarter to two this morning when a tall, well-built gentleman comes out of Orchard Street and made for my cab. I jumps down and opens the door for him. 'You know St. Mary Abbot's Church, Kensington?' he says as he got in. 'Drive me down there and pull up at the gate.' So, of course, I ran him down, and there he got out, give me five bob, and off he went. That's it, sir."

"And when he got out, which way did he go?" asked Mr. Tertius.

"West, sir—along the High Street, past the Town Hall," promptly answered the driver. "And there he crossed the road. I see him cross, because I stopped there a minute or two after he'd got out, tinkering at my engine."

"Can you tell us what this gentleman was like in appearance?" asked Mr. Tertius.

"Well, sir, not so much as regards his face," answered the driver. "I didn't look at him, not particular, in that way—besides, he was wearing one of them overcoats with a big fur collar to it, and he'd the collar turned high up about his neck and cheeks, and his hat—one of them slouched, soft hats, like so many gentlemen wears nowadays sir—was well pulled down. But from what bit I see of him, sir, I should say he was a fresh-coloured gentleman."

"Tall and well built, you say?" observed Mr. Tertius.

"Yes, sir—fine-made gentleman—pretty near six feet, I should have called him," replied the driver. "Little bit inclined to stoutness, like."

Mr. Tertius turned to Peggie.

"I believe you have some recent photographs of Mr. Herapath," he said. "You might fetch them and let me see if our friend here can recognize them. You didn't notice anything else about your fare?" he went on, after Peggie had left the room. "Anything that excited your attention, eh?"

The driver, after examining the pattern of the carpet for one minute and studying the ceiling for another, slowly shook his head. But he then suddenly started into something like activity.

"Yes, there was, sir, now I come to think of it!" he exclaimed. "I hadn't thought of it until now, but now you mention it, there was. I noticed he'd a particularly handsome diamond ring on his left hand—an extra fine one, too, it was."

"Ah!" said Mr. Tertius. "A very fine diamond ring on his left hand? Now, how did you come to see that?"

"He rested that hand on the side of the door as he was getting in, sir, and I noticed how it flashed," answered the driver. "There was a lamp right against us, you see, sir."

"I see," said Mr. Tertius. "He wasn't wearing gloves, then?"

"He hadn't a glove on that hand, sir. He was carrying some papers in it—a sort of little roll of papers."

"Ah!" murmured Mr. Tertius. "A diamond ring—and a little roll of papers." He got up from his chair and put a hand in his pocket. "Now, my friend," he went on, chinking some coins as he withdrew it, "you haven't told this to any one else, I suppose?"

"No, sir," answered the driver. "Came straight here, sir."

"There's a couple of sovereigns for your trouble," said Mr. Tertius, "and there'll be more for you if you do what I tell you to do. At present—that is, until I give you leave—don't say a word of this to a soul. Not even to the police—yet. In fact, not a word to them until I say you may. Keep your mouth shut until I tell you to open it—I shall know where to find you. If you want me, keep an eye open for me in the square outside, or in the street. When the young lady comes back with the photographs, don't mention the ring to her. This is a very queer business, and I don't want too much said just yet. Do as I tell you, and I'll see you're all right. Understand?"

The driver pocketed his sovereigns, and touched his forehead with a knowing look.

"All right, sir," he said. "I understand. Depend on me, sir—I shan't say a word without your leave."

Peggie came in just then with a half a dozen cabinet photographs in her hand. One by one she exhibited them to the driver.

"Do you recognize any of these?" she asked.

The driver shook his head doubtingly until Peggie showed him a half-length of her uncle in outdoor costume. Then his eyes lighted up.

"Couldn't swear as to the features, miss," he exclaimed. "But I'd take my 'davy about the coat and the hat! That's what the gentleman was wearing as I drove this morning—take my Gospel oath on it."

"He recognizes the furred overcoat and the soft hat," murmured Mr. Tertius. "Very good—very good! All right, my man—we are much obliged to you."

He went out into the hall with the driver, and had another word in secret with him before the footman opened the door. As the door closed Mr. Tertius turned slowly back to the study. And as he turned he muttered a word or two and smiled cynically.

"A diamond ring!" he said. "Jacob Herapath never wore a diamond ring in his life!"

Table of Contents

CHAPTER VII

is there a will?

When Triffitt hurried off with his precious budget of news Selwood lingered on the step of the office watching his retreating figure, and wondering about the new idea which the reporter had put into his mind. It was one of those ideas which instantly arouse all sorts of vague, sinister possibilities, but Selwood found himself unable to formulate anything definite out of any of them. Certainly, if Mr. Herapath died at, or before, twelve o'clock midnight, he could not have been in Portman Square at one o'clock in the morning! Yet, according to all the evidence, he had been there, in his own house, in his own study. His coachman had seen him in the act of entering the house; there was proof that he had eaten food and drunk liquor in the house. The doctor must have made a mistake—and yet, Selwood remembered, he had spoken very positively. But if he had not made a mistake?—what then? How could Jacob Herapath be lying dead in his office at Kensington and nibbling at a sandwich in Portman Square at one and the same hour? Clearly there was something wrong, something deeply mysterious, something——

At that point of his surmisings and questionings Selwood heard himself called by Barthorpe Herapath, and he turned to see that gentleman standing in the hall dangling a bunch of keys, which Selwood instantly recognized.

"We have just found these keys," said Barthorpe. "You remember the inspector said he found no keys in my uncle's pockets? We found these pushed away under some loose papers on the desk. It looks as if he'd put them on the desk when he sat down, and had displaced them when he fell out of his chair. Of course, they're his—perhaps you recognize them?"

"Yes," answered Selwood, abruptly. "They're his."

"I want you to come with me while I open his private safe," continued Barthorpe. "At junctures like these there are always things that have got to be done. Now, did you ever hear my uncle speak of his will—whether he'd made one, and, if so, where he'd put it? Hear anything?"

"Nothing," replied Selwood. "I never heard him mention such a thing."

"Well, between ourselves," said Barthorpe, "neither did I. I've done all his legal work for him for a great many years—ever since I began to practice, in fact—and so far as I know, he never made a will. More than once I've suggested that he should make one, but like most men who are in good health and spirits, he always put it off. However, we must look over his papers both here and at Portman Square."

Selwood made no comment. He silently followed Barthorpe into the private room in which his late employer had so strangely met his death. The body had been removed by that time, and everything bore its usual aspect, save for the presence of the police inspector and the detective, who were peering about them in the mysterious fashion associated with their calling. The inspector was looking narrowly at the fastenings of the two windows and apparently debating the chances of entrance and exit from them; the detective, armed with a magnifying glass, was examining the edges of the door, the smooth backs of chairs, even the surface of the desk, presumably for finger-marks.

"I shan't disturb you," said Barthorpe, genially. "Mr. Selwood and I merely wish to investigate the contents of this safe. There's no likelihood of finding what I'm particularly looking for in any of his drawers in that desk," he continued, turning to Selwood. "I knew enough of his habits to know that anything that's in there will be of a purely business nature—referring to the estate. If he did keep anything that's personal here, it'll be in that safe. Now, which is the key? Do you know?"

He handed the bunch of keys to Selwood. And Selwood, who was feeling strangely apathetic about the present proceedings, took them mechanically and glanced carelessly at them. Then he started.

"There's a key missing!" he exclaimed, suddenly waking into interest. "I know these keys well enough—Mr. Herapath was constantly handing them to me. There ought to be six keys here—the key of this safe, the key of the safe at Portman Square, the latch-key for this office, the key of this room, the latch-key of the house, and a key of a safe at the Alpha Safe Deposit place. That one—the Safe Deposit key—is missing."

Barthorpe knitted his forehead, and the two police officials paused in their tasks and drew near the desk at which Selwood was standing.

"Are you certain of that?" asked Barthorpe.

"Sure!" answered Selwood. "As I say, I've been handling these keys every day since I came to Mr. Herapath."

"When did you handle them last?"

"Yesterday afternoon: not so very long before Mr. Herapath went down to the House. That was in Portman Square. He gave them to me to get some papers out of the safe there."

"Was that Safe Deposit key there at that time?"

"They were all there—all six. I'm certain of it," asserted Selwood. "This is the key of this safe," he went on, selecting one.

"Open the safe, then," said Barthorpe. "Another safe at the Alpha, eh?" he continued, musingly. "I never knew he had a safe there. Did you ever know him to use it?"

"I've been to it myself," answered Selwood. "I took some documents there and deposited them, two days ago. There's not very much in this safe," he went on, throwing open the door. "It's not long since I tidied it out—at his request. So far as I know, there are no private papers of any note there. He never made much use of this safe—in my presence, at any rate."

"Well, we'll see what there is, anyhow," remarked Barthorpe. He began to examine the contents of the safe methodically, taking the various papers and documents out one by one and laying them in order on a small table which Selwood wheeled up to his side. Within twenty minutes he had gone through everything, and he began to put the papers back.

"No will there," he murmured. "We'll go on to Portman Square now, Mr. Selwood. After all, it's much more likely that he'd keep his will in the safe at his own house—if he made one. But I don't believe he ever made a will."

Mr. Tertius and Peggie Wynne were still in the study when Barthorpe and Selwood drove up to the house. The driver of the taxi-cab had just gone away, and Mr. Tertius was discussing his information with Peggie. Hearing Barthorpe's voice in the hall he gave her a warning glance.

"Quick!" he said hurriedly. "Attend to what I say! Not a word to your cousin about the man who has just left us. At present I don't want Mr. Barthorpe Herapath to know what he told us. Be careful, my dear—not a word! I'll tell you why later on—but at present, silence—strict silence!"

Barthorpe Herapath came bustling into the room, followed by Selwood, who, as it seemed to Peggie, looked utterly unwilling for whatever task might lay before him. At sight of Mr. Tertius, Barthorpe came to a sudden halt and frowned.

"I don't want to discuss matters further, Mr. Tertius," he said coldly. "I thought I had given you a hint already. My cousin and I have private matters to attend to, and I shall be obliged if you'll withdraw. You've got private rooms of your own in this house, I believe—at any rate, until things are settled—and it will be best if you keep to them."

Mr. Tertius, who had listened to this unmoved, turned to Peggie.

"Do you wish me to go away?" he asked quietly.

Barthorpe turned on him with an angry scowl.

"It's not a question of what Miss Wynne wishes, but of what I order," he burst out. "If you've any sense of fitness, you'll know that until my uncle's will is found and his wishes ascertained I'm master here, Mr. Tertius, and——"

"You're not my master, Barthorpe," exclaimed Peggie, with a sudden flash of spirit. "I know what my uncle's wishes were as regards Mr. Tertius, and I intend to respect them. I've always been mistress of this house since my uncle brought me to it, and I intend to be until I find I've no right to be. Mr. Tertius, you'll please to stop where you are!"

"I intend to," said Mr. Tertius, calmly. "I never had any other intention. Mr. Barthorpe Herapath, I believe, will hardly use force to compel me to leave the room."

Barthorpe bit his lips as he glanced from one to the other.

"Oh!" he said. "So that's how things are? Very good, Mr. Tertius. No, I shan't use physical force. But mind I don't use a little moral force—a slight modicum of that would be enough for you, I'm thinking!"

"Do I understand that you are using threatening language to me?" asked Mr. Tertius, mildly.

Barthorpe sneered, and turned to Selwood.

"We'll open this safe now," he said. "You know which is the key, I suppose," he went on, glaring at Peggie, who had retreated to the hearthrug and was evidently considerably put out by her cousin's behaviour. "I suppose you never heard my uncle mention a will? We've searched his private safe at the office and there's nothing there. Personally, I don't believe he ever made a will—I never heard of it. And I think he'd have told me if——"

Mr. Tertius broke in upon Barthorpe's opinions with a dry cough.

"It may save some unnecessary trouble if I speak at this juncture," he said. "There is a will."

Barthorpe's ruddy cheeks paled in spite of his determined effort to appear unconcerned. He twisted round on Mr. Tertius with a startled eye and twitching lips.

"You—you say there is a will!" he exclaimed. "You say—what do you know about it?"

"When it was made, where it was made, where it now is," answered Mr. Tertius.

"Where it now is!" repeated Barthorpe. "Where it now—is! And where is it, I should like to know?"

Mr. Tertius, who had gone up to Peggie, laid his hand reassuringly on her arm.

"Don't be afraid, my dear," he whispered. "Perhaps," he continued, glancing at Barthorpe, "I had better tell you when and where it was made. About six months ago—in this room. One day Mr. Herapath called me in here. He had his then secretary, Mr. Burchill, with him. He took a document out of a drawer, told us that it was his will, signed it in our joint presence, and we witnessed his signature in each other's presence. He then placed the will in an envelope, which he sealed. I do not know the terms of the will—but I know where the will is."

Barthorpe's voice sounded strangely husky as he got out one word:

"Where?"

Mr. Tertius took Peggie by the elbow and led her across the room to a recess in which stood an ancient oak bureau.

"This old desk," he said, "belonged, so he always told me, to Jacob's great-grandfather. There is a secret drawer in it. Here it is—concealed behind another drawer. You put this drawer out—so—and here is the secret one. And here—where I saw Jacob Herapath put it—is the will."

Barthorpe, who had followed these proceedings with almost irrepressible eagerness, thrust forward a shaking hand. But Mr. Tertius quietly handed the sealed envelope to Peggie.

"This envelope," he remarked, "is addressed to Miss Wynne."

Barthorpe made an effort and controlled himself.

"Open it!" he said hoarsely. "Open it!"

Peggie fumbled with the seal of the envelope and then, with a sudden impulse, passed it to Selwood.

"Mr. Selwood!" she exclaimed imploringly. "You—I can't. You open it, and—"

"And let him read it," added Mr. Tertius.

Selwood, whose nerves had been strung to a high pitch of excitement by this scene, hastily slit open the envelope, and drew out a folded sheet of foolscap paper. He saw at a glance that there was very little to read. His voice trembled slightly as he began a recital of the contents.

"'This is the last will of me, Jacob Herapath, of 500, Portman Square, London, in the County of Middlesex. I give, devise, and bequeath everything of which I die possessed, whether in real or personal estate, absolutely to my niece, Margaret Wynne, now resident with me at the above address, and I appoint the said Margaret Wynne the sole executor of this my will. And I revoke all former wills and codicils. Dated this eighteenth day of April, 1912.

"'Jacob Herapath.'"

Selwood paused there, and a sudden silence fell—to be as suddenly broken by a sharp question from Barthorpe.

"The Witnesses?" he said. "The witnesses!"

Selwood glanced at the further paragraph which he had not thought it necessary to read.

"Oh, yes!" he said. "It's witnessed all right." And he went on reading.

"'Signed by the testator in the presence of us both present at the same time who in his presence and in the presence of each other have hereunto set our names as witnesses.

"'John Christopher Tertius, of 500, Portman Square, London: Gentleman.

"'Frank Burchill, of 331, Upper Seymour Street, London: Secretary.'"

As Selwood finished, he handed the will to Peggie, who in her turn hastily gave it to Mr. Tertius. For a moment nobody spoke. Then Barthorpe made a step forward.

"Let me see that!" he said, in a strangely quiet voice. "I don't want to handle it—hold it up!"

For another moment he stood gazing steadily, intently, at the signatures at the foot of the document. Then, without a word or look, he twisted sharply on his heel, and walked swiftly out of the room and the house.

Table of Contents

CHAPTER VIII

the second witness

If any close observer had walked away with Barthorpe Herapath from the house in Portman Square and had watched his face and noted his manner, that observer would have said that his companion looked like a man who was either lost in a profound day-dream or had just received a shock that had temporarily deprived him of all but the mechanical faculties. And in point of strict fact, Barthorpe was both stunned by the news he had just received and plunged into deep speculation by a certain feature of it. He hurried along, scarcely knowing where he was going—but he was thinking all the same. And suddenly he pulled himself up and found that he had turned down Portman Street and was already in the thick of Oxford Street's busy crowds. A passer-by into whom he jostled in his absent-mindedness snarled angrily, bidding him look where he was going—that pulled Barthorpe together and he collected his wits, asking himself what he wanted. The first thing that met his gaze on this recovery was a little Italian restaurant and he straightway made for the door.

"This is what I want," he muttered. "Some place in which to sit down and think calmly."

He slipped into a quiet corner as soon as he had entered the restaurant, summoned a waiter with a glance, and for a moment concentrated his attention on the bill of fare which the man put before him. That slight mental exercise restored him; when the waiter had taken his simple order and gone away, Barthorpe was fully himself again. And finding himself in as satisfactory a state of privacy as he could desire, with none to overlook or spy on him, he drew from an inner pocket a letter-case which he had taken from Jacob Herapath's private safe at the estate office and into which he had cast a hurried glance before leaving Kensington for Portman Square.

From this letter-case he now drew a letter, and as he unfolded it he muttered a word or two.

"Frank Burchill, 331, Upper Seymour Street," he said. "Um—but not Upper Seymour Street any longer, I think. Now let's see what it all is—what it all means I've got to find out."

The sheet of paper which he was handling was of the sort used by typists, but the letter itself was written by hand, and Barthorpe recognized the penmanship as that of his uncle's ex-secretary, Burchill, second witness to the will which had just been exhibited to him. Then he read, slowly and carefully, what Burchill had written to Jacob Herapath—written, evidently, only a few days previously. For there was the date, plain enough.

"35c, Calengrove Mansions,
"Maida Vale, W.
"*November 11th*, 19—.
"Dear Sir,
"I don't know that I am particularly surprised that you have up to now entirely ignored my letters of the 1st and the 5th instant. You probably think that I am not a person about whom any one need take much trouble; a mean cur, perhaps, who can do no more than snap at a mastiff's heels. I am very well aware (having had the benefit of a year's experience of your character and temperament) that you have very little respect for unmoneyed people and are contemptuous of their ability to interfere with the moneyed. But in that matter you are mistaken. And to put matters plainly, it will pay you far better to keep me a friend than to transform me into an enemy. Therefore I ask you to consider well and deeply the next sentence of this letter—which I will underline.

"I am in full possession of the secret which you have taken such vast pains to keep for fifteen years.

"I think you are quite competent to read my meaning, and I now confidently expect to hear that you will take pleasure in obliging me in the way which I indicated to you in my previous letters.

"Yours faithfully,
"Frank Burchill."

Barthorpe read this communication three times, pausing over every sentence, seeking to read the meanings, the implications, the subtly veiled threat. When he folded the square sheet and replaced it in the letter-case he half spoke one word:

"Blackmail!"

Then, staring in apparent idleness about the little restaurant, with its gilt-framed mirrors, its red, plush-covered seats, its suggestion of foreign atmosphere and custom, he idly drummed the tips of his fingers on the table, and thought. Naturally, he thought of the writer of the letter. Of course, he said to himself, of course he knew Burchill. Burchill had been Jacob Herapath's private secretary for rather more than a year, and it was now about six months since Jacob had got rid of him. He, Barthorpe, remembered very well why Jacob had quietly dismissed Burchill. One day Jacob had said to him, with a dry chuckle:

"I'm getting rid of that secretary of mine—it won't do."

"What won't do?" Barthorpe had asked.

"He's beginning to make eyes at Peggie," Jacob had answered with another chuckle, "and though Peggie's a girl of sense, that fellow's too good looking to have about a house. I never ought to have had him. However—he goes."

Barthorpe, as he ate the cutlets and sipped the half-bottle of claret which the waiter presently brought him, speculated on these facts and memories. He was not very sure about Burchill's antecedents: he believed he was a young man of good credentials and high respectability—personally, he had always wondered why old Jacob Herapath, a practical business man, should have taken as a private secretary a fellow who looked, dressed, spoke, and behaved like a play-actor. As it all came within the scope of things he mused on Burchill and his personal appearance, calling up the ex-secretary's graceful and slender figure, his oval, olive-tinted face, his large, dark, lustrous eyes, his dark, curling hair, his somewhat affected dress, his tall, wide-brimmed hats, his taper fingers, his big, wide-ended cravats. It had once amused Barthorpe—and many other people—to see Jacob Herapath and his secretary together; nevertheless, Jacob had always spoken of Burchill as being thoroughly capable, painstaking, thorough and diligent. His airs and graces Jacob put down as a young man's affectations—yet there came the time when they suited Jacob no longer.

"I catch him talking too much to Peggie," he had added, in that conversation of which Barthorpe was thinking. "Better get rid of him before they pass the too-much stage."

So Burchill had gone, and Barthorpe had heard no more of him until now. But what he had heard now was a revelation. Burchill had witnessed a will of Jacob Herapath's, which, if good and valid and the only will in existence, would leave him, Barthorpe, a ruined man. Burchill had written a letter to Jacob Herapath asking for some favour, reward, compensation, as the price of his silence about a secret. What secret? Barthorpe could not even guess at it—but Burchill had said, evidently knowing what he was talking about, that Jacob Herapath had taken vast pains to keep it for fifteen years.

By the time Barthorpe had finished his lunch he had come to the conclusion that there was only one thing for him to do. He must go straight to Calengrove Mansions and interview Mr. Frank Burchill. In one way or another he must make sure of him, or, rather—though it was really the same thing—sure of what he could tell. And on the way there he would make sure of something else—in order to do which he presently commissioned a taxi-cab and bade its driver go first to 331, Upper Seymour Street.

The domestic who answered Barthorpe's double knock at that house shook her head when he designedly asked for Mr. Frank Burchill. Nobody of that name, she said. But on being assured that there once had been a lodger of that name in residence there, she observed that she would fetch her mistress, and disappeared to return with an elderly lady who also shook her head at sight of the caller.

"Mr. Burchill left here some time ago," she said. "Nearly six months. I don't know where he is."

"Did he leave no address to which his letters were to be sent?" asked Barthorpe, affecting surprise.

"He said there'd be no letters coming—and there haven't been," answered the landlady. "And I've neither seen nor heard of him since he went."

Something in her manner suggested to Barthorpe that she had no desire to renew acquaintance with her former lodger. This sent Barthorpe away well satisfied. It was precisely what he wanted. The three people whom he had left in Portman Square in all probability knew no other address than this at which to seek for Burchill when he was wanted; they would seek him there eventually and get no news. Luckily for himself, Barthorpe knew where he was to be found, and he went straight off up Edgware Road to find him.

Calengrove Mansions proved to be a new block of flats in the dip of Maida Vale; 35c was a top flat in a wing which up to that stage of its existence did not appear to be much sought after by would-be tenants. It was some time before Barthorpe succeeded in getting an answer to his ring and knock; when at last the door was opened Burchill himself looked out upon him, yawning, and in a dressing-gown. And narrowly and searchingly as Barthorpe glanced at Burchill he could not see a trace of unusual surprise or embarrassment in his face. He looked just as any man might look who receives an unexpected caller.

"Oh!" he said. "Mr. Barthorpe Herapath! Come in—do. I'm a bit late—a good bit late, in fact. You see, I'm doing dramatic criticism now, and there was an important _première_ last night at the Hyperion, and I had to do a full column, and so—but that doesn't interest you. Come in, pray."

He led the way into a small sitting-room, drew forward an easy-chair, and reaching down a box of cigarettes from the mantelpiece offered its contents to his visitor. Barthorpe, secretly wondering if all this unconcerned behaviour was natural or merely a bit of acting, took a cigarette and dropped into the chair.

"I don't suppose you thought of seeing me when you opened your door, Burchill?" he remarked good-humouredly, as he took the match which his host had struck for him. "Last man in the world you thought of seeing, eh?"

Burchill calmly lighted a cigarette for himself before he answered.

"Well," he said at last, "I don't know—you never know who's going to turn up. But to be candid, I didn't expect to see you, and I don't know why you've come."

Barthorpe slowly produced the letter-case from his pocket, took Burchill's letter from it, and held it before him.

"That's what brought me here," he said significantly. "That! Of course, you recognize it."

Burchill glanced at the letter without turning a hair. If he was merely acting, thought Barthorpe, he was doing it splendidly, and instead of writing dramatic criticism he ought to put on the sock and buskins himself. But somehow he began to believe that Burchill was not acting. And he was presently sure of it when Burchill laughed—contemptuously.

"Oh!" said Burchill. "Ah! So Mr. Jacob Herapath employs legal assistance—your assistance—in answering me? Foolish—foolish! Or, since that is, perhaps, too strong a word—indiscreet. Indiscreet—and unnecessary. Say so, pray, to Mr. Jacob Herapath."

Barthorpe remained silent a moment; then he put the letter back in the case and gave Burchill a sharp steady look.

"Good gracious, man!" he said quietly. "Are you pretending? Or—haven't you heard? Say—that—to Jacob Herapath? Jacob Herapath is dead!"

Burchill certainly started at that. What was more he dropped his cigarette, and when he straightened himself from picking it up his face was flushed a little.

"Upon my honour!" he exclaimed. "I didn't know. Dead! When? It must have been sudden."

"Sudden!" said Barthorpe. "Sudden? He was murdered!"

There was no doubt that this surprised Burchill. At any rate, he showed all the genuine signs of surprise. He stood staring at Barthorpe for a full minute of silence, and when he spoke his voice had lost something of its usual affectation.

"Murdered?" he said. "Murdered! Are you sure of that? You are? Good heavens!—no, I've heard nothing. But I've not been out since two o'clock this morning, so how could I hear?

Murdered——" he broke off sharply and stared at his visitor. "And you came to me—why?"

"I came to ask you if you remember witnessing my uncle's will," replied Barthorpe promptly. "Give me a plain answer. Do you remember?"

Table of Contents

CHAPTER IX

greek against greek

At this direct question, Burchill, who had been standing on the hearthrug since Barthorpe entered the room, turned away and took a seat in the corner of a lounge opposite his visitor. He gave Barthorpe a peculiarly searching look before he spoke, and as soon as he replied Barthorpe knew that here was a man who was not readily to be drawn.

"Oh," said Burchill, "so I am supposed to have witnessed a will made by Mr. Jacob Herapath, am I?"

Barthorpe made a gesture of impatience.

"Don't talk rot!" he said testily. "A man either knows that he witnessed a will or knows that he didn't witness a will."

"Excuse me," returned Burchill, "I don't agree with that proposition. I can imagine it quite possible that a man may think he has witnessed a will when he has done nothing of the sort. I can also imagine it just as possible that a man may have really witnessed a will when he thought he was signing some much less important document. Of course, you're a lawyer, and I'm not. But I believe that what I have just said is much more in accordance with what we may call the truth of life than what you've said."

"If a man sees another man sign a document and witnesses the signature together with a third man who had been present throughout, what would you say was being done?" asked Barthorpe, sneeringly. "Come, now?"

"I quite apprehend your meaning," replied Burchill. "You put it very cleverly."

"Then why don't you answer my question?" demanded Barthorpe.

Burchill laughed softly.

"Why not answer mine?" he said. "However, I'll ask it in another and more direct form. Have you seen my signature as witness to a will made by Jacob Herapath?"

"Yes," replied Barthorpe.

"Are you sure it was my signature?" asked Burchill.

Barthorpe lifted his eyes and looked searchingly at his questioner. But Burchill's face told him nothing. What was more, he was beginning to feel that he was not going to get anything out of Burchill that Burchill did not want to tell. He remained silent, and again Burchill laughed.

"You see," he said, "I can suppose all sorts of things. I can suppose, for example, that there's such a thing as forging a signature—two signatures—three signatures to a will—or, indeed, to any other document. Don't you think that instead of asking me a direct question like this that you'd better wait until this will comes before the—is it the Probate Court?—and then let some of the legal gentlemen ask me if that—that!—is my signature? I'm only putting it to you, you know. But perhaps you'd like to tell me—all about it?" He paused, looking carefully at Barthorpe, and as Barthorpe made no immediate answer, he went on speaking in a lower, softer tone. "All about it," he repeated insinuatingly. "Ah!"

Barthorpe suddenly flung his cigarette in the hearth with a gesture that implied decision.

"I will!" he exclaimed. "It may be the shortest way out. Very well—listen, then. I tell you my uncle was murdered at his office about—well, somewhere between twelve and three o'clock this morning. Naturally, after the preliminaries were over, I wanted to find out if he'd made a will—naturally, I say."

"Naturally, you would," murmured Burchill.

"I didn't believe he had," continued Barthorpe. "But I examined his safe at the office, and I was going to examine that in his study at Portman Square when Tertius said in the presence of my cousin, myself, and Selwood, your successor, that there was a will, and produced one from a secret drawer in an old bureau——"

"A secret drawer in an old bureau!" murmured Burchill. "How deeply interesting for all of you!—quite dramatic. Yes?"

"Which, on being inspected," continued Barthorpe, "proved to be a holograph——"

"Pardon," interrupted Burchill, "a holograph? Now, I am very ignorant. What is a holograph?"

"A holograph will is a will entirely written in the handwriting of the person who makes it," replied Barthorpe.

"I see. So this was written out by Mr. Jacob Herapath, and witnessed by—whom?" asked Burchill.

"Tertius as first witness, and you as second," answered Barthorpe. "Now then, I've told you all about it. What are you going to tell me? Come—did you witness this will or not? Good gracious, man!—don't you see what a serious thing it is?"

"How can I when I don't know the contents of the will?" asked Burchill. "You haven't told me that—yet."

Barthorpe swallowed an exclamation of rage.

"Contents!" he exclaimed. "He left everything—everything!—to my cousin! Everything to her."

"And nothing to you," said Burchill, accentuating his habitual drawl. "Really, how infernally inconsiderate! Yes—now I see that it is serious. But—only for you."

Barthorpe glared angrily at him and began to growl, almost threateningly. And Burchill spoke, soothingly and quietly.

"Don't," he said. "It does no good, you know. Serious—yes. Most serious—for you, as I said. But remember—only serious for you if the will is—good. Eh?"

Barthorpe jumped to his feet and thrust his hands in his pockets. He began to pace the room.

"Hang me if I know what you mean, Burchill!" he said. "Is that your signature on that will or not?"

"How can I say until I see it?" asked Burchill, with seeming innocence. "Let's postpone matters until then. By the by, did Mr. Tertius say that it was my signature?"

"What do you mean!" exclaimed Barthorpe. "Why, of course, he said that he and you witnessed the will!"

"Ah, to be sure, he would say so," assented Burchill. "Of course. Foolish of me to ask. It's quite evident that we must postpone matters until this will is—what do you call it?—presented, propounded—what is it?—for probate. Let's turn to something else. My letter to your uncle, for instance. Of course, as you've got it, you've read it."

Barthorpe sat down again and stared.

"You're a cool customer, Master Burchill!" he said. "By Jove, you are! You're playing some game. What is it?"

Burchill smiled deprecatingly.

"What's your own?" he asked. "Or, if that's too pointed a question at present, suppose we go back to—my letter? Want to ask me anything about it?"

Barthorpe again drew the letter from the case. He affected to re-read it, while Burchill narrowly watched him.

"What," asked Barthorpe at last, "what was it that you wanted my uncle to oblige you with? A loan?"

"If it's necessary to call it anything," replied Burchill suavely, "you can call it a—well, say a donation. That sounds better—it's more dignified."

"I don't suppose it matters much what it's called," said Barthorpe drily. "I should say, from the tone of your letter, that most people would call it——"

"Yes, but not polite people," interrupted Burchill, "and you and I are—or must be—polite. So we'll say donation. The fact is, I want to start a newspaper—weekly—devoted to the arts. I thought your uncle—now, unfortunately, deceased—would finance it. I didn't want much, you know."

"How much?" asked Barthorpe. "The amount isn't stated in this letter."

"It was stated in the two previous letters," replied Burchill. "Oh, not much. Ten thousand."

"The price of your silence, eh?" suggested Barthorpe.

"Dirt cheap!" answered Burchill.

Barthorpe folded up the letter once more and put it away. He helped himself to another cigarette and lighted it before he spoke again. Then he leaned forward confidentially.

"What is the secret?" he asked.

Burchill stated and assumed an air of virtuous surprise.

"My dear fellow!" he said. "That's against all the rules—all the rules of——"

"Of shady society," sneered Barthorpe. "Confound it, man, what do you beat about the bush so much for? Hang it, I've a pretty good notion of you, and I daresay you've your own of me. Why can't you tell me?"

"You forget that I offered not to tell for—ten thousand pounds," said Burchill. "Therefore I should want quite as much for telling. If you carry ten thousand in cash on you——"

"Is there a secret?" asked Barthorpe. "Sober earnest, now?"

"I have no objection to answering that question," replied Burchill. "There is!"

"And you want ten thousand pounds for it?" suggested Barthorpe.

"Pardon me—I want a good deal more for it, under the present much altered circumstances," said Burchill quietly. "There is an old saying that circumstances alter cases. It's true—they do. I would have taken ten thousand pounds from your uncle to hold my tongue—true. But—the case is altered by his death."

Barthorpe pondered over this definite declaration for a minute or two. Then, lowering his voice, he said:

"Looks uncommonly like—blackmail! And that——"

"Pardon me again," interrupted Burchill. "No blackmail at all—in my view. I happen to possess information of a certain nature, and——"

Barthorpe interrupted in his turn.

"The thing is," he said, "the only thing is—how long are you and I going to beat about the bush? Are you going to tell me if you signed that will I told you of?"

"Certainly not before I've seen it," answered Burchill promptly.

"Will you tell me then?"

"That entirely depends."

"On—what?"

"Circumstances!"

"Have the circumstances got anything to do with this secret?"

"Everything! More than anything—now."

"Now—what?"

"Now that Jacob Herapath is dead. Look here!" continued Burchill, leaning forward and speaking impressively. "Take my counsel. Leave this for the moment and come to see me—now, when? Tonight. Come tonight. I've nothing to do. Come at ten o'clock. Then—I'll be in a position to say a good deal more. How will that do?"

"That'll do," answered Barthorpe after a moment's consideration. "Tonight, here, at ten o 'clock."

He got up and made for the door. Burchill got up too, and for a moment both men glanced at each other. Then Burchill spoke.

"I suppose you've no idea who murdered your uncle?" he said.

"Not the slightest!" exclaimed Barthorpe. "Have you?"

"None! Of course—the police are on the go?"

"Oh, of course!"

"All right," said Burchill. "Tonight, then."

He opened the door for his visitor, nodded to him, as he passed out, and when he had gone sat down in the easy chair which Barthorpe had vacated and for half an hour sat immobile, thinking. At the end of that half-hour he rose, went into his bedroom, made an elaborate toilet, went out, found a taxi-cab, and drove off to Portman Square.

Table of Contents

CHAPTER X

mr. benjamin halfpenny

When Barthorpe Herapath left his cousin, Mr. Tertius, and Selwood in company with the newly discovered will, and walked swiftly out of the house and away from Portman Square, he passed without seeing it a quiet, yet smartly appointed coupé brougham which came round the corner from Portman Street and pulled up at the door which Barthorpe had just quitted. From it at once descended an elderly gentleman, short, stout, and rosy, who bustled up the steps of the Herapath mansion and appeared to fume and fret until his summons was responded to. When the door was opened to him he bustled inside at the same rate, rapped out the inquiry, "Miss Wynne at home?—Miss Wynne at home?" several times without waiting for a reply, and never ceased in his advance to the door of the study, into which he precipitated himself panting and blowing, as if he had run hard all the way from his original starting-point. The three people standing on the hearthrug turned sharply and two of them uttered cries which betokened pleasure mixed with relief.

"Mr. Halfpenny!" exclaimed Peggie, almost joyfully. "How good of you to come!"

"We had only just spoken—were only just speaking of you," remarked Mr. Tertius. "In fact—yes, Mr. Selwood and I were thinking of going round to your offices to see if you were in town."

The short, stout, and rosy gentleman who, as soon as he had got well within the room, began to unswathe his neck from a voluminous white silk muffler, now completed his task and advancing upon Peggie solemnly kissed her on both cheeks, held her away from him, looked at her, kissed her again, and then patted her on the shoulder. This done, he shook hands solemnly with Mr. Tertius, bowed to Selwood, took off his spectacles and proceeded to polish them with a highly-coloured bandana handkerchief which he produced from the tail of his overcoat. This operation concluded, he restored the spectacles to his nose, sat down, placed his hands, palm downwards, on his plump knees and solemnly inspected everybody.

"My dear friends!" he said in a hushed, deep voice. "My dear, good friends! This dreadful, awful, most afflicting news! I heard it but three-quarters of an hour ago—at the office, to which I happened by mere chance, to have come up for the day. I immediately ordered out our brougham and drove here—to see if I could be of any use. You will command me, my dear friends, in anything that I can do. Not professionally, of course. No—in that respect you have Mr. Barthorpe Herapath. But—otherwise."

Mr. Tertius looked at Peggie.

"I don't know whether we shan't be glad of Mr. Halfpenny's professional services?" he said. "The truth is, Halfpenny, we were talking of seeing you professionally when you came in. That's one truth—another is that a will has been found—our poor friend's will, of course."

"God bless me!" exclaimed Mr. Halfpenny. "A will—our poor friend's will—has been found! But surely, Barthorpe, as nephew, and solicitor—eh?"

Again Mr. Tertius looked at Peggie.

"I suppose we'd better tell Mr. Halfpenny everything," he remarked. "Of course, Halfpenny, you'll understand that as soon as this dreadful affair was discovered and the first arrangements had been made, Barthorpe, as only male relative, began to search for a will. He resented any interference from me and was very rude to me, but when he came here and proposed to examine that safe, I told him at once that I knew of a will and where it was, though I didn't know its terms. And I immediately directed him to it, and we found it and read it a few minutes ago with the result that Barthorpe at once quitted the house—you must have passed him in the square."

"God bless us!" repeated Mr. Halfpenny. "I judge from that, then—but you had better show me this document."

Mr. Tertius at once produced the will, and Mr. Halfpenny, rising from his chair, marched across the room to one of the windows where he solemnly half-chanted every word from start to finish. This performance over, he carefully and punctiliously folded the document into its original lines, replaced it in its envelope, and grasping this firmly in his hand, resumed his seat and motioned everybody to attention.

"My dear Tertius!" he said. "Oblige me by narrating, carefully, briefly, your recollection of the circumstances under which your signature to this highly important document was obtained and made."

"Easily done," responded Mr. Tertius. "One night, some months ago, when our poor friend was at work here with his secretary, a Mr. Frank Burchill, he called me into the room, just as Burchill was about to leave. He said: 'I want you two to witness my signature to a paper.' He——"

"A moment," interrupted Mr. Halfpenny. "He said—'a paper.' Did he not say 'my will'?"

"Not before the two of us. He merely said a paper. He produced the paper—that paper, which you now hold. He let us see that it was covered with writing, but we did not see what the writing was. He folded it over, laid it, so folded, on that desk, and signed his name. Then we both signed it in the blank spaces which he indicated: I first, then Burchill. He then put it into an envelope—that envelope—and fastened it up. As regards that part of the proceedings," said Mr. Tertius, "that is all."

"There was, then, another part?" suggested Mr. Halfpenny.

"Yes," replied Mr. Tertius. "There was. Burchill then left—at once. I, too, was leaving the room when Jacob called me back. When we were alone, he said: 'That was my will that you've just witnessed. Never mind what's in it—I may alter it, or some of it, some day, but I don't think I shall. Now look here, I'm going to seal this envelope, and I'll show you where I put it when it's sealed.' He then sealed the envelope in two places, as you see, and afterwards, in my presence, placed it in a secret drawer, which I'll show to you now. And that done, he said: 'There, Tertius, you needn't mention that to anybody, unless I happen to be taken off suddenly.' And," concluded Mr. Tertius, as he motioned Mr. Halfpenny to accompany him to the old bureau, "I never, of course, did mention it until half an hour ago."

Mr. Halfpenny solemnly inspected the secret drawer, made no remark upon it, and reseated himself.

"Now," he said, "this Mr. Frank Burchill—the other witness? He left our old friend?"

"Some little time ago," replied Mr. Tertius.

"Still, we have his address on the will," said Mr. Halfpenny. "I shall call on Mr. Burchill at once—as soon as I leave here. There is, of course, no doubt as to the validity of this will. You said just now that Barthorpe left you as soon as he had seen it. Now, what did Barthorpe say about it?"

"Nothing!" answered Mr. Tertius. "He went away without a word—rushed away, in fact."

Mr. Halfpenny shook his head with profound solemnity.

"I am not in the least surprised to hear that," he observed. "Barthorpe naturally received a great shock. What I am surprised at is—the terms of the will. Nothing whatever to Barthorpe—his only male relative—his only brother's only son. Extraordinary! My dear," he continued, turning to Peggie, "can you account for this? Do you know of anything, any difference between them, anything at all which would make your uncle leave his nephew out of his will?"

"Nothing!" answered Peggie. "And I'm very troubled about it. Does it really mean that I get everything, and Barthorpe nothing?"

"That is the precise state of affairs," answered Mr. Halfpenny. "And it is all the more surprising when we bear in mind that you two are the only relations Jacob Herapath had, and that he was a rich man—a very rich man indeed. However, he doubtless had his reasons. And now, as I conclude you desire me to act for you, I shall take charge of this will and lock it up in my safe as soon as I return to the office. On my way, I shall call at Mr. Burchill's address and just have a word with him. Tertius, you had better come with me. And—yes, there is another thing that I should like to have done. Mr. Selwood—are you engaged on any business?"

"No," replied Selwood, who was secretly speculating on the meaning of the morning's strange events. "I have nothing to attend to."

"Then will you go to Mr. Barthorpe Herapath's office—in Craven Street, I think?—and see him personally and tell him that Mr. Benjamin Halfpenny is in town, has been acquainted with these matters by Mr. Tertius and Miss Wynne, and would esteem it a favour if he would call upon him before five o'clock. Thank you, Mr. Selwood. Now, Tertius, you and I will attend to our business."

Left alone, Peggie Wynne suddenly realized that the world had become a vastly different world to what it had seemed a few short hours before. This room, into which Jacob Herapath, bustling and busy, would never come again, was already a place of dread; nay, the whole house in which she had spent so many years of comfort and luxury suddenly assumed a strange atmosphere of distastefulness. It was true that her uncle had never spent much time in the house. An hour or two in the morning—yes, but by noon he had hurried off to some Committee at the House of Commons, and in session time she had never seen him again that day. But he had a trick of running in for a few minutes at intervals during the day; he would come for a cup of tea; sometimes he would contrive to dine at home; whether he was at home or not, his presence, always alert, masterful, active, seemed to be everywhere in the place. She could scarcely realize that she would never see him again. And as she stood looking at his vacant chair she made an effort to realize what it all really meant to her, and suddenly, for the first time in her life, she felt the meaning of the usually vague term—loneliness. In all practical essentials she was absolutely alone. So far as she knew she had no relations in the world but Barthorpe Herapath—and there was something—something shadowy and undefinable—about Barthorpe which she neither liked nor trusted. Moreover, she had caught a glimpse of Barthorpe's face as he turned from looking at the will and hurried away, and what she had seen had given her a strange feeling of fear and discomfort. Barthorpe, she knew, was not the sort of man to be crossed or thwarted or balked of his will, and now——

"Supposing Barthorpe should begin to hate me because all the money is mine?" she thought. "Then—why, then I should have no one! No one of my own flesh and blood, anyway. Of course, there's Mr. Tertius. But—I must see Barthorpe. I must tell him that I shall insist on sharing—if it's all mine, I can do that. And yet—why didn't Uncle Jacob divide it? Why did he leave Barthorpe—nothing?"

Still pondering sadly over these and kindred subjects Peggie went upstairs to a parlour of her own, a room in which she did as she liked and made into a den after her own taste. There, while the November afternoon deepened in shadow, she sat and thought still more deeply. And she was still plunged in thought when Kitteridge came softly into the room and presented a card. Peggie took it from the butler's salver and glanced half carelessly at it. Then she looked at Kitteridge with some concern.

"Mr. Burchill?" she said. "Here?"

"No, miss," answered Kitteridge. "Mr. Burchill desired me to present his most respectful sympathy, and to say that if he could be of any service to you or to the family, he begged that you would command him. His address is on this card, miss."

"Very kind of him," murmured Peggie, and laid the card aside on her writing-table. When Kitteridge had gone she picked it up and looked at it again. Burchill?—she had been thinking of him only a few minutes before the butler's entrance; thinking a good deal. And her thoughts had been disquieted and unhappy. Burchill was the last man in the world that she wished to have anything to do with, and the fact that his name appeared on Jacob Herapath's will had disturbed her more than she would have cared to admit.

Table of Contents

CHAPTER XI

Mr. Halfpenny, conducting Mr. Tertius to the coupé brougham, installed him in its further corner, got in himself and bade his coachman drive slowly to 331, Upper Seymour Street.

"I said slowly," he remarked as they moved gently away, "because I wanted a word with you before we see this young man. Tertius—what's the meaning of all this?"

Mr. Tertius groaned dolefully and shook his head.

"There is so much, Halfpenny," he answered, "that I don't quite know what you specifically mean by this. Do you mean———"

"I mean, first of all, Herapath's murder," said Mr. Halfpenny. "You think it is a case of murder?"

"I'm sure it's a case of murder—cold, calculated murder," replied Mr. Tertius, with energy. "Vile murder, Halfpenny."

"And, as far as you know, is there no clue?" asked the old lawyer. "There's nothing said or suggested in the newspapers. Haven't you any notion—hasn't Barthorpe any notion?"

Mr. Tertius remained silent for a while. The coupé brougham turned into Upper Seymour Street.

"I think," he said at last, "yes, I think that when we've made this call, I shall ask you to accompany me to my friend Cox-Raythwaite's, in Endsleigh Gardens—you know him, I believe. I've already seen him this morning and told him—something. When we get there, I'll tell it to you, and he shall show you—something. After that, we'll hear what your legal instinct suggests. It is my opinion, Halfpenny—I offer it with all deference, as a layman—that great, excessive caution is necessary. This case is extraordinary—very extraordinary. That is—in my opinion."

"It's an extraordinary thing that Jacob Herapath should have made that will," murmured Mr. Halfpenny reflectively. "Why Barthorpe should be entirely ignored is—to me—marvellous. And—it may be—significant. You never heard of any difference, quarrel, anything of that sort, between him and his uncle?"

"I have not the remotest notion as to what the relations were that existed between the uncle and the nephew," replied Mr. Tertius. "And though, as I have said, I knew that the will was in existence, I hadn't the remotest idea, the faintest notion, of its contents until we took it out of the sealed envelope an hour or so ago. But———" he paused and shook his head meaningly.

"Well?" said Mr. Halfpenny.

"I'm very sure, knowing Jacob as I did, that he had a purpose in making that will," answered Mr. Tertius. "He was not the man to do anything without good reasons. I think we are here."

The landlady of No. 331 opened its door herself to these two visitors. Her look of speculative interest on seeing two highly respectable elderly gentlemen changed to one of inquisitiveness when she heard what they wanted.

"No, sir," she answered. "Mr. Frank Burchill doesn't live here now. And it's a queer thing that during the time he did live here and gave me more trouble than any lodger I ever had, him keeping such strange hours of a night and early morning, he never had nobody to call on him, as I recollect of! And now here's been three gentlemen asking for him within this last hour—you two and another gentleman. And I don't know where Mr. Burchill lives, and don't want, neither!"

"My dear lady!" said Mr. Halfpenny, mildly and suavely. "I am sure we are deeply sorry to disturb you—no doubt we have called you away from your dinner. Perhaps, er, this"—here there was a slight chink of silver in Mr. Halfpenny's hand, presently repeated in one of the landlady's—"will, er, compensate you a little? But we are really anxious to see Mr. Burchill—haven't you any idea where he's gone to live? Didn't he leave an address for any letters that might come here?"

"He didn't, sir—not that he ever had many letters," answered the landlady. "And I haven't the remotest notion. Of course, if I had I'd give the address. But, as I said to the gentleman what was here not so long ago, I've neither seen nor heard of Mr. Burchill since he left—and that's six months since."

Mr. Halfpenny contrived to give his companion a nudge of the elbow.

"Is it, indeed, ma'am?" he said. "Ah! That gentleman who called, now?—I think he must be a friend of ours, who didn't know we were coming. What was he like, now, ma'am?"

"He was a tallish, fine-built gentleman," answered the landlady. "Fresh-coloured, clean-shaved gentleman. And for that matter, he can't be so far away—it isn't more than a quarter of an hour since he was here. I'll ask my girl if she saw which way he went."

"Don't trouble, pray, ma'am, on my account," entreated Mr. Halfpenny. "It's of no consequence. We're deeply obliged to you." He swept off his hat in an old-fashioned obeisance and drew Mr. Tertius away to the coupé brougham. "That was Barthorpe, of course," he said. "He lost no time, you see, Tertius, in trying to see Burchill."

"Why should he want to see Burchill?" asked Mr. Tertius.

"Wanted to know what Burchill had to say about signing the will, of course," replied Mr. Halfpenny. "Well—what next? Do you want me to see Cox-Raythwaite with you?"

Mr. Tertius, who had seemed to be relapsing into a brown study on the edge of the pavement, woke up into some show of eagerness. "Yes, yes!" he said. "Yes, by all means let us go to Cox-Raythwaite. I'm sure that's the thing to do. And there's another man—the chauffeur. But—yes, we'll go to Cox-Raythwaite first. Tell your man to drive to the corner of Endsleigh Gardens—the corner by St. Pancras Church."

Professor Cox-Raythwaite was exactly where Mr. Tertius had left him in the morning, when the two visitors were ushered into his laboratory. And for the second time that day he listened in silence to Mr. Tertius's story. When it was finished, he looked at Mr. Halfpenny, whose solemn countenance had grown more solemn than ever.

"Queer story, isn't it, Halfpenny?" he said laconically. "How does it strike you?"

Mr. Halfpenny slowly opened his pursed-up lips.

"Queer?" he exclaimed. "God bless me!—I'm astounded! I—but let me see these—these things."

"Sealed 'em up not so long ago—just after lunch," remarked the Professor, lifting his heavy bulk out of his chair. "But you can see 'em all right through the glass. There you are!" He led the way to a side-table and pointed to the hermetically-sealed receptacles in which he had safely bestowed the tumbler and the sandwich brought so gingerly from Portman Square by Mr. Tertius. "The tumbler," he continued, jerking a big thumb at it, "will have, of course, to be carefully examined by an expert in finger-prints; the sandwich, so to speak, affords primary evidence. You see—what there is to see, Halfpenny?"

Mr. Halfpenny adjusted his spectacles, bent down, and examined the exhibits with scrupulous, absorbed interest. Again he pursed up his lips, firmly, tightly, as if he would never open them again; when he did open them it was to emit a veritable whistle which indicated almost as much delight as astonishment. Then he clapped Mr. Tertius on the back.

"A veritable stroke of genius!" he exclaimed. "Tertius, my boy, you should have been a Vidocq or a Hawkshaw! How did you come to think of it? For I confess that with all my forty years' experience of Law, I—well, I don't think I should ever have thought of it!"

"Oh, I don't know," said Mr. Tertius, modestly. "I—well, I looked—and then, of course, I saw. That's all!"

Mr. Halfpenny sat down and put his hands on his knees.

"It's a good job you did see, anyway," he said, ruminatively; "an uncommonly good job. Well—you're certain of what we may call the co-relative factor to what is most obvious in that sandwich?"

"Absolutely certain," replied Mr. Tertius.

"And you're equally certain about the diamond ring?"

"Equally and positively certain!"

"Then," said Mr. Halfpenny, rising with great decision, "there is only one thing to be done. You and I, Tertius, must go at once—at once!—to New Scotland Yard. In fact, we will drive straight there. I happen to know a man who is highly placed in the Criminal Investigation Department—we will put our information before him. He will know what ought to be done. In my opinion, it is one of those cases which will require infinite care, precaution, and, for the time being, secrecy—mole's work. Let us go, my dear friend."

"Want me—and these things?" asked the Professor.

"For the time being, no," answered Mr. Halfpenny. "Nor, at present, the taxi-cab driver that Tertius has told us of. We'll merely tell what we know. But take care of these—these exhibits, as if they were the apples of your eyes, Cox-Raythwaite. They—yes, they may hang somebody!"

Half an hour later saw Mr. Halfpenny and Mr. Tertius closeted with a gentleman who, in appearance, resembled the popular conception of a country squire and was in reality as keen a tracker-down of wrong-doers as ever trod the pavement of Parliament Street. And before Mr. Halfpenny had said many words he stopped him.

"Wait a moment," he said, touching a bell at his side, "we're already acquainted, of course, with the primary facts of this case, and I've told off one of our sharpest men to give special attention to it. We'll have him in."

The individual who presently entered and who was introduced to the two callers as Detective-Inspector Davidge looked neither preternaturally wise nor abnormally acute. What he really did remind Mr. Tertius of was a gentleman of the better-class commercial traveller persuasion—he was comfortable, solid, genial, and smartly if quietly dressed. And he and the highly placed gentleman listened to all that the two visitors had to tell with quiet and concentrated attention and did not even exchange looks with each other. In the end the superior nodded as if something satisfied him.

"Very well," he said. "Now the first thing is—silence. You two gentlemen will not breathe a word of all this to any one. As you said just now, Mr. Halfpenny, the present policy is—secrecy. There will be a great deal of publicity during the next few days—the inquest, and so on. We shall not be much concerned with it—the public will say that as usual we are doing nothing. You may think so, too. But you may count on this—we shall be doing a great deal, and within a very short time from now we shall never let Mr. Barthorpe Herapath out of our sight until—we want him."

"Just so," assented Mr. Halfpenny. He took Mr. Tertius away, and when he had once more bestowed him in the coupé brougham, dug him in the ribs. "Tertius!" he said, with something like a dry chuckle. "What an extraordinary thing it is that people can go about the world unconscious that other folks are taking a very close and warm interest in them! Now, I'll lay a pound to a penny that Barthorpe hasn't a ghost of a notion that he's already under suspicion. My idea of the affair, sir, is that he has not the mere phantasm of such a thing. And yet, from now, as our friend there observed, Master Barthorpe, sir, will be watched. Shadowed, Tertius, shadowed!"

Barthorpe Herapath certainly had none of the notions of which Mr. Halfpenny spoke. He spent his afternoon, once having quitted Burchill's flat, in a businesslike fashion. He visited the estate office in Kensington; he went to see the undertaker who had been charged with the funeral arrangements; he called in at the local police-office and saw the inspector and the detective who had first been brought into connection with the case; he made some arrangements with the Coroner's officer about the necessary inevitable inquest. He did all these things in the fashion of a man who has nothing to fear, who is unconscious that other men are already eyeing him with suspicion. And he was quite unaware that when he left his office in Craven Street that evening he was followed by a man who quietly attended him to his bachelor rooms in the Adelphi, who waited patiently until he emerged from them to dine at a neighbouring restaurant, who himself dined at the same place, and who eventually tracked him to Maida Vale and watched him enter Calengrove Mansions.

Table of Contents

CHAPTER XII

for ten per cent

Mr. Frank Burchill welcomed his visitor with easy familiarity—this might have been a mere dropping-in of one friend to another, for the very ordinary purpose of spending a quiet social hour before retiring for the night. There was a bright fire on the hearth, a small smoking-jacket on Burchill's graceful shoulders and fancy slippers on his feet; decanters and glasses were set out on the table in company with cigars and cigarettes. And by the side of Burchill's easy chair was a pile of newspapers, to which he pointed one of his slim white hands as the two men settled themselves to talk.

"I've been reading all the newspapers I could get hold of," he observed. "Brought all the latest editions in with me after dinner. There's little more known, I think, than when you were here this afternoon."

"There's nothing more known," replied Barthorpe. "That is—as far as I'm aware."

Burchill took a sip at his glass and regarded Barthorpe thoughtfully over its rim.

"In strict confidence," he said, "have you got any idea whatever on the subject?"

"None!" answered Barthorpe. "None whatever! I've no more idea of who it was that killed my uncle than I have of the name of the horse that'll win the Derby of year after next! That's a fact. There isn't a clue."

"The police are at work, of course," suggested Burchill.

"Of course!" replied Barthorpe, with an unconcealed sneer. "And a lot of good they are. Whoever knew the police to find out anything, except by a lucky accident?"

"Just so," agreed Burchill. "But then—accidents, lucky or otherwise, will happen. You can't think of anybody whose interest it was to get your esteemed relative out of the way?"

"Nobody!" said Barthorpe. "There may have been somebody. We want to know who the man was who came out of the House with him last night—so far we don't know. It'll all take a lot of finding out. In the meantime——"

"In the meantime, you're much more concerned and interested in the will, eh?" said Burchill.

"I'm much more concerned—being a believer in present necessities—in hearing what you've got to say to me now that you've brought me here," answered Barthorpe, coolly. "What is it?"

"Oh, I've a lot to say," replied Burchill. "Quite a lot. But you'll have to let me say it in my own fashion. And to start with, I want to ask you a few questions. About your family history, for instance."

"I know next to nothing about my family history," said Barthorpe; "but if my knowledge is helpful to what we—or I—want to talk about, fire ahead!"

"Good!" responded Burchill. "Now, just tell me what you know about Mr. Jacob Herapath, about his brother, your father, and about his sister, who was, of course, Miss Wynne's mother. Briefly—concisely."

"Not so much," answered Barthorpe. "My grandfather was a medical man—pretty well known, I fancy—at Granchester, in Yorkshire; I, of course, never knew or saw him. He had three children. The eldest was Jacob, who came to his end last night. Jacob left Granchester for London, eventually began speculating in real estate, and became—what he was. The second was Richard, my father. He went out to Canada as a lad, and did there pretty much what Jacob did here in London——"

"With the same results?" interjected Burchill.

Barthorpe made a wry face.

"Unfortunately, no!" he replied. "He did remarkably well to a certain point—then he made some most foolish and risky speculations in American railroads, lost pretty nearly everything he'd made, and died a poorish man."

"Oh—he's dead, then?" remarked Burchill.

"He's dead—years ago," replied Barthorpe. "He died before I came to England. I, of course, was born out there. I——."

"Never mind you just now," interrupted Burchill. "Keep to the earlier branches of the family. Your grandfather had one other child?"

"A daughter," assented Barthorpe. "I never saw her, either. However, I know that her name was Susan. I also know that she married a man named Wynne—my cousin's father, of course. I don't know who he was or anything about him."

"Nothing?"

"Nothing—nothing at all: My Uncle Jacob never spoke of him to me—except to mention that such a person had once existed. My cousin doesn't know anything about him, either. All she knows is that her father and mother died when she was about—I think—two years old, and that Jacob then took charge of her. When she was six years old, he brought her to live with him. That was about the time I myself came to England."

"All right," said Burchill. "Now, we'll come to you. Tell about yourself. It all matters."

"Well, of course, I don't know what you're getting at," replied Barthorpe. "But I'm sure you do. Myself, eh? Well, I was put to the Law out there in Canada. When my father died—not over well off—I wrote to Uncle Jacob, telling him all about how things were. He suggested that I should come over to this country, finish my legal training here, and qualify. He also promised—if I suited him—to give me his legal work. And, of course, I came."

"Naturally," said Burchill. "And that's—how long ago?"

"Between fifteen and sixteen years," answered Barthorpe.

"Did Jacob Herapath take you into his house?" asked Burchill, continuing the examination which Barthorpe was beginning to find irksome as well as puzzling. "I'm asking all this for good reasons—it's necessary, if you're to understand what I'm going to tell you."

"Oh, as long as you're going to tell me something I don't mind telling you anything you like to ask," replied Barthorpe. "That's what I want to be getting at. No—he didn't take me into the house. But he gave me a very good allowance, paid all my expenses until I got through my remaining examinations and stages, and was very decent all around. No—I fixed up in the rooms which I've still got—a flat in the Adelphi."

"But you went a good deal to Portman Square?"

"Why, yes, a good deal—once or twice a week, as a rule."

"Had your cousin—Miss Wynne—come there then?"

"Yes, she'd just about come. I remember she had a governess. Of course, Peggie was a mere child then—about five or six. Must have been six, because she's quite twenty-one now."

"And—Mr. Tertius?"

Burchill spoke the name with a good deal of subtle meaning, and Barthorpe suddenly looked at him with a rising comprehension.

"Tertius?" he answered. "No—Tertius hadn't arrived on the scene then. He came—soon after."

"How soon after?"

"I should say," replied Barthorpe, after a moment's consideration, "I should say—from my best recollection—a few months after I came to London. It was certainly within a year of my coming."

"You remember his coming?"

"Not particularly. I remember that he came—at first, I took it, as a visitor. Then I found he'd had rooms of his own given him, and that he was there as a permanency."

"Settled down—just as he has been ever since?"

"Just! Never any difference that I've known of, all these years."

"Did Jacob ever tell you who he was?"

"Never! I never remember my uncle speaking of him in any particular fashion—to me. He was simply—there. Sometimes, you saw him; sometimes, you didn't see him. At times, I mean, you'd meet him at dinner—other times, you didn't."

Burchill paused for a while; when he asked his next question he seemed to adopt a more particular and pressing tone.

"Now—have you the least idea who Tertius is?" he asked.

"Not the slightest!" affirmed Barthorpe. "I never have known who he is. I never liked him—I didn't like his sneaky way of going about the house—I didn't like anything of him—and he never liked me. I always had a feeling—a sort of intuition—that he resented my presence—in fact, my existence."

"Very likely," said Burchill, with a dry laugh. "Well—has it ever struck you that there was a secret between Tertius and Jacob Herapath?"

Barthorpe started. At last they were coming to something definite.

"Ah!" he exclaimed. "So—that's the secret you mentioned in that letter?"

"Never mind," replied Burchill. "Answer my question."

"No, then—it never did strike me."

"Very well," said Burchill. "There is a secret."

"There is?"

"There is! And," whispered Burchill, rising and coming nearer to his visitor, "it's a secret that will put you in possession of the whole of the Herapath property! And—I know it."

Barthorpe had by this time realized the situation. And he was thinking things over at a rapid rate. Burchill had asked Jacob Herapath for ten thousand pounds as the price of his silence; therefore——

"And, of course, you want to make something out of your knowledge?" he said presently.

"Of course," laughed Burchill. He opened a box of cigars, selected one and carefully trimmed the end before lighting it. "Of course!" he repeated. "Who wouldn't? Besides, you'll be in a position to afford me something when you come into all that."

"The will?" suggested Barthorpe.

Burchill threw the burnt-out match into the fire.

"The will," he said slowly, "will be about as valuable as that—when I've fixed things up with you. Valueless!"

"You mean it?" exclaimed Barthorpe incredulously. "Then—your signature?"

"Look here!" said Burchill. "The only thing between us is—terms! Fix up terms with me, and I'll tell you the whole truth. And then—you'll see!"

"Well—what terms?" demanded Barthorpe, a little suspiciously. "If you want money down——"

"You couldn't pay in cash down what I want, nor anything like it," said Burchill. "I may want an advance that you can pay—but it will only be an advance. What I want is ten per cent. on the total value of Jacob Herapath's property."

"Good heavens!" exclaimed Barthorpe. "Why I believe he'll cut up for a good million and a half!"

"That's about the figure—as I've reckoned it," assented Burchill. "But you'll have a lot left when you've paid me ten per cent."

Barthorpe fidgeted in his chair.

"When did you find out this secret?" he asked.

"Got an idea of it just before I left Jacob, and worked it all out, to the last detail, after I left," replied Burchill. "I tell you this for a certainty—when I've told you all I know, you'll know for an absolute fact, that the Herapath property is—yours!"

"Well!" said Barthorpe. "What do you want me to do?"

Burchill moved across to a desk and produced some papers.

"I want you to sign certain documents," he said, "and then I'll tell you the whole story. If the story's no good, the documents are no good. How's that?"

"That'll do!" answered Barthorpe. "Let's get to business."

It was one o'clock in the morning when Barthorpe left Calengrove Mansions. But the eyes that had seen him enter saw him leave, and the shadow followed him through the sleeping town until he, too, sought his own place of slumber.

Table of Contents

CHAPTER XIII

adjourned

Ever since Triffitt had made his lucky scoop in connection with the Herapath Mystery he had lived in a state of temporary glory, with strong hopes of making it a permanent one. Up to the morning of the event, which gave him a whole column of the *Argus* (big type, extra leaded), Triffitt, as a junior reporter, had never accomplished anything notable. As he was fond of remarking, he never got a chance. Police-court cases—county-court cases—fires—coroners' inquests—street accidents—they were all exciting enough, no doubt, to the people actively concerned in them, but you never got more than twenty or thirty lines out of their details. However, the chance did come that morning, and Triffitt made the most of it, and the news editor (a highly exacting and particular person) blessed him moderately, and told him, moreover, that he could call the Herapath case his own. Thenceforth Triffitt ate, drank, smoked, and slept with the case; it was the only thing he ever thought of. But at half-past one on the afternoon of the third day after what one may call the actual start of the affair, Triffitt sat in a dark corner of a tea-shop in Kensington High Street, munching ham sandwiches, sipping coffee, and thinking lugubriously, if not despairingly. He had spent two and a half hours in the adjacent Coroner's Court, listening to all that was said in evidence about the death of Jacob Herapath, and he had heard absolutely nothing that was not quite well known to him when the Coroner took his seat, inspected his jurymen, and opened the inquiry. Two and a half hours, at the end of which the court adjourned for lunch—and the affair was just as mysterious as ever, and not a single witness had said a new thing, not a single fresh fact had been brought forward out of which a fellow could make good, rousing copy!

"Rotten!" mumbled Triffitt into his cup. "Extra rotten! Somebody's keeping something back—that's about it!"

Just then another young gentleman came into the alcove in which Triffitt sat disconsolate—a pink-cheeked young gentleman, who affected a tweed suit of loud checks and a sporting coat, and wore a bit of feather in the band of his rakish billycock. Triffitt recognized him as a fellow-scribe, one of the youthful bloods of an opposition journal, whom he sometimes met on the cricket-field; he also remembered that he had caught a glimpse of him in the Coroner's Court, and he hastened to make room for him.

"Hullo!" said Triffitt.

"What-ho!" responded the pink young gentleman. He beckoned knowingly to a waitress, and looked at her narrowly when she came. "Got such a thing as a muffin?" he asked.

"Muffins, sir—yes, sir," replied the waitress, "Fresh muffins."

"Pick me out a nice, plump, newly killed muffin" commanded Triffitt's companion. "Leave it in its natural state—that is to say, cold—split it in half put between the halves a thick, generous slice of that cold ham I see on your counter, and produce it with a pot of fresh—and very hot—China tea. That's all."

"Plenty too, I should think!" muttered Triffitt. "Fond of indigestion, Carver?"

"I don't think you've ever been in Yorkshire, have you, Triffitt?" asked Mr. Carver, settling himself comfortably. "You haven't had that pleasure?—well, if you'd ever gone to a football match on a Saturday afternoon in a Yorkshire factory district, you'd have seen men selling muffin-and-ham sandwiches—fact! And I give you my word that if you want something to fill you up during the day, something to tide over the weary wait between breakfast and dinner, a fat muffin with a thick slice of ham is the best thing I know."

"I don't want anything to fill me up," grunted Triffitt. "I want something cheering—at present. I've been listening with all my ears for something new in that blessed Herapath case all the morning, and, as you know, there's been nothing!"

"Think so?" said Carver. "Um—I should have said there was a good deal, now."

"Nothing that I didn't know, anyway," remarked Triffitt. "I got all that first thing; I was on the spot first."

"Oh, it was you, was it?" said Carver, with professional indifference. "Lucky man! So you've only been hearing——"

"A repetition of what I'd heard before," answered Triffitt. "I knew all that evidence before I went into court. Caretaker—police—folks from Portman Square—doctor—all the lot!

And I guess there'll be nothing this afternoon—the thing'll be adjourned."

"Oh, that's of course," assented Carver, attacking his muffin sandwich. "There'll be more than one adjournment of this particular inquest, Triffitt. But aren't you struck by one or two points?"

"I'm struck by this," replied Triffitt. "If what the police-surgeon says—and you noticed how positive he was about it—if what he says is true, that old Herapath was shot, and died, at, or just before (certainly not after, he positively asserted), twelve o'clock midnight, it was not he who went to Portman Square!"

"That, of course, is obvious," said Carver. "And it's just as obvious that whoever went to Portman Square returned from Portman Square to that office. Eh?"

"That hasn't quite struck me," replied Triffitt. "How is it just as obvious?"

"Because whoever went to Portman Square went in old Herapath's fur-trimmed coat and his slouch hat, and the fur trimmed coat and slouch hat were found in the office," answered Carver. "It's absolutely plain, that. I put it like this. The murderer, having settled his man, put on his victim's coat and hat, took his keys, went to Portman Square, did something there, went back to the office, left the coat and hat, and hooked it. That, my son, is a dead certainty. There's been little—if anything—made of all that before the Coroner, and it's my impression, Triffitt, that somebody—somebody official, mind you—is keeping something back. Now," continued Carver, dropping his voice to a confidential whisper, "I'm only doing a plain report of this affair for our organ of light and leading, but I've read it up pretty well, and there are two things I want to know, and I'll tell you what, Triffitt, if you like to go in with me at finding them out—two can always work better than one—I'm game!"

"What are the two things?" asked Triffitt, cautiously. "Perhaps I've got 'em in mind also."

"The first's this," replied Carver. "Somebody—some taxi-cab driver or somebody of that sort—must have brought the man who personated old Jacob Herapath back to, or to the neighbourhood of, the office that morning. How is it that somebody hasn't been discovered? You made a point of asking for him in the *Argus*. Do you know what I think? I think he has been discovered, and he's being kept out of the way. That's point one."

"Good!" muttered Triffitt. "And point two?"

"Point two is—where is the man who came out of the House of Commons with Jacob Herapath that night, the man that the coachman Mountain described? In my opinion," asserted Carver, "I believe that man's been found, too, and he's being kept back."

"Good again!" said Triffitt. "It's likely. Well, I've a point. You heard the evidence about old Herapath's keys? Yes—well, where's the key of that safe that he rented at the Safe Deposit place. That young secretary, Selwood, swore that it was on the little bunch the day of the murder, that he saw it at three o'clock in the afternoon. What did Jacob Herapath do with it between then and the time of the murder?"

"Yes—that's a great point," asserted Carver. "We may hear something of that this afternoon—perhaps of all these points."

But when they went back to the densely crowded court it was only to find that they—and an expectant public—were going to hear nothing more for that time. As soon as the court re-assembled, there was some putting together of heads on the part of the legal gentlemen and the Coroner; there were whisperings and consultations and noddings and veiled hints, palpable enough to everybody with half an eye; then the Coroner announced that no further evidence would be taken that day, and adjourned the inquest for a fortnight. Such of the public as had contrived to squeeze into the court went out murmuring, and Triffitt and Carver went out too and exchanged meaning glances.

"Just what I expected!" said Carver. "I reckon the police are at the bottom of all that. A fortnight today we'll be hearing something good—something sensational."

"I don't want to wait until a fortnight today," growled Triffitt. "I want some good, hot stuff—now!"

"Then you'll have to find it for yourself, very soon," remarked Carver. "Take my tip—you'll get nothing from the police."

Triffitt was well aware of that. He had talked to two or three police officials and detectives that morning, and had found them singularly elusive and uncommunicative. One of them was the police-inspector who had been called to the Herapath Estate Office on the discovery of the murder; another was the detective who had accompanied him. Since the murder Triffitt had kept in touch with these two, and had found them affable and ready to talk; now, however, they had suddenly curled up into a dry taciturnity, and there was nothing to be got out of them.

"Tell you what it is," he said suddenly. "We'll have to go for the police!"

"How go for the police?" asked Carver doubtfully.

"Throw out some careful hints that the police know more than they'll tell at present," answered Triffitt, importantly. "That's what I shall do, anyhow—I've got *carte blanche* on our rag, and I'll make the public ear itch and twitch by breakfast-time tomorrow morning! And after that, my boy, you and I'll put our heads together, as you suggest, and see if we can't do a bit of detective work of our own. See you tomorrow at the usual in Fleet Street."

Then Triffitt went along to the *Argus* office, and spent the rest of the afternoon in writing up a breezy and brilliant column about the scene at the inquest, intended to preface the ordinary detailed report. He wound it up with an artfully concocted paragraph in which he threw out many thinly veiled hints and innuendoes to the effect that the police were in possession of strange and sensational information and that ere long such a dramatic turn would be given to this Herapath Mystery that the whole town would seethe with excitement. He preened his feathers gaily over this accomplishment, and woke earlier than usual next morning on purpose to go out before breakfast and buy the *Argus*. But when he opened that enterprising journal he found that his column had been woefully cut down, and that the paragraph over which he had so exercised his brains was omitted altogether. Triffitt had small appetite for breakfast that morning, and he went early to the office and made haste to put himself in the way of the news editor, who grinned at sight of him.

"Look here, Master Triffitt," said the news editor, "there's such a thing as being too smart—and too previous. I was a bit doubtful about your prognostications last night, and I rang up the C.I.D. about 'em. Don't do it again, my son!—you mean well, but the police know their job better than you do. If they want to keep quiet for a while in this matter, they've good reasons for it. So—no more hints. See?"

"So they do know something?" muttered Triffitt sourly. "Then I was right, after all!"

"You'll be wrong, after all, if you stick your nose where it isn't wanted," said the news editor. "Just chuck the inspired prophet game for a while, will you? Keep to mere facts; you'll be alarming the wrong people, if you don't. Off you go now! and do old Herapath's funeral—it's at noon, at Kensal Green. There'll be some of his fellow M.P.'s there, and so on. Get their names—make a nice, respectable thing of it on conventional lines. And no fireworks! This thing's to lie low at present."

Triffitt went off to Kensal Green, scowling and cogitating. Of course the police knew something! But—what? What they knew would doubtless come out in time, but Triffitt had a strong desire to be beforehand with them. In spite of the douche of cold water which the news editor had just administered, Triffitt knew his *Argus*. If he could fathom the Herapath Mystery in such a fashion as to make a real great, smashing, all-absorbing feature of a sensational discovery, the *Argus* would throw police precaution and official entreaties to the first wind that swept down Fleet Street. No!—he, Triffitt, was not to be balked. He would do his duty—he would go and see Jacob Herapath buried, but he would also continue his attempt to find out how it was that that burial came to be. And as he turned into the cemetery and stared at its weird collection of Christian and pagan monuments he breathed a fervent prayer to the Goddesses of Chance and Fortune to give him what he called "another look-in."

Table of Contents

CHAPTER XIV

the scottish verdict

If Triffitt had only known it, the Goddesses of Chance and Fortune were already close at hand, hovering lovingly and benignly above the crown of his own Trilby hat. Triffitt, of course, did not see them, nor dream that they were near; he was too busily occupied in taking stock of the black-garmented men who paid the last tribute of respect (a conventional phrase which he felt obliged to use) to Jacob Herapath. These men were many in number; some of them were known to Triffitt, some were not. He knew Mr. Fox-Crawford, an Under-Secretary of State, who represented the Government; he knew Mr. Dayweather and Mr. Encilmore, and Mr. Camford and Mr. Wallburn; they were all well-known members of Parliament. Also, he knew Mr. Barthorpe Herapath, walking at the head of the procession of mourners. Very soon he had quite a lengthy list of names; some others, if necessary, he could get from Selwood, whom he recognized as the cortège passed him by. So for the time being he closed his note-book and drew back beneath the shade of a cypress-tree, respectfully watching. In the tail-end of the procession he knew nobody; it was made up, he guessed, of Jacob Herapath's numerous clerks from the estate offices, and——

But suddenly Triffitt saw a face in that procession. The owner of that face was not looking at Triffitt; he was staring quietly ahead, with the blank, grave demeanour which people affect when they go to funerals. And it was as well that he was not looking at Triffitt, for Triffitt, seeing that face, literally started and even jumped a little, feeling as if the earth beneath him suddenly quaked.

"Gad!" exclaimed Triffitt under his breath. "It is! It can't be! Gad, but I'm certain it is! Can't be mistaken—not likely I should ever forget him!"

Then he took off the Trilby hat, which he had resumed after the coffin had passed, and he rubbed his head as men do when they are exceedingly bewildered or puzzled. After which he unobtrusively followed the procession, hovered about its fringes around the grave until the last rites were over, and eventually edged himself up to Selwood as the gathering was dispersing. He quietly touched Selwood's sleeve.

"Mr. Selwood!" he whispered. "Just a word. I know a lot of these gentlemen—the M.P.'s and so on—but there are some I don't know. Will you oblige me, now?—I want to get a full list. Who are the two elderly gentlemen with Mr. Barthorpe Herapath—relatives, eh?"

"No—old personal friends," answered Selwood, good-naturedly turning aside with the little reporter. "One is Mr. Tertius—Mr. J. C. Tertius—a very old friend of the late Mr.

Herapath's; the other is Mr. Benjamin Halfpenny, the solicitor, also an old friend."

"Oh, I know of his firm," said Triffitt, busily scribbling. "Halfpenny and Farthing, of course—odd combination, isn't it? And that burly gentleman behind them, now—who's he?"

"That's Professor Cox-Raythwaite, the famous scientist," answered Selwood. "He's also an old friend. The gentleman he's speaking to is Sir Cornelius Debenham, chairman of the World Alliance Association, with which Mr. Herapath was connected, you know."

"I know—I know," answered Triffitt, still busy. "Those two behind him, now—middle-aged parties?"

"One's Mr. Frankton, the manager, and the other's Mr. Charlwood, the cashier, at the estate office," replied Selwood.

"They'll go down in staff and employees," said Triffitt. "Um—I've got a good list. By the by, who's the gentleman across there—just going up to the grave—the gentleman who looks like an actor? Is he an actor?"

"That? Oh!" answered Selwood. "No—that's Mr. Frank Burchill, who used to be Mr. Herapath's secretary—my predecessor."

"Oh!" responded Triffitt. He had caught sight of Carver a few yards off, and he hurried his notebook into his pocket, and bustled off. "Much obliged to you, Mr. Selwood," he said with a grin. "Even we with all our experience, don't know everybody, you know—many thanks." He hastened over to Carver who was also busy pencilling, and drew him away into the shelter of a particularly large and ugly monument. "I say!" he whispered. "Here's something! Shove that book away now—I've got all the names—and attend to me a minute. Don't look too obtrusively—but do you see that chap—looks like an actor—who is just coming away from the graveside—tall, well-dressed chap?"

Carver looked across. His face lighted up.

"I know that man," he said. "I've seen him at the club—he's been in once or twice, though he's not a member. He does theatre stuff for the *Magnet*. His name's Burchill."

Triffitt dropped his friend's arm.

"Oh!" he said. "So you know him—by sight, anyhow? And his name's Burchill, eh? Very good. Let's get."

He walked Carver out of the cemetery, down the Harrow Road, and turned into the saloon bar of the first tavern that presented itself.

"I'm going to have some ale and some bread and cheese," he observed, "and if you'll follow suit, Carver, we'll sit in that corner, and I'll tell you something that'll make your hair curl. Two nice plates of bread and cheese, and two large tankards of your best bitter ale, if you please," he continued, approaching the bar and ringing a half-crown on it. "Yes, Carver, my son—that will curl your hair for you. And," he went on, when they had carried their simple provender over to a quiet corner, "about that chap now known as Burchill—Burchill. Mr.—Frank—Burchill; late secretary to the respected gentleman whose mortal remains have just been laid to rest. Ah!"

"What's the mystery?" asked Carver, setting down his tankard. "Seems to be one, anyway. What about Burchill?"

"Speak his name softly," answered Triffitt. "Well, my son, I suddenly saw—him—this morning, and I just as suddenly remembered that I'd seen him before!"

"You had, eh?" said Carver. "Where?"

Triffitt sank his voice to a still lower whisper.

"Where?" he said. "Where? In the dock!"

Carver arrested the progress of a lump of bread and cheese and turned in astonishment.

"In the dock?" he exclaimed. "That chap? Good heavens! When—where?"

"It's a longish story," answered Triffitt. "But you've got to hear it if we're going into this thing—as we are. Know, then, that I have an aunt—Eliza. My aunt—maternal aunt—Eliza is married to a highly respectable Scotsman named Kierley, who runs a flour-mill in the ancient town of Jedburgh, which is in the county of Roxburgh, just over the Border. And it's just about nine years (I can tell the exact date to a day if I look at an old diary) that Mr. and Mrs. Kierley were good enough to invite me to spend a few weeks in Bonnie Scotland. And the first night of my arrival Kierley told me that I was in luck, for within a day or two there was going to be a grand trial before the Lords Justiciar—Anglicé, judges. A trial of a man for murder!"

"Great Scott!" said Carver. "Murder, eh? And"—he nodded his head in the direction of the adjacent cemetery. "Him?"

"Let me explain a few legal matters," said Triffitt, disregarding the question. "Then you'll get the proper hang of things. In Scotland, law's different in procedure to ours. The High Court of Justiciary is fixed permanently at Edinburgh, but its judges go on circuit so many times a year to some of the principal towns, where they hold something like our own assizes. Usually, only one judge sits, but in cases of special importance there are two, and two came to Jedburgh, this being a case of very special importance, and one that was arousing a mighty amount of interest. It was locally known as the Kelpies' Glen Case, and by that name it got into all the papers—we could find it, of course, in our own files."

"I'll turn it up," observed Carver.

"By all means," agreed Triffitt; "but I'll give you an outline of it just now. Briefly, it was this. About eleven years ago, there was near the town of Jedburgh a man named Ferguson, who kept an old-established school for boys. He was an oldish chap, married to a woman a good deal younger than himself, and she had a bit of a reputation for being overfond of the wine of the country. According to what the Kierleys told me, old Ferguson used to use the tawse on her sometimes, and they led a sort of cat-and-dog life. Well, about the time I'm talking about, Ferguson got a new undermaster; he only kept one. This chap was an Englishman—name of Bentham—Francis Bentham, to give him his full patronymic, but I don't know where he came from—I don't think anybody did."

"F. B., eh?" muttered Carver. "Same initials as——"

"Precisely," said Triffitt, "and—to anticipate—same man. But to proceed in due order. Old Ferguson died rather suddenly—but in quite an above-board and natural fashion, about six months after this Bentham came to him. The widow kept on the school, and retained Bentham's services. And within half a year of the demise of her first husband, she took Bentham for her second."

"Quick work!" remarked Carver.

"And productive of much wagging of tongues, you may bet!" said Triffitt. "Many things were said—not all of them charitable. Well, this marriage didn't mend the lady's manners. She still continued, now and then, to take her drops in too generous measure. Rumour had it that the successor to Ferguson followed his predecessor's example and corrected his wife in the good, old-fashioned way. It was said that the old cat-and-dog life was started again by these two. However, before they'd been married a year, the lady ended that episode by quitting life for good. She was found one night lying at the foot of the cliff in the Kelpies' Glen—with a broken neck."

"Ah!" said Carver. "I begin to see."

"Now, that Kelpies' Glen," continued Triffitt, "was a sort of ravine which lay between the town of Jedburgh and the school. It was traversed by a rough path which lay along the top of one side of it, amongst trees and crags. At one point, this path was on the very edge of a precipitous cliff; from that edge there was a sheer drop of some seventy or eighty feet to a bed of rocks down below, on the edge of a brawling stream. It was on these rocks that Mrs. Bentham's body was found. She was dead enough when she was discovered, and the theory was that she had come along the path above in a drunken condition, had fallen over the low railings which fenced it in, and so had come to her death."

"Precisely," assented Carver, nodding his head with wise appreciation. "Her alcoholic tendencies were certainly useful factors in the case."

"Just so—you take my meaning," agreed Triffitt. "Well, at first nobody saw any reason to doubt this theory, for the lady had been seen staggering along that path more than once. But she had a brother, a canny Scot who was not over well pleased when he found that his sister—who had come into everything that old Ferguson left, which was a comfortable bit—had made a will not very long before her death in which she left absolutely everything to her new husband, Francis Bentham. The brother began to inquire and to investigate—and to cut the story short, within a fortnight of his wife's death, Bentham was arrested and charged with her murder."

"On what evidence?" asked Carver.

"Precious little!" answered Triffitt. "Indeed next to none. Still, there was some. It was proved that he was absent from the house for half an hour or so about the time that she would be coming along that path; it was also proved that certain footprints in the clay of the path were his. He contended that he had been to look for her; he proved that he had often been to look for her in that way; moreover, as to the footprints, he, like everybody in the house, constantly used that path in going to the town."

"Aye, to be sure," said Carver. "He'd a good case, I'm thinking."

"He had—and so I thought at the time," continued Triffitt. "And so a good many folks thought—and they, and I, also thought something else, I can tell you. I know what the verdict of the crowded court would have been!"

"What?" asked Carver.

"Guilty!" exclaimed Triffitt. "And so far as I'm concerned, I haven't a doubt that the fellow pushed her over the cliff. But opinion's neither here nor there. The only thing that mattered, my son, was the jury's verdict!"

"And the jury's verdict was—what?" demanded Carver.

Triffitt winked into his empty tankard and set it down with a bang.

"The jury's verdict, my boy," he answered, "was one that you can only get across the Border. It was '*Not Proven*'!"

Table of Contents

CHAPTER XV

young brains

Carver, who had been listening intently to the memory of a bygone event, pushed away the remains of his frugal lunch, and shook his head as he drew out a cigarette-case.

"By gad, Triff, old man!" he said. "If I'd been that chap I'd rather have been hanged, I think. Not proven, eh?—whew! That meant——"

"Pretty much what the folk in court and the mob outside thought," asserted Triffitt. "That scene outside, after the trial, is one of my liveliest recollections. There was a big crowd there—

chiefly women. When they heard the verdict there was such yelling and hooting as you never heard in your life! You see, they were all certain about the fellow's guilt, and they wanted him to swing. If they could have got at him, they'd have lynched him. And do you know, he actually had the cheek to leave the court by the front entrance, and show himself to that crowd! Then there was a lively scene—stones and brickbats and the mud of the street began flying. Then the police waded in—and they gave Mr. Francis Bentham pretty clearly to understand that there must be no going home for him, or the folks would pull his roof over his head. And they forced him back into the court, and got him away out of the town on the quiet—and I reckon he's never shown his face in that quarter of the globe since."

"That will?" asked Carver. "Did it stand good—did he get the woman's money?"

"He did. My aunt told me afterwards that he employed some local solicitor chap—writers, as they call 'em there—to wind everything up, convert everything into cash, for him. Oh, yes!" concluded Triffitt. "He got the estate, right enough. Not an awful lot, you know—a thousand or two—perhaps three—but enough to go adventuring with elsewhere."

"You're sure this is the man?" asked Carver.

"As certain as that I'm myself!" answered Triffitt. "Couldn't mistake him—even if it is nine years ago. It's true I was only a nipper then—sixteen or so—but I'd all my wits about me, and I was so taken with him in the dock, and with his theatrical bearing there—he's a fine hand at posing—that I couldn't forget or mistake him. Oh, he's the man! I've often wondered what had become of him."

"And now you find out that he's up till recently been secretary to Jacob Herapath, M.P., and is just now doing dramatic criticism for the *Magnet*," observed Carver. "Well, Triffitt, what do you make of it?"

Triffitt, who had filled and lighted an old briarwood pipe, puffed solemnly and thoughtfully for a while.

"Well," he said, "nobody can deny that there's a deep mystery about Jacob Herapath's death. And knowing what I do about this Bentham or Burchill, and that he's recently been secretary to Jacob Herapath, I'd just like to know a lot more. And—I mean to!"

"Got any plan of campaign?" asked Carver.

"I have!" affirmed Triffitt with sublime confidence. "And it's this—I'm going to dog this thing out until I can go to our boss and tell him that I can force the hands of the police! For the police are keeping something dark, my son, and I mean to find out what it is. I got a quencher this morning from our news editor, but it'll be the last. When I go back to the office to write out this stuff, I'm going to have that extremely rare thing with any of our lot—an interview with the old man."

"Gad!—I thought your old man was unapproachable!" exclaimed Carver.

"To all intents and purposes, he is," assented Triffitt. "But I'll see him—and today. And after that—but you'll see. Now, as to you, old man. You're coming in with me at this, of course—not on behalf of your paper, but on your own. Work up with me, and if we're successful, I'll promise you a post on the *Argus* that'll be worth three times what you're getting now. I know what I'm talking about—unapproachable as our guv'nor is, I've sized him up, and if I make good in this affair, he'll do anything I want. Stick to Triffitt, my son, and Triffitt'll see you all serene!"

"Right-oh!" said Carver. "I'm on. Well, and what am I to do, first?"

"Two things," responded Triffitt. "One of 'em's easy, and can be done at once. Get me— diplomatically—this man Burchill's, or Bentham's, present address. You know some *Magnet* chaps—get it out of them. Tell 'em you want to ask Burchill's advice about some dramatic stuff—say you've written a play and you're so impressed by his criticisms that you'd like to take his counsel."

"I can do that," replied Carver. "As a matter of fact, I've got a real good farce in my desk. And the next?"

"The next is—try to find out if there's any taxi-cab driver around the Portman Square district who took a fare resembling old Herapath from anywhere about there to Kensington on the night of the murder," said Triffitt. "There must be some chap who drove that man, and if we've got any brains about us we can find him. If we find him, and can get him to talk—well, we shall know something."

"It'll mean money," observed Carver.

"Never mind," said Triffitt, confident as ever. "If it comes off all right with our boss, you needn't bother about money, my son! Now let's be going Fleet Street way, and I'll meet you tonight at the usual—say six o'clock."

Arrived at the *Argus* office and duly seated at his own particular table, Triffitt, instead of proceeding to write out his report of the funeral ceremony of the late Jacob Herapath, M.P., wrote a note to his proprietor, which note he carefully sealed and marked "Private." He carried this off to the great man's confidential secretary, who stared at it and him.

"I suppose this really is of a private nature?" he asked suspiciously. "You know as well as I do that Mr. Markledew'll make me suffer if it isn't."

"Soul and honour, it's of the most private!" affirmed Triffitt, laying a hand on his heart. "And of the highest importance, too, and I'll be eternally grateful if you'll put it before him as soon as you can."

The confidential secretary took another look at Triffitt, and allowed himself to be reluctantly convinced of his earnestness.

"All right!" he said. "I'll shove it under his nose when he comes in at four o'clock."

Triffitt went back to his work, excited, yet elated. It was no easy job to get speech of Markledew. Markledew, as everybody in Fleet Street knew, was a man in ten thousand. He was not only sole proprietor of his paper, but its editor and manager, and he ruled his office and his employees with a rod of iron—chiefly by silence. It was usually said of him that he never spoke to anybody unless he was absolutely obliged to do so—certain it was that all his orders to the various heads were given out pretty much after the fashion of a drill sergeant's commands to a squad of well-trained, five-month recruits, and that monosyllables were much more in his mouth than even brief admonitions and explanations. If anybody ever did manage to approach Markledew, it was always with fear and trembling. A big, heavy, lumbering man, with a face that might have been carved out of granite, eyes that bored through an opposing brain, and a constant expression of absolute, yet watchful immobility, he was a trying person to tackle, and most men, when they did tackle him, felt as if they might be talking to the Sphinx and wondered if the tightly-locked lips were ever going to open. But all men who ever had anything to do with Markledew were well aware that, difficult as he was of access, you had only got to approach him with something good to be rewarded for your pains in full measure.

At ten minutes past four Triffitt, who had just finished his work, lifted his head to see a messenger-boy fling open the door of the reporter's room and cast his eyes round. A shiver shot through Triffitt's spine and went out of his toes with a final sting.

"Mr. Markledew wants Mr. Triffitt!"

Two or three other junior reporters who were scribbling in the room glanced at Triffitt as he leapt to obey the summons. They hastened to make kindly comments on this unheard-of episode in the day's dull routine.

"Pale as a fair young bride!" sighed one. "Buck up, Triff!—he won't eat you."

"I hear your knees knocking together, Triff," said another. "Brace yourself!"

"Markledew," observed a third, "has decided to lay down the sceptre and to instal Triff in the chair of rule. Ave, Triffitt, Imperator!—be merciful to the rest of us."

Triffitt consigned them to the nether regions and hurried to the presence. The presence was busied with its secretary and kept Triffitt standing for two minutes, during which space he recovered his breath. Then the presence waved away secretary and papers with one hand, turned its awful eyes upon him, and rapped out one word:

"Now!"

Triffitt breathed a fervent prayer to all his gods, summoned his resolution and his powers, and spoke. He endeavoured to use as few words as possible, to be lucid, to make his points, to show what he was after—and, driving fear away from him, he kept his own eyes steadily fixed on those penetrating organs which confronted him. And once, twice, he saw or thought he saw a light gleam of appreciation in those organs; once, he believed, the big head nodded as if in agreement. Anyhow, at the end of a quarter of an hour (unheard-of length for an interview with Markledew!) Triffitt had neither been turned out nor summarily silenced; instead, he had come to what he felt to be a good ending of his pleas and his arguments, and the great man was showing signs of speech.

"Now, attend!" said Markledew, impressively. "You'll go on with this. You'll follow it up on the lines you suggest. But you'll print nothing except under my personal supervision. Make certain of your facts. Facts!—understand! Wait."

He pulled a couple of slips of paper towards him, scribbled a line or two on each, handed them to Triffitt, and nodded at the door.

"That'll do," he said. "When you want me, let me know. And mind—you've got a fine chance, young man."

Triffitt could have fallen on the carpet and kissed Markledew's large boots. But knowing Markledew, he expressed his gratitude in two words and a bow, and sped out of the room. Once outside, he hastened to send the all-powerful notes. They were short and sharp, like Markledew's manner, but to Triffitt of an inexpressible sweetness, and he walked on air as he went off to other regions to present them.

The news editor, who was by nature irascible and whom much daily worry had rendered more so, glared angrily as Triffitt marched up to his table. He pointed to a slip of proof which lay, damp and sticky, close by.

"You've given too much space to that Herapath funeral," he growled. "Take it away and cut it down to three-quarters."

Triffitt made no verbal answer. He flung Markledew's half-sheet of notepaper before the news editor, and the news editor, seeing the great man's sprawling caligraphy, read, wonderingly:—

"Mr. Triffitt is released from ordinary duties to pursue others under my personal supervision. J. M."

The news editor stared at Triffitt as if that young gentleman had suddenly become an archangel.

"What's this mean?" he demanded.

"Obvious—and sufficient," retorted Triffitt. And he turned, hands in pockets, and strolled out, leaving the proof lying unheeded. That was the first time he had scored off his news editor, and the experience was honey-like and intoxicating. His head was higher than ever as he sought the cashier and handed Markledew's other note to him. The cashier read it over mechanically.

"Mr. Triffitt is to draw what money he needs for a special purpose. He will account to me for it. J. M."

The cashier calmly laid the order aside and looked at its deliverer.

"Want any now?" he asked apathetically. "How much?"

"Not at present," replied Triffitt. "I'll let you know when I do."

Then he went away, got his overcoat, made a derisive and sphinx-like grin at his fellow-reporters, and left the office to find Carver.

Table of Contents

CHAPTER XVI

nameless fear

If Triffitt had stayed in Kensal Green Cemetery a little longer, he would have observed that Mr. Frank Burchill's presence at the funeral obsequies of the late Jacob Herapath was of an eminently modest, unassuming, and retiring character. He might, as an ex-secretary of the dead man, have claimed to walk abreast of Mr. Selwood, and ahead of the manager and cashier from the estate office; instead, he had taken a place in the rear ranks of the procession, and in it he remained until the close of the ceremony. Like the rest of those present, he defiled past the grave at which the chief mourners were standing, but he claimed no recognition from and gave no apparent heed to any of them; certainly none to Barthorpe Herapath. Also, like all the rest, he went away at once from the cemetery, and after him, quietly and unobtrusively, went a certain sharp-eyed person who had also been present, not as a mourner, but in the character of a casual stroller about the tombs and monuments, attracted for the moment by the imposing cortège which had followed the dead man to his grave.

Another sharp-eyed person made it his business to follow Barthorpe Herapath when he, too, went away. Barthorpe had come to the ceremony unattended. Selwood, Mr. Tertius, Professor Cox-Raythwaite, and Mr. Halfpenny had come together. These four also went away together. Barthorpe, still alone, re-entered his carriage when they had driven off. The observant person of the sharp eyes, hanging around the gates, heard him give his order:

"Portman Square!"

The four men who had preceded him were standing in the study when Barthorpe drove up to the house—standing around Peggie, who was obviously ill at ease and distressed. And when Barthorpe's voice was heard in the hall, Mr. Halfpenny spoke in decisive tones.

"We must understand matters at once," he said. "There is no use in beating about the bush. He has refused to meet or receive me so far—now I shall insist upon his saying plainly whatever he has to say. You, too, my dear, painful as it may be, must also insist."

"On—what?" asked Peggie.

"On his saying what he intends—if he intends—I don't know what he intends!" answered Mr. Halfpenny, testily. "It's most annoying, and we can't——"

Barthorpe came striding in, paused as he glanced around, and affected surprise.

"Oh!" he said. "I came to see you, Peggie—I did not know that there was any meeting in progress."

"Barthorpe!" said Peggie, looking earnestly at him. "You know that all these gentlemen were Uncle Jacob's friends—dear friends—and they are mine. Don't go away—Mr. Halfpenny wants to speak to you."

Barthorpe had already half turned to the door. He turned back—then turned again.

"Mr. Halfpenny can only want to speak to me on business," he said, coldly. "If Mr. Halfpenny wants to speak to me on business, he knows where to find me."

He had already laid a hand on the door when Mr. Halfpenny spoke sharply and sternly.

"Mr. Barthorpe Herapath!" he said. "I know very well where to find you, and I have tried to find you and to get speech with you for two days—in vain. I insist, sir, that you speak to us— or at any rate to your cousin—you are bound to speak, sir, out of common decency!"

"About what?" asked Barthorpe. "I came to speak to my cousin—in private."

"There is a certain something, sir," retorted Mr. Halfpenny, with warmth, "about which we must speak in public—such a public, at any rate, as is represented here and now. You know what it is—your uncle's will!"

"What about my uncle's will—or alleged will?" asked Barthorpe with a sneer.

Mr. Halfpenny appeared to be about to make a very angry retort, but he suddenly checked himself and looked at Peggie.

"You hear, my dear?" he said. "He says—alleged will!"

Peggie turned to Barthorpe with an appealing glance.

"Barthorpe!" she exclaimed. "Is that fair—is it generous? Is it just—to our uncle's memory? You know that is his will—what doubt can there be about it?"

Barthorpe made no answer. He still stood with one hand on the door, looking at Mr. Halfpenny. And suddenly he spoke.

"What do you wish to ask me?" he said.

"I wish to ask you a plain question," replied Mr. Halfpenny. "Do you accept this will, and are you going to act on your cousin's behalf? I want your plain answer."

Barthorpe hesitated a moment before replying. Then he made as if to open the door.

"I decline to discuss the matter of the alleged will," he answered. "I decline—especially," he continued, lifting a finger and pointing at Mr. Tertius, "especially in the presence of that man!"

"Barthorpe!" exclaimed Peggie, flushing at the malevolence of the tone and gesture. "How dare you! In my house——"

Barthorpe suddenly laughed. Once again he turned to the door—and this time he opened it.

"Just so—just so!" he said. "Your house, my dear cousin—according to the alleged will."

"Which will be proved, sir," snapped out Mr. Halfpenny. "As you refuse, or seem to do so, I shall act for your cousin—at once."

Barthorpe opened the door wide, and as he crossed the threshold, turned and gave Mr. Halfpenny a swift glance.

"Act!" he said. "Act!—if you can!"

Then he walked out and shut the door behind him, and Mr. Halfpenny turned to the others.

"The will must be proved at once," he said decisively. "Alleged—you all heard him say alleged! That looks as if—um! My dear Tertius, you have no doubt whatever about the proper and valid execution of this important document—now in my safe. None?"

"How can I have any doubt about what I actually saw?" replied Mr. Tertius. "I can't have any doubt, Halfpenny! I saw Jacob sign it; I signed it myself; I saw young Burchill sign it; we all three saw each other sign. What more can one want?"

"I must see this Mr. Burchill," remarked Mr. Halfpenny. "I must see him at once. Unfortunately, he left no address at the place we called at. He will have to be discovered."

Peggie coloured slightly as she turned to Mr. Halfpenny.

"Is it really necessary to see Mr. Burchill personally?" she asked with a palpable nervousness which struck Selwood strangely. "Must he be found?"

"Absolutely necessary, my dear," replied Mr. Halfpenny. "He must be found, and at once."

Mr. Tertius uttered an exclamation of annoyance.

"Dear, dear!" he said. "I noticed the young man at the cemetery just now—I ought really to have pointed him out to you—most forgetful of me!"

"I have Mr. Burchill's address," said Peggie, with an effort. "He left his card here on the day of my uncle's death—the address is on it. And I put it in this drawer."

Selwood watched Peggie curiously, and with a strange, vague sense of uneasiness as she went over to a drawer in Jacob Herapath's desk and produced the card. He had noticed a slight tremor in her voice when she spoke of Burchill, and her face, up till then very pale, had coloured at the first mention of his name. And now he was asking himself why any reference to this man seemed to disturb her, why——

But Mr. Halfpenny cut in on his meditations. The old lawyer held up the card to the light and slowly read out the address.

"Ah! Calengrove Mansions, Maida Vale," he said. "Um—quarter of an hour's drive. Tertius—you and I will go and see this young fellow at once."

Mr. Tertius turned to Professor Cox-Raythwaite.

"What do you think of this, Cox-Raythwaite?" he asked, almost piteously. "I mean—what do you think's best to be done?"

The Professor, who had stood apart with Selwood during the episode which had just concluded, pulling his great beard and looking very big and black and formidable, jerked his thumb in the direction of the old lawyer.

"Do what Halfpenny says," he growled. "See this other witness. And—but here, I'll have a word with you in the hall."

He said good-bye in a gruffly affectionate way to Peggie, patted her shoulder and her head as if she were a child, and followed the two other men out. Peggie, left alone with Selwood, turned to him. There was something half-appealing in her face, and Selwood suddenly drove his hands deep into his pockets, clenched them there, and put a tight hold on himself.

"It's all different!" exclaimed Peggie, dropping into a chair and clasping her hands on her knees. "All so different! And I feel so utterly helpless."

"Scarcely that," said Selwood, with an effort to speak calmly. "You've got Mr. Tertius, and Mr. Halfpenny, and the Professor, and—and if there's anything—anything I can do, don't you know, why, I——"

Peggie impulsively stretched out a hand—and Selwood, not trusting himself, affected not to see it. To take Peggie's hand at that moment would have been to let loose a flood of words which he was resolved not to utter just then, if ever. He moved across to the desk and pretended to sort and arrange some loose papers.

"We'll—all—all—do everything we can," he said, trying to keep any tremor out of his voice. "Everything you know, of course."

"I know—and I'm grateful," said Peggie. "But I'm frightened."

Selwood turned quickly and looked sharply at her.

"Frightened?" he exclaimed. "Of what?"

"Of something that I can't account for or realize," she replied. "I've a feeling that everything's all wrong—and strange. And—I'm frightened of Mr. Burchill."

"What!" snapped Selwood. He dropped the papers and turned to face her squarely. "Frightened of—Burchill? Why?"

"I—don't—know," she answered, shaking her head. "It's more an idea—something vague. I was always afraid of him when he was here—I've been afraid of him ever since. I was very much afraid when he came here the other day."

"You saw him?" asked Selwood.

"I didn't see him. He merely sent up that card. But," she added, "I was afraid even then."

Selwood leaned back against the desk, regarding her attentively.

"I don't think you're the sort to be afraid without reason," he said. "Of course, if you have reason, I've no right to ask what it is. All the same, if this chap is likely to annoy you, you've only to speak and—and——"

"Yes?" she said, smiling a little. "You'd——"

"I'll punch his head and break his neck for him!" growled Selwood. "And—and I wish you'd say if you have reasons why I should. Has—has he annoyed you?"

"No," answered Peggie. She regarded Selwood steadily for a minute; then she spoke with sudden impulse. "When he was here," she said, "I mean before he left my uncle, he asked me to marry him."

Selwood, in spite of himself, could not keep a hot flush from mounting to his cheek.

"And—you?" he said.

"I said no, of course, and he took my answer and went quietly away," replied Peggie. "And that—that's why I'm frightened of him."

"Good heavens! Why?" demanded Selwood. "I don't understand. Frightened of him because he took his answer, went away quietly, and hasn't annoyed you since? That—I say, that licks me!"

"Perhaps," she said. "But, you see, you don't know him. It's just because of that—that quiet—that—oh, I don't quite know how to explain!—that—well, silence—that I'm afraid—yes, literally afraid. There's something about him that makes me fear. I used to wish that my uncle had never employed him—that he had never come here. And—I'd rather be penniless than that my uncle had ever got him—him!—to witness that will!"

Selwood found no words wherewith to answer this. He did not understand it. Nevertheless he presently found words of another sort.

"All right!" he muttered doggedly. "I'll watch him—or, I'll watch that he—that—well, that no harm comes to—you know what I mean, don't you?"

"Yes," murmured Peggie, and once more held out an impulsive hand. But Selwood again pretended to see nothing, and he began another energetic assault upon the papers which Jacob Herapath would never handle again.

CHAPTER XVII

the law

Once within a taxi-cab and on their way to Maida Vale, Mr. Halfpenny turned to his companion with a shake of the head which implied a much mixed state of feeling.

"Tertius!" he exclaimed. "There's something wrong! Quite apart from what we know, and from what we were able to communicate to the police, there's something wrong. I feel it—it's in the air, the—the whole atmosphere. That fellow Barthorpe is up to some game. What? Did you notice his manner, his attitude—everything? Of course!—who could help it? He—has some scheme in his head. Again I say—what?"

Mr. Tertius stirred uneasily in his seat and shook his head.

"You haven't heard anything from New Scotland Yard?" he asked.

"Nothing—so far. But they are at work, of course. They'll work in their own way. And," continued Mr. Halfpenny, with a grim chuckle, "you can be certain of this much, Tertius—having heard what we were able to tell them, having seen what we were able to put before them, with respect to the doings of that eventful night, they won't let Master Barthorpe out of their ken—not they! It is best to let them pursue their own investigations in their own manner—they'll let us know what's been done, sure enough, at the right time."

"Yes," assented Mr. Tertius. "Yes—so I gather—I am not very conversant with these things. I confess there's one thing that puzzles me greatly though, Halfpenny. That's the matter of the man who came out of the House of Commons with Jacob that night. You remember that the coachman, Mountain, told us—and said at the inquest also—that he overheard what Jacob said to that man—'The thing must be done at once, and you must have everything ready for me at noon tomorrow,' or words to that effect. Now that man must be somewhere at hand—he must have read the newspapers, know all about the inquest—why doesn't he come forward?"

Mr. Halfpenny chuckled again and patted his friend's arm.

"Ah!" he said. "But you don't know that he hasn't come forward! The probability is, Tertius, that he has come forward, and that the people at New Scotland Yard are already in possession of whatever story he had to tell. Oh, yes, I quite expect that—I also expect to hear, eventually, another piece of news in relation to that man."

"What's that?" asked Mr. Tertius.

"Do you remember that, at the inquest, Mountain, the coachman, said that there was another bit of evidence he had to give which he'd forgotten to tell Mr. Barthorpe when he questioned him? Mountain"—continued Mr. Halfpenny—"went on to say that while Jacob Herapath and the man stood talking in Palace Yard, before Jacob got into his brougham, Jacob took some object from his waistcoat pocket and handed it, with what looked like a letter, to the man? Eh?"

"I remember very well," replied Mr. Tertius.

"Very good," said Mr. Halfpenny. "Now I believe that object to have been the key of Jacob's safe at the Safe Deposit, which, you remember, could not be found, but which young Selwood affirmed had been in Jacob's possession only that afternoon. The letter I believe to have been a formal authority to the Safe Deposit people to allow the bearer to open that safe. I've thought all that out," concluded Mr. Halfpenny, with a smile of triumph, "thought it out carefully, and it's my impression that that's what we shall find when the police move. I believe that man has revealed himself to the police, has told them—whatever it is he has to tell, and that his story probably throws a vast flood of light on the mystery. So I say—let us not at present concern ourselves with the actual murder of our poor friend: the police will ferret that out! What we're concerned with is—the will! That will, Tertius, must be proved, and at once."

"I am as little conversant with legal matters as with police procedure," observed Mr. Tertius. "What is the exact course, now, in a case of this sort?"

"The exact procedure, my dear sir," replied Mr. Halfpenny, dropping into his best legal manner, and putting the tips of his warmly-gloved fingers together in front of his well-filled overcoat, "the exact procedure is as follows. Barthorpe Herapath is without doubt the heir-at-law of his deceased uncle, Jacob Herapath. If Jacob had died intestate Barthorpe would have taken what we may call everything, for his uncle's property is practically all in the shape of real estate, in comparison to which the personalty is a mere nothing. But there is a will, leaving everything to Margaret Wynne. If Barthorpe Herapath intends to contest the legality of that will——"

"Good heavens, is that possible?" exclaimed Mr. Tertius. "He can't!"

"He can—if he wishes," replied Mr. Halfpenny, "though at present I don't know on what possible grounds. But, if he does, he can at once enter a caveat in the Probate Registry. The effect of that—supposing he does it—will be that when I take the will to be proved, progress will be stopped. Very well—I shall then, following the ordinary practice, issue and serve upon Barthorpe Herapath a document technically known as a 'warning.' On service of this warning, Barthorpe, if he insists upon his opposition, must enter an appearance. There will then be an opportunity for debate and attempt at agreement between him and ourselves. If that fails, or does not take place, I shall then issue a writ to establish the will. And that being done, why, then, my dear sir, the proceedings—ah, the proceedings would follow—substantially—the—er—usual course of litigation in this country."

"And that," asked Mr. Tertius, deeply interested and wholly innocent, "that would be—— ?"

"Well, there are two parties in this case—supposed case," continued Mr. Halfpenny, "Barthorpe Herapath, Margaret Wynne. After the issue of the writ I have just spoken of, each party would put in his or her pleas, and the matter would ultimately go to trial in the Probate Division of the High Court, most likely before a judge and a special jury."

"And how long would all this take?" asked Mr. Tertius.

"Ah!—um!" replied Mr. Halfpenny, tapping the tips of his gloves together. "That, my dear sir, is a somewhat difficult question to answer. I believe that all readers of the newspapers are aware that our Law Courts are somewhat congested—the cause lists are very full. The time which must elapse before a case can actually come to trial varies, my dear Tertius, varies enormously. But if—as in the matter we are supposing would probably be the case—if all the parties concerned were particularly anxious to have the case disposed of without delay, the trial might be arrived at within three or four months—that is, my dear sir, if the Long Vacation did not intervene. But—speaking generally—a better, more usual, more probable estimate would be, say six, seven, eight, or nine months."

"So long?" exclaimed Mr. Tertius. "I thought that justice was neither denied, sold, nor delayed!"

"Justice is never denied, my good friend, nor is it sold," replied Mr. Halfpenny, oracularly. "As to delay, ah, well, you know, if people will be litigants—and I assure you that nothing is so pleasing to a very large number of extraordinary persons who simply love litigation—a little delay cannot be avoided. However, we will hope that we shall have no litigation. Our present job is to get that will proved, and so far I see no difficulty. There is the will—we have the witnesses. At least, there are you, and we're hoping to see t'other in a few minutes. By the by, Tertius, what sort of fellow is this Burchill?"

Mr. Tertius considered his answer to this question.

"Well, I hardly know," he said at last. "Of course, I have rarely seen much of Jacob's secretaries. This man—he's not quite a youngster, Halfpenny—struck me as being the sort of person who might be dangerous."

"Ah!" exclaimed Mr. Halfpenny. "Dangerous! God bless me! Now, in what way, Tertius?"

"I don't quite know," replied Mr. Tertius. "He, somehow, from what I saw of him, suggested, I really don't know how, a certain atmosphere of, say—I'm trying to find the right words—cunning, subtlety, depth. Yes—yes, I should say he was what we commonly call—or what is commonly called in vulgar parlance—deep. Deep!"

"You mean—designing?" suggested Mr. Halfpenny.

"Exactly—designing," assented Mr. Tertius. "It—it was the sort of idea he conveyed, you know."

"Don't like the sound of him," said Mr. Halfpenny, "However, he's the second witness and we must put up with the fact. And here we are at these Calengrove Mansions, and let's hope we haven't a hundred infernal steps to climb, and that we find the fellow in."

The fellow was in. And the fellow, who had now discarded his mourning suit for the purple and fine linen which suggested Bond Street, was just about to go out, and was in a great hurry, and said so. He listened with obvious impatience while Mr. Tertius presented his companion.

"I wished to see you about the will of the deceased Jacob Herapath, Mr. Burchill," said Mr. Halfpenny "The will which, of course, you witnessed."

Burchill, who was gathering some books and papers together, and had already apologized for not being able to ask his callers to sit down, answered in an off-hand, bustling fashion.

"Of course, of course!" he replied. "Mr. Jacob Herapath's will, eh? Oh, of course, yes. Anything I can do, Mr. Halfpenny, of course—perhaps you'll drop me a line and make an appointment at your office some day—then I'll call, d'you see?"

"You remember the occasion, and the will, and your signature?" said Mr. Halfpenny, contriving to give Mr. Tertius a nudge as he put this direct question.

"Oh, I remember everything that ever happened in connection with my secretaryship to Mr. Jacob Herapath!" replied Burchill, still bustling. "I shall be ready for anything whenever I'm wanted, Mr. Halfpenny—pleased to be of service to the family, I'm sure. Now, you must really pardon me, gentlemen, if I hurry you and myself out—I've a most important engagement and I'm late already. As I said—drop me a line for an appointment, Mr. Halfpenny, and I'll come to you. Now, good-bye, good-bye!"

He had got them out of his flat, shaken hands with them, and hurried off before either elderly gentleman could get a word in, and as he flew towards the stairs Mr. Halfpenny looked at Mr. Tertius and shook his head.

"That beggar didn't want to talk," he said. "I don't like it."

"But he said that he remembered!" exclaimed Mr. Tertius. "Wasn't that satisfactory?"

"Anything but satisfactory, the whole thing," replied the old lawyer. "Didn't you notice that the man avoided any direct reply? He said 'of course' about a hundred times, and was as ambiguous, and non-committal, and vague, as he could be. My dear Tertius, the fellow was fencing!"

Mr. Tertius looked deeply distressed.

"You don't think——" he began.

"I might think a lot when I begin to think," said Mr. Halfpenny as they slowly descended the stairs from the desert solitude of the top floor of Calengrove Mansions. "But there's one thought that strikes me just now—do you remember what Burchill's old landlady at Upper Seymour Street told us?"

"That Barthorpe Herapath had been to inquire for Burchill?—yes," replied Mr. Tertius. "You're wondering——"

"I'm wondering if, since then, Barthorpe has found him," said Mr. Halfpenny. "If he has—if there have been passages between them—if——"

He paused half-way down the stairs, stood for a moment or two in deep thought and then laid his hand on his friend's arm.

"Tertius!" he said gravely. "That will must be presented for probate at once! I must lose no time. Come along—let me get back to my office and get to work. And do you go back to Portman Square and give the little woman your company."

Mr. Tertius went back to Portman Square there and then, and did what he could to make the gloomy house less gloomy. Instead of retreating to his own solitude he remained with Peggie, and tried to cheer her up by discussing various plans and matters of the future. And he was taking a quiet cup of tea with her at five o'clock when Kitteridge came in with a telegram for him. He opened it with trembling fingers and read:

"*Barthorpe entered caveat in Probate Registry at half-past three this afternoon.—Halfpenny.*"

Table of Contents

CHAPTER XVIII

the rosewood box

Mr. Tertius dropped the telegram on the little table at which he and Peggie were sitting, and betrayed his feelings with a deep groan. Peggie, who was just about to give him his second cup of tea, set down her teapot and jumped to his side.

"Oh, what is it!" she exclaimed. "Some bad news? Please——"

Mr. Tertius pulled himself together and tried to smile.

"You must forgive me, my dear," he said, with a feeble attempt to speak cheerily. "I—the truth is, I think I have lived in such a state of ease and—yes, luxury, for so many years that I am not capable of readily bearing these trials and troubles. I'm ashamed of myself—I must be braver—not so easily affected."

"But—the telegram?" said Peggie.

Mr. Tertius handed it to her with a dismal shake of his head.

"I suppose it's only what was to be expected, after all that Halfpenny told me this afternoon," he remarked. "But I scarcely thought it would occur so soon. My dear, I am afraid you must prepare yourself for a great deal of unpleasantness and worry. Your cousin seems to be determined to give much trouble. Extraordinary!—most extraordinary! My dear, I confess I do not understand it."

Peggie had picked up the telegram and was reading it with knitted brow.

"'Barthorpe entered caveat in Probate Registry at half-past three this afternoon,'" she slowly repeated. "But what does that mean, Mr. Tertius? Something to do with the will?"

"A great deal to do with the will, I fear!" replied Mr. Tertius, lugubriously. "A caveat, my dear, is some sort of process—I'm sure I don't know whether it's given by word of mouth, or if it's a document—by which the admission to probate of a dead person's last will and testament can be stopped. In plain language," continued Mr. Tertius, "your cousin Barthorpe has been to the Probate Registry and done something to prevent Mr. Halfpenny from proving the will. It is a wicked action on his part—and, considering that he is a solicitor, and that he saw the will with his own eyes, it is, as I have previously remarked, most extraordinary!"

"And all this means—what?" asked Peggie.

"It means that there will be legal proceedings," groaned Mr. Tertius. "Long, tedious, most annoying and trying proceedings! Perhaps a trial—we may have to go to court and give evidence. I dread it!—I am, as I said, so used to a life of ease and freedom from anxiety that anything of this sort distresses me unspeakably. I fear I am degenerating into cowardice!"

"Nonsense!" said Peggie. "It is merely that this sort of thing is disturbing. And we are not going to be afraid of Barthorpe. Barthorpe is very foolish. I meant—always have meant, ever since I heard about the will—to share with him, for there's no law against that. But if Barthorpe wants to upset the will altogether and claim everything, I shall fight him. And if I win—as I suppose I shall—I shall make him do penance pretty heavily before he's forgiven. However, that's all in the future. What I don't understand about the present is—how can that will be upset? Mr. Halfpenny says it's duly and properly executed, witnessed, and so on—how can Barthorpe object to it?"

Mr. Tertius put down his cup and rose.

"Your cousin, Barthorpe, my dear, is, I regret to say, a deep man," he replied. "He has some scheme in his head. This," he went on, picking up the telegram and placing it in his pocket, "this is the first step in that scheme. Well, it is perhaps a relief to know that he has taken it: we shall now know where we are and what has to be done."

"Quite so," said Peggie. "But there is another matter, Mr. Tertius, which seems to be forgotten in this of the will. Pray, what is Barthorpe doing, what is anybody doing, about solving the mystery of my uncle's death? Everybody says he was murdered—who is doing anything to find the murderer?"

Mr. Tertius, who had advanced as far as the door on his way out of the room, came back to Peggie's side in a fashion suggestive of deep mystery, walking on the tips of his toes and putting a finger to his lips as he drew near his chair.

"My dear!" he said, bending down to her and speaking in a tone fully as indicative of mystery as his tip-toe movement, "a great deal is being done—but in the strictest secrecy! Most important investigations, my dear!—the police, the detective police, you know. The word at present—to put it into one word, vulgar, but expressive—the word is 'Mum'! Silence, my dear— the policy of the mole—underground working, you know. From what I am aware of, and from what our good friend Halfpenny tells me, and believes, I gather that a result will be attained which will be surprising."

"So long as justice is done," remarked Peggie. "That is all I want—all we ought to aim at. I don't care twopence about surprising or sensational discoveries—I want to see my uncle's murderer properly punished."

She shed a few more quiet tears over Jacob Herapath's untoward fate when Mr. Tertius had left her and fell to thinking about him. The thoughts which came presently led her to go to the dead man's room—a simple, spartan-like chamber which she had not entered since his death. She had a vague sense of wanting to be brought into touch with him through the things which had been his, and for a while she wandered aimlessly about the room, laying a hand now and then on the objects which she knew he must have handled the last time he had occupied the room—his toilet articles, the easy chair in which he always sat for a few minutes every night, reading a little before going to bed, the garments which hung in his wardrobe, anything on which his fingers had rested. And as she wandered about she noted, not for the first nor the hundredth time, how Jacob Herapath had gathered about him in this room a number of objects connected with his youth. The very furniture, simple, homely stuff, had once stood in his mother's bedroom in a small cottage in a far-off country. On the walls were portraits of his father and mother—crude things painted by some local artist; there, too, were some samplers worked by his mother in her girlhood, flanked by some faded groups of flowers which she had painted about the same time. Jacob Herapath had brought all these things to his grand house in Portman Square years before, and had cleared a room of fine modern furniture and fittings to make space for them. He had often said to Peggie, when she grew old enough to understand, that he liked to wake in a morning and see the old familiar things about him which he had known as a child. For one object in that room he had a special veneration and affection—an old rosewood workbox, which had belonged to his mother, and to her mother before her. Once he had allowed Peggie to inspect it, to take from it the tray lined with padded green silk, to examine the various nooks and corners contrived by the eighteenth-century cabinetmaker—some disciple, maybe, of Chippendale or Sheraton—to fit the tarnished silver thimbles on to her own fingers, to wonder at the knick-knacks of a departed age, and to laugh over the scent of rose and lavender which hung about the skeins and spools. And he had told her that when he died the rosewood box should be hers—as long as he lived, he said, it must stand on his chest of drawers, so that he could see it at least twice a day.

Jacob Herapath was dead now, and buried, and the rosewood box and everything else that had been his had passed to Peggie—as things were, at any rate. She presently walked up to the queer old chest of drawers, and drew the rosewood box towards her and lifted the lid. It was years since Jacob had shown it to her, and she remembered the childish delight with which she had lifted out the tray which lay on the top and looked into the various compartments beneath it. Now she opened the box again, and lifted the tray—and there, lying bold and uncovered before her eyes, she saw a letter, inscribed with one word in Jacob Herapath's well-known handwriting—"Peggie."

If Jacob Herapath himself had suddenly appeared before her in that quiet room, the girl could scarcely have felt more keenly the strange and subtle fear which seized upon her as she realized that what she was staring at was probably some message to herself. It was some time before she dared to lay hands on this message—when at last she took the letter out of the box her fingers trembled so much that she found a difficulty in opening the heavily-sealed envelope. But she calmed herself with a great effort, and carrying the half-sheet of note-paper, which she drew from its cover, over to the window, lifted it in the fading light and read the few lines which Jacob Herapath had scrawled there.

"If anything ever happens suddenly to me, my will, duly executed and witnessed by Mr. Tertius and Mr. Frank Burchill, is in a secret drawer of my old bureau which lies behind the third small drawer on the right-hand side.

"Jacob Herapath."

That was all—beyond a date, and the date was a recent one. "If anything ever happens suddenly"—had he then felt some fear, experienced any premonition, of a sudden happening? Why had he never said anything to her, why?

But Peggie realized that such questions were useless at that time—that time was pre-eminently one of action. She put the letter back in the rosewood box, took the box in her arms, and carrying it off to her own room, locked it up in a place of security. And that had scarcely been done when Kitteridge came seeking her and bringing with him a card: Mr. Frank Burchill's card, and on it scribbled a single line: "Will you kindly give me a few minutes?"

Peggie considered this request in one flash of thought, and turned to the butler.

"Where is Mr. Burchill?" she asked. "In the study? Very well, I will come down to him in a few minutes."

She made a mighty effort to show herself calm, collected, and indifferent, when she presently went down to the study. But she neither shook hands with the caller, nor asked him to sit; instead she marched across to the hearthrug and regarded him from a distance.

"Yes, Mr. Burchill?" she said quietly. "You wish to see me?"

She looked him over steadily as she spoke, and noted a certain air of calm self-assurance about him which struck her with a vague uneasiness. He was too easy, too quiet, too entirely businesslike to be free from danger. And the bow which he gave her was, to her thinking, the height of false artifice.

"I wished to see you and to speak to you, with your permission," he answered. "I beg you to believe that what I have—what I desire to say is to be said by me with the deepest respect, the most sincere consideration. I have your permission to speak? Then I beg to ask you if—I speak with deep courtesy!—if the answer which you made to a certain question of mine some time ago is—was—is to be—final?"

"So final that I am surprised that you should refer to the matter," replied Peggie. "I told you so at the time."

"Circumstances have changed," he said. "I am at a parting of the ways in life's journey. I wish to know—definitely—which way I am to take. A ray of guiding light from you——"

"There will be none!" said Peggie sharply. "Not a gleam. This is waste of time. If that is all you have to say——"

The door of the study opened, and Selwood, who was still engaged about the house, came in. He paused on the threshold, staring from one to the other, and made as if to withdraw. But Peggie openly smiled on him.

"Come in, Mr. Selwood," she said. "I was just going to ask Kitteridge to find you. I want to see both you and Mr. Tertius."

Then she turned to Burchill, who stood, a well-posed figure in his fine raiment, still watching her, and made him a frigid bow.

"There is no more to say on that point—at any time," she said quietly. "Good day. Mr. Selwood, will you ring the bell?"

Burchill executed another profound and self-possessed bow. He presently followed the footman from the room, and Peggie, for the first time since Jacob Herapath's death, suddenly let her face relax and burst into a hearty laugh.

Table of Contents

CHAPTER XIX

That evening Triffitt got Burchill's address from Carver, and next day he drew a hundred pounds from the cashier of the *Argus* and went off to Calengrove Mansions. In his mind there was a clear and definite notion. It might result in something; it might come to nothing, but he was going to try it. Briefly, it was that if he wished—as he unfeignedly did wish—to find out anything about Burchill, he must be near him; so near, indeed, that he could keep an eye on him, acquaint himself with his goings and comings, observe his visitors, watch for possible openings, make himself familiar with Burchill's daily life. It might be a difficult task; it might be an easy task—in any case, it was a task that must be attempted. With Markledew's full consent and approval behind him and Markledew's money-bags to draw upon, Triffitt felt equal to attempting anything.

The first thing was to take a quiet look at Burchill's immediate environment. Calengrove Mansions turned out to be one of the smaller of the many blocks of residential flats which have of late years arisen in such numbers in the neighbourhood of Maida Vale and St. John's Wood. It was an affair of some five or six floors, and judging from what Triffitt could see of it from two sides, it was not fully occupied at that time, for many of its windows were uncurtained, and there was a certain air of emptiness about the upper storeys. This fact was not unpleasing to Triffitt; it argued that he would have small difficulty in finding a lodgment within the walls which sheltered the man he wanted to watch. And in pursuance of his scheme, which, as a beginning, was to find out exactly where Burchill was located, he walked into the main entrance and looked about him, hoping to find an address-board. Such a board immediately caught his eye, affixed to the wall near the main staircase. Then Triffitt saw that the building was divided into five floors, each floor having some three or four flats. Those on the bottom floors appeared to be pretty well taken; the names of their occupants were neatly painted in small compartments on the board. Right at the top was the name Mr. Frank Burchill—and on that floor, which evidently possessed three flats, there were presumably no other occupants, for the remaining two spaces relating to it were blank.

Triffitt took all this in at a glance; another glance showed him a door close by on which was painted the word "Office." He pushed this open and walked inside, to confront a clerk who was the sole occupant. To him, Triffitt, plunging straight into business, gently intimated that he was searching for a convenient flat. The clerk immediately began to pull out some coloured plans, labelled first, second, third floors.

"About what sized flat do you require?" he asked. He had already looked Triffitt well over, and as Triffitt, in honour of the occasion, had put on his smartest suit and a new overcoat, he decided that this was a young man who was either just married or about to be married. "Do you want a family flat, or one for a couple without family, or——"

"What I want," answered Triffitt readily, "is a bachelor flat—for myself. And—if possible—furnished."

"Oh!" said the clerk. "Just so. I happen to have something that will suit you exactly—that is, if you don't want to take it for longer than three or four months." He pulled forward another plan, labelled "Fifth Floor," and pointed to certain portions, shaded off in light colours. "One of our tenants, Mr. Stillwater," he continued, "has gone abroad for four months, and he'd be glad to let his flat, furnished, in his absence. That's it—it contains, you see, a nice sitting-room, a bedroom, a bathroom, and a small kitchen—all contained within the flat, of course. It is well and comfortably furnished, and available at once."

Triffitt bent over the plan. But he was not looking at the shaded portion over which the clerk's pencil was straying; instead he was regarding the fact that across the corresponding portion of the plan was written in red ink the words, "Mr. Frank Burchill." The third portion was blank; it, apparently, was unlet.

"That is really about the size of flat I want," said Triffitt, musingly. "What's the rent of that, now?"

"I can let that to you for fifty shillings a week," answered the clerk. "That includes everything—there's plate, linen, glass, china, anything you want. Slight attendance can be arranged for with our caretaker's wife—that is, she can cook breakfast, and make beds, and do more, if necessary. Perhaps you would like to see this flat?"

Triffitt followed the clerk to the top of the house. The absent Mr. Stillwater's rooms were comfortable and pleasant; one glance around them decided Triffitt.

"This place will suit me very well," he said. "Now I'll give you satisfactory references about myself, and pay you a month's rent in advance, and if that's all right to you, I'll come in today. You can ring up my references on your 'phone, and then, if you're satisfied, we'll settle the rent, and I'll see the caretaker's wife about airing that bed."

Within half an hour Triffitt was occupant of the flat, the cashier of the *Argus* having duly telephoned that he was a thoroughly dependable and much-respected member of its staff, and Triffitt himself having handed over ten pounds as rent for the coming month, he interviewed the caretaker's wife, went to a neighbouring grocer's shop and ordered a stock of necessaries wherewith to fill his larder, repaired to his own lodgings and brought away all that he wanted in the way of luggage, books, and papers, and by the middle of the afternoon was fairly settled in his new quarters. He spent an hour in putting himself and his belongings straight—and then came the question what next?

He was there for a special purpose—that special purpose was to acquaint himself as thoroughly as possible with the doings of Frank Burchill. Burchill was there—he was almost on the point of saying, in the next cell!—there, in the flat across the corridor; figuratively, within touch, if it were not for sundry divisions of brick, mortar, and the like. Burchill's door was precisely opposite his own; there was an advantage in that fact. And in Triffitt's outer door (all these flats, he discovered—that is, if they were all like his own, possessed double doors) there was a convenient letter slit, by manipulating which he could, if he chose, keep a perpetual observation on the other opposite. But Triffitt did not propose to sit with his eye glued to that letter slit all day—it might be useful at times, and for some special purpose, but he had wider views. And the first thing to do was to make an examination, geographical and exhaustive, of his own surroundings: Triffitt had learnt, during his journalistic training, that attention to details is one of the most important things in life.

The first thing that had struck Triffitt in this respect was that there was no lift in this building. He had remarked on that to the clerk, and the clerk had answered with a shrug of the shoulders that it was a mistake and one for which the proprietor was already having to pay. However, Triffitt, bearing in mind what job he was on, was not displeased that the lift had been omitted—it is sometimes an advantage to be able to hang over the top rail of a staircase and watch people coming up from below. He stored that fact in his mental reservoirs. And now that he had got into his rooms, he proceeded to seek for more facts. First, as to the rooms themselves—he wanted to know all about them, because he had carefully noticed, while looking at the plan of that floor in the office downstairs, that Burchill's flat was arranged exactly like his own. And Triffitt's flat was like this—you entered through a double door into a good-sized sitting-room, out of which two other rooms led—one went into a small kitchen and pantry; the other into the bedroom, at the side of which was a little bathroom. The windows of the bedroom opened on to a view of the street below; those of the sitting-room on to a square of garden, on the lawn of which tenants might disport themselves, more or less sadly, with tennis or croquet in summer.

Triffitt looked out of his sitting-room windows last of all. He then perceived with great joy that in front of them was a balcony, and that this balcony stretched across the entire front of the house. There were, in fact, balconies to all five floors—the notion being, of course, that occupants could whenever they pleased sit out there in such sunlight as struggled between their own roof and the tall buildings opposite. It immediately occurred to Triffitt that here was an easy way of making a call upon your next door neighbour; instead of crossing the corridor and knocking at his door, you had nothing to do but walk along the balcony and tap at his window. Filled with this thought Triffitt immediately stepped out on his balcony and inspected the windows of his own and the next flat. He immediately saw something which filled him with a great idea. Both windows were fitted with patent ventilators, let into the top panes. Now, supposing one of these ventilators was fully open, and two people were talking within the room in even the ordinary tones of conversation—would it not be possible for an eavesdropper outside to hear a good deal, if not everything, of what was said? The idea was worth thinking over, anyway, and Triffitt retired indoors to ruminate over it and over much else.

For two or three days nothing happened. Twice Triffitt met Burchill on the stairs—Burchill, of course, did not know him from Adam, and gave him no more than the mere glance he would have thrown at any other ordinary young man. Triffitt, however, gave Burchill more than a passing look—unobtrusively. Certainly he was the man whom he had seen in the dock nine years before in that far-off Scottish town—there was little appreciable alteration in his appearance, except that he was now very smartly dressed. There were peculiarities about the fellow, said Triffitt, which you couldn't forget—certainly, Frank Burchill was Francis Bentham.

But on the third day, two things happened—one connected directly with Triffitt's new venture, the other not. The first was that as Triffitt was going down the stairs that afternoon, on his way to the office, at which he kept looking in now and then, although he was relieved from regular attendance and duty, he met Barthorpe Herapath coming up. Triffitt thanked his lucky stars that the staircase was badly lighted, and that this was an unusually gloomy November day. True, Barthorpe had only once seen him, that he knew of—that morning at the estate office, when he, Triffitt, had asked Selwood for information—but then, some men have sharp memories for faces, and Barthorpe might recognize him and wonder what an *Argus* man was doing there in Calengrove Mansions. So Triffitt quickly pulled the flap of the Trilby hat about his nose, and sank his chin lower into the turned-up collar of his overcoat, and hurried past the tall figure. And Barthorpe on his part never looked at the reporter—or if he did, took no more heed of him than of the balustrade at his side.

"That's one thing established, anyway!" mused Triffitt as he went his way. "Barthorpe Herapath is in touch with Burchill. The dead man's nephew and the dead man's ex-secretary—um! Putting their heads together—about what?"

He was still pondering this question when he reached the office and found a note from Carver who wanted to see him at once. Triffitt went round to the *Magnet* and got speech with Carver in a quiet corner. Carver went straight to his point.

"I've got him," he said, eyeing his fellow-conspirator triumphantly.

"Got—who?" demanded Triffitt.

"That taxi-cab chap—you know who I mean," answered Carver. "Ran him down at noon today."

"No!" exclaimed Triffitt. "Gad! Are you sure, though?—is it certain he's the man you were after?"

"He's the chap who drove a gentleman from near Portman Square to just by St. Mary Abbot church at two o'clock on the morning of the Herapath murder," replied Carver. "That's a dead certainty! I risked five pounds on it, anyway, for which I'll trouble you. I went on the lines of rounding up all the cabbies I could find who were as a rule on night duty round about that quarter, and bit by bit I got on to this fellow, and, as I say, I gave him a fiver for just telling me a mere bit. And it's here—he's already given some information to that old Mr. Tertius—you know—and Tertius commanded him to keep absolutely quiet until the moment came for a move. Well, that moment has not come yet, evidently—the chap hasn't been called on since, anyhow— and when I mentioned money he began to prick his ears. He's willing to tell—for money—if we keep dark what he tells us. The truth is, he's out to get what he can out of anybody. If you make it worth his while, he'll tell."

"Aye!" said Triffitt. "But the question is, what has he got to tell? What does he know?— actually know?"

"He knows," replied Carver, "he actually knows who the man was that he drove that morning! He didn't know who he was when he first gave information to Tertius, but he knows now, and, as I say, he's willing to sell his knowledge—in private."

Table of Contents

CHAPTER XX

the diamond ring

Triffitt considered Carver's report during a moment of mutual silence. If he had consulted his own personal inclination he would have demanded to be led straight to the taxi-cab driver. But Triffitt knew himself to be the expender of the Markledew money, and the knowledge made him unduly cautious.

"It comes to this," he said at last, "this chap knows something which he's already told to this Mr. Tertius. Mr. Tertius has in all probability already told it to the people at New Scotland Yard. They, of course, will use the information at their own time and in their own way. But what we want is something new—something startling—something good!"

"I tell you the fellow's got all that," said Carver. "He knows the man whom he drove that morning. Isn't that good enough?"

"Depend upon how I can bring it out," answered Triffitt. "Well, when can I see this chap?"

"Tonight—seven o'clock," replied Carver. "I fixed that, in anticipation."

"And—where?" demanded Triffitt.

"I'll go with you—it's to be at a pub near Orchard Street," said Carver. "Better bring money with you—he'll want cash."

"All right," agreed Triffitt. "But I'm not going to throw coin about recklessly. I shall want value."

Carver laughed. Triffitt's sudden caution amused him.

"I reckon people have to buy pigs in pokes in dealing with this sort of thing, Triff," he said. "But whether the chap's information's good for much or not, I'm certain it's genuine. Well, come round here again at six-thirty."

Triffitt, banknotes in pocket, went round again at six-thirty, and was duly conducted Oxford Street way by Carver, who eventually led him into a network of small streets, in which the mews and the stable appeared to be conspicuous features, and to the bar-parlour of a somewhat dingy tavern, at that hour little frequented. And at precisely seven o'clock the door of the parlour opened and a face showed itself, recognized Carver, and grinned. Carver beckoned the face into a corner, and having formally introduced his friend Triffitt, suggested liquid refreshment. The face assented cordially, and having obscured itself for a moment behind a pint pot, heaved a sigh of gratification, and seemed desirous of entering upon business.

"But it ain't, of course, to go no further—at present," said the owner of the face. "Not into no newspapers nor nothing, *at* present. I don't mind telling you young gents, if it's made worth my while, of course, but as things is, I don't want the old gent in Portman Square to know as how I've let on—d'ye see? Of course, I ain't seen nothing of him never since I called there, and he gave me a couple o' quid, and told me to expect more—only the more's a long time o' coming, and if I do see my way to turning a honest penny by what I knows, why, then, d'ye see——"

"I see, very well," assented Triffitt. "And what might your idea of an honest penny be, now?"

The taxi-cab driver silently regarded his questioner. He had already had a five-pound note out of Carver, who carried a small fund about him in case of emergency; he was speculating on his chances of materially increasing this, and his eyes grew greedy.

"Well, now, guv'nor, what's your own notion of that?" he asked at last. "I'm a poor chap, you know, and I don't often get a chance o' making a bit in this way. What's it worth—what I can tell, you know—to you? This here young gentleman was keen enough about it this afternoon, guv'nor."

"Depends," answered Triffitt. "You'd better answer a question or two. First—you haven't told the old gentleman in Portman Square—Mr. Tertius—any more than what you told my friend here you'd told him?"

"Not a word more, guv'nor! 'Cause why—I ain't seen him since."

"And you've told nothing to the police?"

"The police ain't never come a-nigh me, and I ain't been near them. What the old chap said was—wait! And I've waited and ain't heard nothing."

"Wherefore," observed Triffitt sardonically, "you want to make a bit."

"Ain't no harm in a man doing his best for his-elf, guv'nor, I hope," said the would-be informant. "If I don't look after myself, who's a-going to look after me—I asks you that, now?"

"And I ask you—how much?" said Triffitt. "Out with it!"

The taxi-cab driver considered, eyeing his prospective customer furtively.

"The other gent told you what it is I can tell, guv'nor?" he said at last. "It's information of what you might call partik'lar importance, is that."

"I know—you can tell the name of the man whom you drove that morning from the corner of Orchard Street to Kensington High Street," replied Triffitt. "It may be important—it mayn't. You see, the police haven't been in any hurry to approach you, have they? Come now, give it a name?"

The informant summoned up his resolution.

"Cash down—on the spot, guv'nor?" he asked.

"Spot cash," replied Triffitt. "On this table!"

"Well—how would a couple o' fivers be, now?" asked the anxious one. "It's good stuff, guv'nor."

"A couple of fivers will do," answered Triffitt. "And here they are." He took two brand-new, crackling five-pound notes from his pocket, folded them up, laid them on the table, and set a glass on them. "Now, then!" he said. "Tell your tale—there's your money when it's told."

The taxi-cab driver eyed the notes, edged his chair further into the half-lighted corner in which Triffitt and Carver sat, and dropped his voice to a whisper.

"All right, guv'nor," he said. "Thanking you. Then it's this here—the man what I drove that morning was the nephew!"

"You mean Mr. Barthorpe Herapath?" said Triffitt, also in a whisper.

"That's him—that's the identical, sir! Of course," continued the informant, "I didn't know nothing of that when I told the old gent in Portman Square what I did tell him. Now, you see, I wasn't called at that inquest down there at Kensington—after what I'd told the old gent, I expected to be, but I wasn't. All the same, there's been a deal of talk around about the corner of Orchard Street, and, of course, there is them in that quarter as knows all the parties concerned, and this man Barthorpe, as you call him, was pointed out to me as the nephew—nephew to him as was murdered that night. And then, of course, I knew it was him as I took up at two o'clock that morning."

"How did you know?" asked Triffitt.

The taxi-cab driver held up a hand and tapped a brass ring on its third finger.

"Where I wears that ring, gentlemen," he said triumphantly, "he wears a fine diamond—a reg'lar swell 'un. That morning, when he got into my cab, he rested his hand a minute on the door, and the light from one o' the lamps across the street shone full on the stone. Now, then, when this here Barthorpe was pointed out to me in Orchard Street, a few days ago, as the nephew of Jacob Herapath, he was talking to another gentleman, and as they stood there he lighted a cigar, and when he put his hand up, I see that ring again—no mistaking it, guv'nor! He was the man. And, from what I've read, it seems to me it was him as put on his uncle's coat and hat after the old chap was settled, and——"

"If I were you, I'd keep those theories to myself—yet awhile, at any rate," said Triffitt. "In fact—I want you to. Here!" he went on, removing the glass and pushing the folded banknotes towards the taxi-cab driver, "put those in your pocket. And keep your mouth shut about having seen and told me. I shan't make any use—public use, anyway—of what you've said, just yet. If the old gentleman, Tertius, comes to you, or the police come along with or without him, you can tell 'em anything you like—everything you've told me if you please—it doesn't matter, now. But you're on no account to tell them that I've seen you and that you've spilt to me—do you understand?"

The informant understood readily enough, and promised with equal readiness, even going so far as to say that that would suit him down to the ground.

"All right," said Triffitt, "keep a still tongue as regards me, and there'll be another fiver for you. Now, Carver, we'll get."

Outside Triffitt gave his companion's arm a confidential squeeze.

"Things are going well!" he said. "I wasn't a bit surprised at what that fellow told me—I expected it. What charms me is that Barthorpe Herapath, who is certainly to be strongly suspected, is in touch with Burchill—I didn't tell you that I met him on the stairs at Calengrove Mansions this afternoon. Of course, he was going to see my next-door neighbour! What about, friend Carver?"

"If you could answer your own last question, we should know something," replied Carver.

"We know something as it is," said Triffitt. "Enough for me to tell Markledew, anyway. I don't see so far into all this, myself, but Markledew's the sort of chap who can look through three brick walls and see a mole at work in whatever's behind the third, and he'll see something in what I tell him, and I'll do the telling as soon as he comes down tomorrow morning."

Markledew listened to Triffitt's story next day in his usual rapt silence. The silence remained unbroken for some time after Triffitt had finished. And eventually Markledew got up from his elbow-chair and reached for his hat.

"You can come with me," he said. "We'll just ride as far as New Scotland Yard."

Triffitt felt himself turning pale. New Scotland Yard! Was he then to share his discoveries with officials? In spite of his awful veneration for the great man before him he could not prevent two words of despairing ejaculation escaping from his lips.

"The police!"

"Just so—the police," answered Markledew, calmly. "I mean to work this in connection with them. No need to alarm yourself, young man—I know what you're thinking. But you won't lose any 'kudos'—I'm quite satisfied with you so far. But we can't do without the police—and they may be glad of even a hint from us. Now run down and get a taxi-cab and I'll meet you outside."

Triffitt had never been within the mazes of New Scotland Yard in his life, and had often wished that business would take him there. It was very soon plain to him, however, that his proprietor knew his way about the Criminal Investigation Department as well as he knew the *Argus* office. Markledew was quickly closeted with the high official who had seen Mr. Halfpenny and Mr. Tertius a few days previously; while they talked, Triffitt was left to kick his heels in a waiting-room. When he was eventually called in, he found not only the high official and Markledew, but another man whose name was presently given to him as Davidge.

"Mr. Davidge," observed the high official, "is in charge of this case. Will you just tell him your story?"

It appeared to Triffitt that Mr. Davidge was the least impressionable, most stolid man he had ever known. Davidge showed no sign of interest; Triffitt began to wonder if anything could ever surprise him. He listened in dead silence to all that the reporter had to say; when Triffitt had finished he looked apathetically at his superior.

"I think, sir, I will just step round to Mr. Halfpenny's office," he remarked. "Perhaps Mr. Triffitt will accompany me?—then he and I can have a bit of a talk."

Triffitt looked at Markledew: Markledew nodded his big head.

"Go with him," said Markledew. "Work with him! He knows what he's after."

Davidge took Triffitt away to Mr. Halfpenny's office—on the way thither he talked about London fogs, one of which had come down that morning. But he never mentioned the business in hand until—having left Triffitt outside while he went in—he emerged from Mr. Halfpenny's room. Then he took the reporter's arm and led him away, and his manner changed to one of interest and even enthusiasm.

"Well, young fellow!" he said, leading Triffitt down the street, "you're the chap I wanted to get hold of!—you're a godsend. And so you really have a flat next to that occupied by the person whom we'll refer to as F. B., eh?"

"I have," answered Triffitt, who was full of wonderment.

"Good—good!—couldn't be better!" murmured the detective. "Now then—I dare say you'd be quite pleased if I called on you at your flat—quietly and unobtrusively—at say seven o'clock tonight, eh?"

"Delighted!" answered Triffitt. "Of course!"

"Very good," said Davidge. "Then at seven o'clock tonight I shall be there. In the meantime—not a word. You're curious to know why I'm coming? All right—keep your curiosity warm till I come—I'll satisfy it. Tonight, mind, young man—seven, sharp!"

Then he gave Triffitt's arm a squeeze and winked an eye at him, and at once set off in one direction, while the reporter, mystified and inquisitive, turned in another.

Table of Contents

CHAPTER XXI

the deserted flat

When Triffitt had fairly separated from the detective and had come to reckon up the events of that morning he became definitely conscious of one indisputable fact. The police knew more than he did. The police were in possession of information which had not come his way. The police were preparing some big *coup*. Therefore—the police would get all the glory.

This was not what Triffitt had desired. He had wanted to find things out for himself, to make a grand discovery, to be able to go to Markledew and prove his case. Markledew could then have done what he pleased; it had always been in Triffitt's mind that Markledew would in all probability present the result of his reporter's labours to the people at Scotland Yard. But Markledew had become somewhat previous—he had insisted that Triffitt should talk to the Scotland Yard folk at this early—in Triffitt's view, much too early—stage of the proceedings. And Triffitt had felt all the time he was talking that he was only telling the high official and the apathetic Davidge something that they already knew. He had told them about his memories of Bentham and the Scottish murder trial—something convinced him that they were already well acquainted with that story. He had narrated the incident of the taxi-cab driver: he was sure that they were quite well aware that the man who had been driven from Orchard Street to St. Mary Abbot church that morning after the murder was Barthorpe Herapath. Their cold eyes and polite, yet almost chillingly indifferent manner had convinced Triffitt that they were just listening to something with which they were absolutely familiar. Never a gleam of interest had betrayed itself in their stolid official faces until he had referred to the fact that he himself was living in a flat next door to Burchill's. Then, indeed, the detective had roused himself almost to eagerness, and now he was coming to see him, Triffitt, quietly and unobtrusively. Why?

"All the same," mused Triffitt, "I shall maybe prove a small cog in the bigger mechanism, and that's something. And Markledew was satisfied, anyway, so far. And if I don't get something out of that chap Davidge tonight, write me down an ass!"

From half-past six that evening, Triffitt, who had previously made some ingenious arrangements with the slit of his letter-box, by which he could keep an eye on the corridor outside, kept watch on Burchill's door—he had an instinctive notion that Davidge, when he arrived, would be glad to know whether the gentleman opposite was in or out. At a quarter to seven Burchill went out in evening dress, cloak, and opera hat, making a fine figure as he struck the light of the corridor lamp. And ten minutes later Triffitt heard steps coming along the corridor and he opened the door to confront Davidge and another man, a quiet-looking, innocent-visaged person. Davidge waved a hand towards his companion.

"Evening, Mr. Triffitt," said he. "Friend of mine—Mr. Milsey. You'll excuse the liberty, I'm sure."

"Glad to see both of you," answered Triffitt, cordially. He led the way into his sitting-room, drew chairs forward, and produced refreshments which he had carefully laid in during the afternoon in preparation. "Drop of whisky and soda, gentlemen?" he said, hospitably. "Let me help you. Will you try a cigar?"

"Very kind of you," replied Davidge. "A slight amount of the liquid'll do us no harm, but no cigars, thank you, Mr. Triffitt. Cigars are apt to leave a scent, an odour, about one's clothes, however careful you may be, and we don't want to leave any traces of our presence where we're going, do we, Jim?"

"Not much," assented Mr. Milsey, laconically. "Wouldn't do."

Triffitt handed round the glasses and took a share himself.

"Ah!" he said. "That's interesting! And where are you going, now—if one may ask?"

Davidge nodded his desires for his host's good health, and then gave him a wink.

"We propose to go in there," he said with a jerk of his thumb towards Burchill's flat. "It's what I've been wanting to do for three or four days, but I didn't see my way clear without resorting to a lot of things—search-warrant, and what not—and it would have meant collusion with the landlord here, and the clerk downstairs, and I don't know what all, so I put it off a bit. But when you told me that you'd got this flat, why, then, I saw my way! Of course, I've been familiar with the lie of these flats for a week—I saw the plans of 'em downstairs as soon as I started on to this job."

"You've been on this job from the beginning, then—in connection with him?" exclaimed Triffitt, nodding towards the door.

"We've never had him out of our sight since I started," replied Davidge, coolly, "except when he's been within his own four walls—where we're presently going. Oh, yes—we've watched him."

"He's out now," remarked Triffitt.

"We know that," said Davidge. "We know where he's gone. There's a first night, a new play, at the Terpsichoreum—he's gone there. He's safe enough till midnight, so we've plenty of time. We just want to have a look around his little nest while he's off it, d'you see?"

"How are you going to get in?" asked Triffitt.

Davidge nodded towards the window of the sitting-room.

"By way of that balcony," he answered. "I told you I knew all about how these flats are arranged. That balcony's mighty convenient, for the window'll not be any more difficult than ordinary."

"It'll be locked, you know," observed Triffitt, with a glance at his own. "Mine is, anyway, and you can bet his will be, too."

"Oh—that doesn't matter," said Davidge, carelessly. "We're prepared. Show Mr. Triffitt your kit, Jim—all pals here."

The innocent-looking Mr. Milsey, who, during this conversation, had mechanically sipped at his whisky and soda and reflectively gazed at the various pictures with which the absent Mr. Stillwater had decorated the walls of his parlour, plunged a hand into some deep recess in his overcoat and brought out an oblong case which reminded Triffitt of nothing so much as those Morocco or Russian-leather affairs in which a knife, a fork, and a spoon repose on padded blue satin and form an elegant present to a newly-born infant. Mr. Milsey snapped open the lid of his case, and revealed, instead of spoon or fork or knife a number of shining keys, of all sorts and sizes and strange patterns, all of delicate make and of evidently superior workmanship. He pushed the case across the table to the corner at which Triffitt was sitting, and Davidge regarded it fondly in transit.

"Pretty things, ain't they?" he said. "Good workmanship there! There's not very much that you could lock up—in the ordinary way of drawers, boxes, desks, and so on—that Milsey there couldn't get into with the help of one or other of those little friends—what, Jim?"

"Nothing!—always excepting a safe," assented Mr. Milsey.

"Well, we don't suppose our friend next door keeps an article of that description on his premises," said Davidge cheerfully. "But we expect he's got a desk, or a private drawer, or something of that nature in which we may find a few little matters of interest and importance—it's curious, Mr. Triffitt—we're constantly taking notice of it in the course of our professional duties—it's curious how men will keep by them bits of paper that they ought to throw into the fire, and objects that they'd do well to cast into the Thames! Ah!—I've known one case in which a mere scrap of a letter hanged a man, and another in which a bit of string got a chap fifteen years of the very best—fact, sir! You never know what you may come across during a search."

"You're going to search his rooms?" asked Triffitt.

"Something of that sort," replied Davidge. "Just a look round, you know, and a bit of a peep into his private receptacles."

"Then—you're suspecting him in connection with this——" began Triffitt.

Davidge stopped him with a look, and slowly drank off the contents of his glass. Then he rose.

"We'll talk of those matters later," he said significantly. "Now that my gentleman's safely away I think we'll set to work. It'll take a bit of time. And first of all, Mr. Triffitt, we'll examine your balcony door—I know enough about these modern flats to know that everything's pretty much alike in them as regards fittings, and if your door's easy to open, so will the door of the next be. Now we'll just let Jim there go outside with his apparatus, and we'll lock your balcony door on him, and then see if he finds any difficulty in getting in. To it, Jim!"

Mr. Milsey, thus adjured, went out on the balcony with his little case and was duly locked out. Within two minutes he opened the door and stepped in with a satisfied grin.

"Easy as winking!" said Mr. Milsey. "It's what you might call one of your penny plain locks, this—and t'other'll be like it. No difficulty about this job, anyway."

"Then we'll get to work," said Davidge. "Mr. Triffitt, I can't ask you to come with us, because that wouldn't be according to etiquette. Sit you down and read your book and smoke your pipe and drink your drop—and maybe we'll have something to tell you when our job's through."

"You've no fear of interruption?" asked Triffitt, who would vastly have preferred action to inaction. "Supposing—you know how things do and will turn out sometimes—supposing he came back?"

Davidge shook his head and smiled grimly and knowingly.

"No," he said. "He'll not come back—at least, if he did, we should be well warned. I've more than one man at work on this job, Mr. Triffitt, and if his lordship changed the course of his arrangements and returned this way, one of my chaps would keep him in conversation while another hurried up here to give us the office by a few taps on the outer door. No!—we're safe enough. Sit you down and don't bother about us. Come on, Jim—we'll get to it."

Triffitt tried to follow the detective's advice—he was just then deep in a French novel of the high-crime order, and he picked it up when the two men had gone out on the balcony and endeavoured to get interested in it. But he speedily discovered that the unravelling of crime on paper was nothing like so fascinating as the actual participation in detection of crime in real life, and he threw the book aside and gave himself up to waiting. What were those two doing in Burchill's rooms? What were they finding? What would the result be?

Certainly Davidge and his man took their time. Eight o'clock came and went—nine o'clock, ten o'clock followed and sped into the past, and they were still there. It was drawing near to eleven, and they had been in those rooms well over three hours, when a slight sound came at Triffitt's window and Davidge put his head in, to be presently followed by Milsey. Milsey looked as innocent as ever, but it seemed to Triffitt that Davidge looked grave.

"Well?" said Triffitt. "Any luck?"

Davidge drew the curtains over the balcony window before he turned and answered this question.

"Mr. Triffitt," he said, when at last he faced round, "you'll have to put us up for the night. After what I've found, I'm not going to lose sight, or get out of touch with this man. Now listen, and I'll tell you, at any rate, something. Tomorrow morning at ten o'clock there's to be a sort of informal inquiry at Mr. Halfpenny's office into the matter of a will of the date of Jacob Herapath's—all the parties concerned are going to meet there, and I know that this man Burchill is to be present. I don't propose to lose sight of him after he returns here tonight until he goes to that office—what happens after he's once there, you shall see. So Milsey and I'll just have to trouble you to let me stop here for the night. You can go to your bed, of course—we'll sit up. I'll send Milsey out to buy a bit of supper for us—I dare say he'll find something open close by."

"No need," Triffitt hastened to say. "I've a cold meat pie, uncut, and plenty of bread, and cheese. And there's bottled ale, and whisky, and I'll get you some supper ready at once. So"—he went on, as he began to bustle about—"you did find—something?"

Davidge rubbed his hands and winked first at Milsey and then at Triffitt.

"Wait till tomorrow!" he said. "There'll be strange news for you newspaper gentlemen before tomorrow night."

Table of Contents

CHAPTER XXII

yea and nay

Mr. Halfpenny, face to face with the fact that Barthorpe Herapath meant mischief about the will, put on his thinking-cap and gave himself up to a deep and serious consideration of the matter. He thought things over as he journeyed home to his house in the country; he spent an evening in further thought; he was still thinking when he went up to town next morning. The result of his cogitations was that after giving certain instructions in his office as to the next steps to be taken towards duly establishing Jacob Herapath's will, he went round to Barthorpe Herapath's office and asked to see him.

Barthorpe himself came out of his private room and showed some politeness in ushering his caller within. His manner seemed to be genuinely frank and unaffected: Mr. Halfpenny was considerably puzzled by it. Was Barthorpe playing a part, or was all this real? That, of course, must be decided by events: Mr. Halfpenny was not going to lose any time in moving towards them, whatever they might turn out to be. He accordingly went straight to the point.

"My dear sir," he began, bending confidentially towards Barthorpe, who had taken a seat at his desk and was waiting for his visitor to speak, "you have entered a caveat against the will in the Probate Registry."

"I have," answered Barthorpe, with candid alacrity. "Of course!"

"You intend to contest the matter?" inquired Mr. Halfpenny.

"Certainly!" replied Barthorpe.

Mr. Halfpenny gathered a good deal from the firm and decisive tone in which this answer was made. Clearly there was something in the air of which he was wholly ignorant.

"You no doubt believe that you have good reason for your course of action," he observed.

"The best reasons," said Barthorpe.

Mr. Halfpenny ruminated a little, silently.

"After all," he said at last, "there are only two persons really concerned—your cousin, Miss Wynne, and yourself. I propose to make an offer to you."

"Always willing to be reasonable, Mr. Halfpenny," answered Barthorpe.

"Very good," said Mr. Halfpenny. "Of course, I see no possible reason for doubting the validity of the will. From our side, litigation must go on in the usual course. But I have a proposal to make to you. It is this—will you meet your cousin at my office, with all the persons— witnesses to the will, I mean—and state your objections to the will? In short, let us have what we may call a family discussion about it—it may prevent much litigation."

Barthorpe considered this suggestion for a while.

"What you really mean is that I should come to your offices and tell my cousin and you why I am fighting this will," he said eventually. "That it?"

"Practically—yes," assented Mr. Halfpenny.

"Whom do you propose to have present?" asked Barthorpe.

"Yourself, your cousin, myself, the two witnesses, and, as a friend of everybody concerned, Professor Cox-Raythwaite," replied Mr. Halfpenny. "No one else is necessary."

"And you wish me to tell, plainly, why I refuse to believe that the will is genuine?" asked Barthorpe.

"Certainly—yes," assented Mr. Halfpenny.

Barthorpe hesitated, eyeing the old lawyer doubtfully.

"It will be a painful business—for my cousin," he said.

"If—I really haven't the faintest notion of what you mean!" exclaimed Mr. Halfpenny. "But if—if it will be painful for your cousin to hear this—whatever it is—in private, it would be much more painful for her to hear it in public. I gather, of course, that you have some strange revelation to make. Surely, it would be most considerate to her to make it in what we may call the privacy of the family circle, Cox-Raythwaite and myself."

"I haven't the least objection to Cox-Raythwaite's presence, nor yours," said Barthorpe. "Very good—I'll accept your proposal—it will, as you say, save a lot of litigation. Now— when?"

"Today is Tuesday," said Mr. Halfpenny. "What do you say to next Friday morning, at ten o'clock?"

"Friday will do," answered Barthorpe. "I will be there at ten o'clock. I shall leave it to you to summon all the parties concerned. By the by, have you Burchill's address?"

"I have," replied Mr. Halfpenny. "I will communicate with him at once."

Barthorpe nodded, rose from his seat, and walked with his visitor towards the door of his private room.

"Understand, Mr. Halfpenny," he said, "I'm agreeing to this to oblige you. And if the truth is very painful to my cousin, well, as you say, it's better for her to hear it in private than in a court of justice. All right, then—Friday at ten."

Mr. Halfpenny went back to his own office, astonished and marvelling. What on earth were these revelations which Barthorpe hinted at—these unpleasant truths which would so wound and hurt Peggie Wynne? Could it be possible that there really was some mystery about that will of which only Barthorpe knew the secret? It was incomprehensible to Mr. Halfpenny that any man could be so cool, so apparently cocksure about matters as Barthorpe was unless he felt absolutely certain of his own case. What that case could be, Mr. Halfpenny could not imagine—the only thing really certain was that Barthorpe seemed resolved on laying it bare when Friday came.

"God bless me!—it's a most extraordinary complication altogether!" mused Mr. Halfpenny, once more alone in his own office. "It's very evident to me that Barthorpe Herapath is absolutely ignorant that he's suspected, and that the police are at work on him! What a surprise for him if the thing comes to a definite head, and—but let us see what Friday morning brings."

Friday morning brought Barthorpe to Mr. Halfpenny's offices in good time. He came alone; a few minutes after his arrival Peggie Wynne, nervous and frightened, came, attended by Mr. Tertius and Professor Cox-Raythwaite. All these people were at once ushered into Mr. Halfpenny's private room, where polite, if constrained, greetings passed. At five minutes past ten o'clock Mr. Halfpenny looked at Barthorpe.

"We're only waiting for Mr. Burchill," he remarked. "I wrote to him after seeing you, and I received a reply from him in which he promised to be here at ten this morning. It's now——"

But at that moment the door opened to admit Mr. Frank Burchill, who, all unconscious of the fact that more than one pair of sharp eyes had followed him from his flat to Mr. Halfpenny's office, and that their owners were now in the immediate vicinity, came in full of polite self-assurance, and executed formal bows while he gracefully apologised to Mr. Halfpenny for being late.

"It's all right, all right, Mr. Burchill," said the old lawyer, a little testy under the last-comer's polite phrases, all of which he thought unnecessary. "Five or ten minutes won't make any great difference. Take a seat, pray: I think if we all sit around this centre table of mine it will be more convenient. We can begin at once now, Mr. Barthorpe Herapath—I have already given strict instructions that we are not to be disturbed, on any account. My dear—perhaps you will sit here by me?—Mr. Tertius, you sit next to Miss Wynne—Professor——"

Mr. Halfpenny's dispositions of his guests placed Peggie and her two companions on one side of a round table; Barthorpe and Burchill at the other—Mr. Halfpenny himself sat at the head. And as soon as he had taken his own seat, he looked at Barthorpe.

"This, of course," he began, "is a quite informal meeting. We are here, as I understand matters, to hear why you, Mr. Barthorpe Herapath, object to your late uncle's will, and why you intend to dispute it. So I suppose the next thing to do will be to ask you to state your grounds."

But Barthorpe shook his head with a decisive motion.

"No," he answered. "Not at all! The first thing to do, Mr. Halfpenny, in my opinion, is to hear what is to be said in favour of the will. The will itself, I take it, is in your possession. I have seen it—I mean, I have seen the document which purports to be a will of the late Jacob Herapath—so I admit its existence. Two persons are named on that document as witnesses: Mr.

Tertius, Mr. Burchill. They are both present now; at your request. I submit that the proper procedure is to question them both as to the circumstances under which this alleged will was made."

"I have no objections to that," answered Mr. Halfpenny. "I have no objection—neither, I am sure, has Miss Wynne—to anything you propose. Well, we take it for granted that this document exists—it is, of course, in my safe keeping. Every person has seen it, one time or another. We have here the two gentlemen who witnessed Jacob Herapath's signature and each other's. So I will first ask the elder of the two to tell us what he recollects of the matter. Now, Mr. Tertius?"

Mr. Tertius, who since his arrival had shown as much nervousness as would probably have signalised his appearance in a witness-box, started at this direct appeal.

"You—er, wish me——" he began, with an almost blank stare at Mr. Halfpenny. "You want me to——"

"Come, come!" said Mr. Halfpenny. "This is as I have already said, an informal gathering. We needn't have any set forms or cut-and-dried procedure. I want you—we all want you—to tell us what you remember about the making of Jacob Herapath's will. Tell us in your own way, in whatever terms you like. Then we shall hear what your fellow-witness has to say."

"Perhaps you'll let me suggest something," broke in Barthorpe, who had obviously been thinking matters over. "Lay the alleged will on the table before you, Mr. Halfpenny—question the two opposed witnesses on it. That will simplify things."

Mr. Halfpenny considered this proposition for a moment or two; then having whispered to Peggie and received her assent, he went across to a safe and presently returned with the will, which he placed on a writing-pad that lay in front of him.

"Now, Mr. Tertius," he said. "Look at this will, which purports to have been made on the eighteenth day of April last. I understand that Jacob Herapath called you into his study on the evening of that day and told you that he wanted you and Mr. Burchill, his secretary, to witness his signature to a will which he had made—had written out himself. I understand also that you did witness his signature, attached your own, in Mr. Herapath's presence and Mr. Burchill's presence, and that Mr. Burchill's signature was attached under the same conditions. Am I right in all this?"

"Quite right," replied Mr. Tertius. "Quite!"

"Is this the document which Jacob Herapath produced?"

"It is—certainly."

"Was it all drawn out then?—I am putting these questions to you quite informally."

"It was all written out, except the signatures. Jacob showed us that it was so written, though he did not allow us to see the wording. But he showed us plainly that there was nothing to do but to sign. Then he laid it on the desk, covered most of the sheet of paper with a piece of blotting paper and signed his name in our presence—I stood on one side of him, Mr. Burchill on the other. Then Mr. Burchill signed in his place—beneath mine."

"And this," asked Mr. Halfpenny, pointing to the will, "this is your signature?"

"Most certainly!" answered Mr. Tertius.

"And this," continued Mr. Halfpenny, "is Jacob Herapath's?—and this Mr. Burchill's? You have no doubt about it?"

"No more than that I see and hear you," replied Mr. Tertius. "I have no doubt."

Mr. Halfpenny turned from Mr. Tertius to Barthorpe Herapath. But Barthorpe's face just then revealed nothing. Therefore the old lawyer turned towards Burchill. And suddenly a sharp idea struck him. He would settle one point to his own satisfaction at once, by one direct question.

And so he—as it were by impulse—thrust the will before and beneath Burchill's eyes, and placed his finger against the third signature.

"Mr. Burchill," he said, "is that your writing?"

Burchill, calm and self-possessed, glanced at the place which Mr. Halfpenny indicated, and then lifted his eyes, half sadly, half deprecatingly.

"No!" he replied, with a little shake of the head;"No, Mr. Halfpenny, it is not!"

Table of Contents

CHAPTER XXIII

the accusation

The old lawyer, who had bent forward across the table in speaking to Burchill, pulled himself up sharply on receiving this answer, and for a second or two stared with a keen, searching gaze at the man he had questioned, who, on his part, returned the stare with calm assurance. A deep silence had fallen on the room; nothing broke it until Professor Cox-Raythwaite suddenly began to tap the table with the ends of his fingers. The sound roused Mr. Halfpenny to speech and action. He bent forward again towards Burchill, once more laying a hand on the will.

"That is not your signature?" he asked quietly.

Burchill shook his head—this time with a gesture of something very like contempt.

"It is not!" he answered.

"Did you see the late Jacob Herapath write—that?"

"I did not!"

"Did you see Mr. Tertius write—that?"

"I did not!"

"Have you ever seen this will, this document, before?"

"Never!"

Mr. Halfpenny drew the will towards himself with an impatient movement and began to replace it in the large envelope from which it had been taken.

"In short, you never assisted at the execution of this document—never saw Jacob Herapath make any will—never witnessed any signature of his to this?" he said testily. "That's what you really say—what you affirm?"

"Just so," replied Burchill. "You apprehend me exactly."

"Yet you have just heard what Mr. Tertius says! What do you say to that, Mr. Burchill?"

"I say nothing to that, Mr. Halfpenny. I have nothing to do with what Mr. Tertius says. I have answered your questions."

"Mr. Tertius says that he and you saw Jacob Herapath sign that document, saw each other sign it! What you say now gives Mr. Tertius the direct lie, and——"

"Pardon me, Mr. Halfpenny," interrupted Burchill quietly. "Mr. Tertius may be under some strange misapprehension; Mr. Tertius may be suffering from some curious hallucination. What I say is—I did not see the late Jacob Herapath sign that paper; I did not sign it myself; I did not see Mr. Tertius sign it; I have never seen it before!"

Mr. Halfpenny made a little snorting sound, got up from his chair, picked up the envelope which contained the will, walked over to his safe, deposited the envelope in some inner receptacle, came back, produced his snuff-box, took a hearty pinch of its contents, snorted again, and looked hard at Barthorpe.

"I don't see the least use in going on with this!" he said. "We have heard what Mr. Tertius, as one witness, says; we have heard what Mr. Frank Burchill, as the other witness, says. Mr. Tertius says that he saw the will executed in Mr. Burchill's presence; Mr. Burchill denies that in the fullest and most unqualified fashion. Why waste more time? We had better separate."

But Barthorpe laughed, maliciously.

"Scarcely!" he said. "You brought us here. It was your own proposal. I assented. And now that we are here, and you have heard—what you have heard—I'm going to have my say. You have gone, all along, Mr. Halfpenny, on the assumption that the piece of paper which you have just replaced in your safe is a genuine will. That's what you've said—I believe it's what you say now. I don't say so!"

"What do you say it is, then?" demanded Mr. Halfpenny.

Barthorpe slightly lowered his voice.

"I say it's a forgery!" he answered. "That, I hope, is plain language. A forgery—from the first word to its last."

"Oh!" exclaimed Mr. Halfpenny, a little sneeringly. "And who's the forger, pray?"

"That man, there!" said Barthorpe, suddenly pointing to Mr. Tertius. "He's the forger! I accuse him to his face of forging every word, every letter of it from the first stroke to the final one. And I'll give you enough evidence to prove it—enough evidence, at any rate, to prove it to any reasonable man or before a judge and jury. Forgery, I tell you!"

Mr. Halfpenny sat down again and became very calm and judicial. And he had at once to restrain Peggie Wynne, who during Barthorpe's last speech had manifested signs of a desire to speak, and had begun to produce a sealed packet from her muff.

"Wait, my dear," said Mr. Halfpenny. "Do not speak just now—you shall have an opportunity later—leave this to me at present. So you say you can prove that this will is a forgery, Mr. Barthorpe Herapath?" he continued, turning to the other side of the table. "Very well—since I suggested that you should come here, you shall certainly have the opportunity. But just allow me to ask Mr. Tertius a question—Tertius, you have heard what Mr. Frank Burchill has just said?"

"I have!" replied Mr. Tertius. "And—I am amazed!"

"You stand by what you said yourself? You gave us a perfectly truthful account of the execution of the will?"

"I stand by every word I said. I gave you—will give it again, anywhere!—a perfectly truthful account of the circumstances under which the will was signed and witnessed. I have made no mistakes—I am under no hallucination. I am—astonished!"

Mr. Halfpenny turned to Barthorpe with a wave of the hand.

"We are at your disposal, Mr. Barthorpe Herapath," he said. "I leave the rest of these proceedings to you. You have openly and unqualifiedly accused Mr. Tertius of forging the will which we have all seen, and have said you can prove your accusations. Perhaps you'd better do it. Mind you!" he added, with a sudden heightening of tone, "mind you, I'm not asking you to prove anything. But if I know Tertius—and I think I do—he won't object to your saying anything you like—we shall, perhaps, get at the truth by way of what you say. So—say on!"

"You're very kind," retorted Barthorpe. "I shall say on! But—I warned you—what I've got to say will give a good deal of pain to my cousin there. It would have been far better if you'd kept her out of this—still, she'd have had to hear it sooner or later in a court of justice——"

"It strikes me we shall have to hear a good deal in a court of justice—as you say, sooner or later," interrupted Mr. Halfpenny, dryly. "So I don't think you need spare Miss Wynne. I should advise you to go on, and let us become acquainted with what you've got to tell us."

"Barthorpe!" said Peggie, "I do not mind what pain you give me—you can't give me much more than I've already been given this morning. But I wish"—she turned appealingly to Mr. Halfpenny and again began to draw the sealed packet from her muff—"I do wish, Mr. Halfpenny, you'd let me say something before——"

"Say nothing, my dear, at present," commanded Mr. Halfpenny, firmly. "Allow Mr. Barthorpe Herapath to have his say. Now, sir!" he went on, with a motion of his hand towards the younger solicitor. "Pray let us hear you."

"In my own fashion," retorted Barthorpe. "You're not a judge, you know. Very good—if I give pain to you, Peggie, it's not my fault. Now, Mr. Halfpenny," he continued, turning and pointing contemptuously to Mr. Tertius, "as this is wholly informal, I'll begin with an informal yet pertinent question, to you. Do you know who that man really is?"

"I believe that gentleman, sir, to be Mr. John Christopher Tertius, and my very good and much-esteemed friend," replied Mr. Halfpenny, with asperity.

"Pshaw!" sneered Barthorpe. He turned to Professor Cox-Raythwaite. "I'll put the same question to you?" he said. "Do you know who he is?"

"And I give you the same answer, sir," answered the professor.

"No doubt!" said Barthorpe, still sneeringly. "The fact is, neither of you know who he is. So I'll tell you. He's an ex-convict. He served a term of penal servitude for forgery—forgery, do you hear? And his real name is not Tertius. What it is, and who he really is, and all about him, I'm going to tell you. Forger—ex-convict—get that into your minds, all of you. For it's true!"

Mr. Tertius, who had started visibly as Barthorpe rapped out the first of his accusations, and had grown paler as they went on, quietly rose from his chair.

"Before this goes further, Halfpenny," he said, "I should like to have a word in private with Miss Wynne. Afterwards—and I shan't detain her more than a moment—I shall have no objection to hearing anything that Mr. Barthorpe Herapath has to say. My dear!—step this way with me a moment, I beg."

Mr. Halfpenny's private room was an apartment of considerable size, having in it two large recessed windows. Into one of these Mr. Tertius led Peggie, and there he spoke a few quiet words to her. Barthorpe Herapath affected to take no notice, but the other men, watching them closely, saw the girl start at something which Mr. Tertius said. But she instantly regained her self-possession and composure, and when she came back to the table her face, though pale, was firm and resolute. And Barthorpe looked at her then, and his voice, when he spoke again, was less aggressive and more civil.

"It's not to my taste to bring unpleasant family scandals into public notice," he said, "and that's why I rather welcomed your proposal that we should discuss this affair in private, Mr. Halfpenny. And now for what I've got to tell you. I shall have to go back a long way in our family history. My late uncle, Jacob Herapath, was the eldest of the three children of his father, Matthew Herapath, who was a medical practitioner at Granchester in Yorkshire—a small town on the Yorkshire and Lancashire border. The three children were Jacob, Richard, and Susan. With the main outlines of Jacob Herapath's career I believe we are all fairly well acquainted. He came to London as a youth, and he prospered, and became what we know him to have been. Richard, my father, went out to Canada, when he was very young, settled there, and there he died.

"Now we come to Susan, the only daughter. Susan Herapath, at the age of twenty, married a man named Wynne—Arthur John Wynne, who at that time was about twenty-five years of age, was the secretary and treasurer of a recently formed railway—a sort of branch railway on the coast, which had its head office at Southampton, a coast town. In Southampton, this Arthur John Wynne and his wife settled down. At the end of a year their first child was born—my cousin Margaret, who is here with us. When she—I am putting all this as briefly as I can—when she was about eighteen months old a sad affair happened. Wynne, who had been living in a style very much above his position, was suddenly arrested on a charge of forgery. Investigations proved that he had executed a number of most skilful and clever forgeries, by which he had defrauded his employers of a large—a very large—amount of money. He was sent for trial to the assizes at Lancaster, he was found guilty, and he was sentenced to seven years' penal servitude. And almost at once after the trial his wife died.

"Here my late uncle, Jacob Herapath, came forward. He went north, assumed possession and guardianship of the child, and took her away from Southampton. He took her into Buckinghamshire and there placed her in the care of some people named Bristowe, who were farmers near Aylesbury and whom he knew very well. In the care of Mrs. Bristowe, the child remained until she was between six and seven years old. Then she was removed to Jacob Herapath's own house in Portman Square, where she has remained ever since. My cousin, I believe, has a very accurate recollection of her residence with the Bristowes, and she will remember being brought from Buckinghamshire to London at the time I have spoken of."

Barthorpe paused for a moment and looked at Peggie. But Peggie, who was listening intently with downcast head, made no remark, and he presently continued.

"Now, not so very long after that—I mean, after the child was brought to Portman Square—another person came to the house as a permanent resident. His name was given to the servants as Mr. Tertius. The conditions of his residence were somewhat peculiar. He had rooms of his own; he did as he liked. Sometimes he joined Jacob Herapath at meals; sometimes he did not. There was an air of mystery about him. What was it? I will tell you in a word—the mystery or its secret, was this—the man Tertius, who sits there now, was in reality the girl's father! He was Arthur John Wynne, the ex-convict—the clever forger!"

Table of Contents

CHAPTER XXIV

cold steel

The two men who formed what one may call the alien and impartial audience at that table were mutually and similarly impressed by a certain feature of Barthorpe Herapath's speech—its exceeding malevolence. As he went on from sentence to sentence, his eyes continually turned to Mr. Tertius, who sat, composed and impassive, listening, and in them was a gleam which could not be mistaken—the gleam of bitter, personal dislike. Mr. Halfpenny and Professor Cox-Raythwaite both saw that look and drew their own conclusions, and when Barthorpe spat out his last words, the man of science turned to the man of law and muttered a sharp sentence in Latin which no one else caught. And Mr. Halfpenny nodded and muttered a word or two back before he turned to Barthorpe.

"Even supposing—mind, I only say supposing—even supposing you are correct in all you say—and I don't know that you are," he said, "what you have put before us does nothing to prove that the will which we have just inspected is not what we believe it to be—we, at any rate—the valid will of Jacob Herapath. You know as well as I do that you'd have to give stronger grounds than that before a judge and jury."

"I'll give you my grounds," answered Barthorpe eagerly. He bent over the table in his eagerness, and the old lawyer suddenly realized that Barthorpe genuinely believed himself to be in the right. "I'll give you my grounds without reserve. Consider them—I'll check them off, point by point—you can follow them:

"First. It was well known—to me, at any rate, that my uncle Jacob Herapath, had never made a will.

"Second. Is it not probable that if he wanted to make a will he would have employed me, who had acted as his solicitor for fifteen years?

"Third. I had a conversation with him about making a will just under a year ago, and he then said he'd have it done, and he mentioned that he should divide his estate equally between me and my cousin there.

"Fourth. Mr. Burchill here absolutely denies all knowledge of this alleged will.

"Fifth. My uncle's handwriting, as you all know, was exceedingly plain and very easy to imitate. Burchill's handwriting is similarly plain—of the copperplate sort—and just as easy to imitate.

"Sixth. That man across there is an expert forger! I have the account of his trial at Lancaster Assizes—the evidence shows that his work was most expert. Is it likely that his hand should have lost its cunning—even after several years?

"Seventh. That man there had every opportunity of forging this will. With his experience and knowledge it would be a simple matter to him. He did it with the idea of getting everything into the hands of his own daughter, of defrauding me of my just rights. Since my uncle's death he has made two attempts to see Burchill privately—why? To square him, of course! And——"

Mr. Tertius, who had been gazing at the table while Barthorpe went through these points, suddenly lifted his head and looked at Mr. Halfpenny. His usual nervousness seemed to have left him, and there was something very like a smile of contempt about his lips when he spoke.

"I think, Halfpenny," he said quietly, "I really think it is time all this extraordinary farce—for it is nothing less!—came to an end. May I be permitted to ask Mr. Barthorpe Herapath a few questions?"

"So far as I am concerned, as many as you please, Tertius," replied Mr. Halfpenny. "Whether he'll answer them or not is another matter. He ought to."

"I shall answer them if I please, and I shall not answer them if I don't want to," said Barthorpe sullenly. "You can put them, anyway. But they'll make no difference—I know what I'm talking about."

"So do I," said Mr. Tertius. "And really, as we come here to get at the truth, it will be all the better for everybody concerned if you do answer my questions. Now—you say I am in reality Arthur Wynne, the father of your cousin, the brother-in-law of Jacob Herapath. What you have said about Arthur John Wynne is unfortunately only too true. It is true that he erred and was punished—severely. In due course he went to Portland. I want to ask you what became of him afterwards?—you say you have full knowledge."

"You mean, what became of you afterwards," sneered Barthorpe. "I know when you left Portland. You left it for London—and you came to London to be sheltered, under your assumed name, by Jacob Herapath."

"No more than that?" asked Mr. Tertius.

"That's enough," answered Barthorpe. "You left Portland in April, 1897; you came to London when you were discharged; in June of that year you'd taken up your residence under

Jacob Herapath's roof. And it's no use your trying to bluff me—I've traced your movements!"

"With the aid, no doubt, of Mr. Burchill there," observed Mr. Tertius, dryly. "But——"

Burchill drew himself up.

"Sir!" he exclaimed. "That is an unwarrantable assumption, and——"

"Unwarrantable assumptions, Mr. Burchill, appear to be present in great quantity," interrupted Mr. Tertius, with an air of defiance which surprised everybody. "Don't you interrupt me, sir!—I'll deal with you before long in a way that will astonish you. Now, Mr. Barthorpe Herapath," he went on, turning to that person with determination, "I will astonish you somewhat, for I honestly believe you really have some belief in what you say. I am not Arthur John Wynne. I am what I have always been—John Christopher Tertius, as a considerable number of people in this town can prove. But I knew Arthur John Wynne. When he left Portland he came to me here in London—at the suggestion of Jacob Herapath. I then lived in Bloomsbury—I had recently lost my wife. I took Wynne to live with me. But he had not long to live. If you had searched into matters more deeply, you would have found that he got his discharge earlier than he would have done in the usual course, because of his health. As a matter of fact, he was very ill when he came to me, and he died six weeks after his arrival at my house. He is buried in the churchyard of the village from which he originally came—in Wales—and you can inspect all the documents relating to his death, and see his grave if you care to. After his death, for reasons into which I need not go, I went to live with Jacob Herapath. It was his great desire—and mine—that Wynne's daughter, your cousin, should never know her father's sad history. But for you she never would have known it! And—that is a plain answer to what you have had to allege against me. Now, sir, let me ask you a plain question. Who invented this cock-and-bull story? You don't reply—readily? Shall I assist you by a suggestion? Was it that man who sits by you—Burchill? For Burchill knows that he has lied vilely and shamelessly this morning—Burchill knows that he did see Jacob Herapath sign that will—Burchill knows that that will was duly witnessed by himself and by me in the presence of each other and of the testator! God bless my soul!" exclaimed Mr. Tertius, thumping the table vehemently. "Why, man alive, your cousin Margaret has a document here which proves that that will is all right—a document written by Jacob Herapath himself! Bring it out, my dear—confound these men with an indisputable proof!"

But before Peggie could draw the packet from her muff, Burchill had risen and was showing signs of retreat. And Barthorpe, now pale with anger and perplexity, had risen too—and he was looking at Burchill.

Mr. Halfpenny looked at both men. Then he pointed to their chairs. "Hadn't you better sit down again?" he said. "It seems to me that we're just arriving at the most interesting stage of these proceedings."

Burchill stepped towards the door.

"I do not propose to stay in company in which I am ruthlessly insulted," he said. "It is, of course, a question of my word against Mr. Tertius's. We shall see. As for the present, I do."

"Stop!" said Barthorpe. He moved towards Burchill, motioning him towards the window in which Peggie and Mr. Tertius had spoken together. "Here—a word with you!"

But Burchill made for the door, and Mr. Halfpenny nudged Professor Cox-Raythwaite.

"I say—stop!" exclaimed Barthorpe. "There's some explanation——"

He was about to lay a hand on the door when Mr. Halfpenny touched a bell which stood in front of him on the table. And at its sharp sound the door opened from without, and Burchill fell back at what he saw—fell back upon Barthorpe, who looked past him, and started in his turn.

"Great Scot!" said Barthorpe. "Police!"

Davidge came quickly and quietly in—three other men with him. And in the room from which they emerged Barthorpe saw more men, many more men, and with them an eager, excited face which he somehow recognized—the face of the little *Argus* reporter who had asked him and Selwood for news on the morning after Jacob Herapath's murder.

But Barthorpe had no time to waste thoughts on Triffitt. He suddenly became alive to the fact that two exceedingly strong men had seized his arms; that two others had similarly seized Burchill. The pallor died out of his face and gave place to a dull glow of anger.

"Now, then?" he growled. "What's all this!"

"The same for both of you, Mr. Herapath," answered Davidge, cheerfully and in business-like fashion. "I'll charge both you and Mr. Burchill formally when we've got you to the station. You're both under arrest, you know. And I may as well warn you———"

"Nonsense!" exclaimed Barthorpe. "Arrest!—on what charge?"

"Charge will be the same for both," answered Davidge coolly. "The murder of Jacob Herapath."

A dead silence fell on the room. Then Peggie Wynne cried out, and Barthorpe suddenly made a spring at Burchill.

"You villain!" he said in a low concentrated voice. "You've done me, you devil! Let me get my hands on———"

The other men, Triffitt on their heels, came bustling into the room, obedient to Davidge's lifted finger.

"Put the handcuffs on both of 'em," commanded Davidge. "Can't take any chances, Mr. Herapath, if you lose your temper—the other gentleman———"

It was at that moment that the other gentleman took his chance. While Barthorpe Herapath had foolishly allowed himself to become warm and excited, Burchill had remained cool and watchful and calculating. And now in the slight diversion made by the entrance of the other detectives, he suddenly and adroitly threw off the grasp of the men who held him, darted through the open door on to the stairs, and had vanished before Davidge could cry out. Davidge darted too, the other police darted, Mr. Halfpenny smote his bell and shouted to his clerks. But the clerks were downstairs, out of hearing, and the police were fleshy men, slow of movement, while Burchill was slippery as an eel and agile as an athlete. Moreover, Burchill, during his secretaryship to Jacob Herapath, had constantly visited Mr. Halfpenny's office, and was as well acquainted with its ins and outs as its tenant; he knew where, in those dark stairs there was a side stair which led to a private door in a neighbouring alley. And while the pursuers blundered this way and that, he calmly slipped out to freedom, and, in a couple of minutes was mingling with the crowds in a busy thoroughfare, safe for that time.

Then Davidge, cursing his men and his luck, took Barthorpe Herapath away, and Triffitt rushed headlong to Fleet Street, seething with excitement and brimming with news.

Table of Contents

CHAPTER XXV

professional analysis

The *Argus* came out in great style next morning, and it and Triffitt continued to give its vast circle of readers a similar feast of excitement for a good ten days. Triffitt, in fact, went almost foodless and sleepless; there was so much to do. To begin with, there was the daily hue and cry after Burchill, who had disappeared as completely as if his familiar evil spirits had carried him bodily away from the very door of Halfpenny and Farthing's office. Then there was the bringing up of Barthorpe Herapath before the magistrate at Bow Street, and the proceedings at the adjourned coroner's inquest. It was not until the tenth day that anything like a breathing space came. But the position of affairs on that tenth day was a fairly clear one. The coroner's jury had returned a verdict of wilful murder against Barthorpe Herapath and Frank Burchill; the magistrate had committed Barthorpe for trial; the police were still hunting high and low for Burchill. And there was scarcely a soul who had heard the evidence before the coroner and the magistrate who did not believe that both the suspected men were guilty and that both—when Burchill had been caught—would ere long stand in the Old Bailey dock and eventually hear themselves sentenced to the scaffold.

One man, however, believed nothing of the sort, and that man was Professor Cox-Raythwaite. His big, burly form had been very much in evidence at all the proceedings before coroner and magistrate. He had followed every scrap of testimony with the most scrupulous care; he had made notes from time to time; he had given up his leisure moments, and stolen some from his proper pursuits, to a deep consideration of the case as presented by the police. And on the afternoon which saw Barthorpe committed to take his trial, he went away from Bow Street, alone, thinking more deeply than ever. He walked home to his house in Endsleigh Gardens, head bent, hands clasped behind his big back, the very incarnation of deep and ponderous musing. He shut himself in his study; he threw himself into his easy chair before his hearth; he remained smoking infinite tobacco, staring into vacancy, until his dinner-bell rang. He roused himself to eat and drink; then he went out into the street, bought all the evening newspapers he could lay hands on, and, hailing a taxi-cab, drove to Portman Square.

Peggie, Mr. Tertius, and Selwood had just dined; they were sitting in a quiet little parlour, silent and melancholy. The disgrace of Barthorpe's arrest, of the revelations before coroner and magistrate, of his committal on the capital charge, had reduced Peggie to a state of intense misery; the two men felt hopelessly unable to give her any comfort. To both, the entrance of Cox-Raythwaite came as a positive relief.

Cox-Raythwaite, shown into the presence of these three, closed the door in a fashion which showed that he did not wish to be disturbed, came silently across the room, and drew a chair into the midst of the disconsolate group. His glance round commanded attention.

"Now, my friends," he said, plunging straight into his subject, "if we don't wish to see Barthorpe hanged, we've just got to stir ourselves! I've come here to begin the stirring."

Peggie looked up with a sudden heightening of colour. Mr. Tertius slowly shook his head.

"Pitiable!" he murmured. "Pitiable, most pitiable! But the evidence, my dear Cox-Raythwaite, the evidence! I only wish——"

"I've been listening to all the evidence that could be brought before coroner's jury and magistrate in police court," broke in the Professor. "Listening with all my ears until I know every scrap of it by heart. And for four solid hours this afternoon I've been analysing it. I'm going to analyse it to you—and then I'll show you why it doesn't satisfy me. Give me your close attention, all of you."

He drew a little table to his elbow, laid his bundle of papers upon it, and began to talk, checking off his points on the tips of his big, chemical-stained fingers.

"Now," he said, "we'll just go through the evidence which has been brought against these two men, Barthorpe and Burchill, which evidence has resulted in Barthorpe being committed for trial and in the police's increased anxiety to lay hold of Burchill. The police theory, after all, is a very simple one—let's take it and their evidence point by point.

"1. The police say that Jacob Herapath came to his death as the result of a conspiracy between his nephew Barthorpe Herapath and Frank Burchill.

"2. They say that the proof that that conspiracy existed is found in certain documents discovered by Davidge at Burchill's flat, in which documents Barthorpe covenants to pay Burchill ten per cent. of the value of the Herapath property if and when he, Barthorpe, comes into it.

"3. The police argue that this conspiracy to murder Jacob Herapath and upset the will was in existence before November 12th—in other words that the idea of upsetting the will came first, and that the murder arose out of it.

"4. In support of this they have proved that Barthorpe was in close touch with Burchill as soon as the murder was committed—afternoon of the same day, at any rate—and therefore presumably had been in close touch with him previously.

"5. They have proved to the full a certain matter about which there is no doubt—that Barthorpe was at the estate office about the time at which, according to medical evidence, his uncle was murdered, that he subsequently put on his uncle's coat and hat and visited this house, and afterwards returned to the estate office. That, I say, is certain—and it is the most damning thing against Barthorpe.

"6. According to the police, then, Barthorpe was the actual murderer, and Burchill was an accessory before the fact. There is no evidence that Burchill was near the estate office that night. But that, of course, doesn't matter—if, as the police suggest, there is evidence that the conspiracy to kill Jacob Herapath existed before November 12th, then it doesn't matter at all whether Burchill took an active part in it or not—he's guilty as accessory."

The Professor here paused and smote his bundle of papers. Then he lifted and wagged one of his great fingers.

"But!" he exclaimed. "But—but—always a but! And the but in this case is a mighty one. It's this—did that conspiracy exist before November 12th? Did it—did it? It's a great point—it's a great point. Now, we all know that this morning, before he was committed, Barthorpe, much against the wishes of his legal advisers, insisted, forcibly insisted, on making a statement. It's in the evening papers here, verbatim. I'll read it to you carefully—you heard him, all of you, but I want you to hear it again, read slowly. Consider it—think of it carefully—remember the circumstances under which it's made!"

He turned to the table, selected a newspaper, and read:

"'The accused, having insisted, in spite of evident strong dissuasion from his counsel, upon making a statement, said: "I wish to tell the plain and absolute truth about my concern with this affair. I have heard the evidence given by various witnesses as to my financial position. That evidence is more or less true. I lost a lot of money last winter in betting and gambling. I was not aware that my position was known to my uncle until one of these witnesses revealed that my uncle had been employing private inquiry agents to find it out. I was meaning, when his death occurred, to make a clean breast to him. I was on the best of terms with him—whatever he may have known, it made no difference that I ever noticed in his behaviour to me. I was not aware that my uncle had made a will. He never mentioned it to me. About a year ago, there was some joking conversation between us about making a will, and I said to him that he ought to do it, and give me the job, and he replied, laughingly, that he supposed he would have to, some time. I solemnly declare that on November 12th I hadn't the ghost of a notion that he had made a will.

""""On November 12th last, about five o'clock in the afternoon, I received a note from my uncle, asking me to meet him at his estate office, at midnight. I had often met him there at that time—there was nothing unusual about such an appointment. I went there, of course—I walked there from my flat in the Adelphi. I noticed when I got there that my uncle's brougham was being slowly driven round the square across the road. The outer door of the office was slightly open. I was surprised. The usual thing when I made late calls was for me to ring a bell which sounded in my uncle's private room, and he then came and admitted me. I went in, and down the hall, and I then saw that the door of his room was also open. The electric light was burning. I went in. I at once saw my uncle—he was lying between the desk and the hearth, quite dead. There was a revolver lying near. I touched his hand and found it was quite warm.

""""I looked round, and seeing no sign of any struggle, I concluded that my uncle had shot himself. I noticed that his keys were lying on the desk. His fur-collared overcoat and slouch hat were thrown on a sofa. Of course, I was much upset. I went outside, meaning, I believe, to call the caretaker. Everything was very still in the house. I did not call. I began to think. I knew I was in a strange position. I knew my uncle's death would make a vast difference to me. I was next of kin. I wanted to know how things stood—how I was left. Something suggested itself to me. I think the overcoat and hat suggested it. I put on the hat and coat, took the keys from the table, and the latch-key of the Portman Square house from my uncle's waistcoat pocket, turned out the light, went out, closed both doors, went to the brougham, and was driven away. I saw very well that the coachman didn't know me at all—he thought I was his master.

""""I have heard the evidence about my visit to Portman Square. I stopped there some time. I made a fairly complete search for a will and didn't find anything. It is quite true that I used one of the glasses, and ate a sandwich, and very likely I did bite into another. It's true, too, that I have lost two front teeth, and that the evidence of that could be in the sandwich. All that's true—I admit it. It's also quite true that I got the taxi-cab at two o'clock at the corner of Orchard Street and drove back to Kensington. I re-entered the office; everything was as I'd left it. I took off the coat and hat, put the keys under some loose papers on the table, turned out the light and went home to my flat.

""""Now I wish to tell the absolute, honest truth about Burchill and the will. When I heard of and saw the will, after Mr. Tertius produced it, I went to see Burchill at his flat. I had never seen him, never communicated with him in any way whatever since he had left my uncle's service until that afternoon. I had got his address from a letter which I found in a pocket-book of my uncle's, which I took possession of when the police and I searched his effects. I went to see Burchill about the will, of course. When I said that a will had been found he fenced with me. He would only reply ambiguously. Eventually he asked me, point-blank, if I would make it worth his while if he aided me in upsetting the will. I replied that if he could—which I doubted—I would. He told me to call at ten o'clock that night. I did so. He then told me what I had never suspected—that Mr. Tertius was, in reality, Arthur John Wynne, a convicted forger. He gave me his proofs, and I was fool enough to believe them. He then suggested that it would be the easiest thing in the world, considering Wynne's record, to prove that he had forged the will for his daughter's benefit. He offered to aid in this if I would sign documents giving him ten per cent. of the total value of my uncle's estate, and I was foolish enough to consent, and to sign. I solemnly declare that the entire suggestion about upsetting the will came from Burchill, and that there was no conspiracy between us of any sort whatever previous to that night. Whatever may happen, I've told this court the absolute, definite truth!'"

Professor Cox-Raythwaite folded up the newspaper, laid it on the little table, and brought his big hand down on his knee with an emphatic smack.

"Now, then!" he said. "In my deliberate, coldly reasoned opinion, that statement is true! If they hang Barthorpe, they'll hang an innocent man. But——"

Table of Contents

CHAPTER XXVI

the remand prison

Mr. Tertius broke the significant silence which followed. He shook his head sadly, and sighed deeply.

"Ah, those buts!" he said. "As you remarked just now, Cox-Raythwaite, there is always a but. Now, this particular one—what is it?"

"Let me finish my sentence," responded the Professor. "I say, I do not believe Barthorpe to be guilty of murder, though guilty enough of a particularly mean, dirty, and sneaking conspiracy to defraud his cousin. Yes, innocent of murder—but it will be a stiff job to prove his innocence. As things stand, he'll be hanged safe enough! You know what our juries are, Tertius—evidence such as that which has been put before the coroner and the magistrate will be quite sufficient to damn him at the Old Bailey. Ample!"

"What do you suggest, then?" asked Mr. Tertius.

"Suggestion," answered the Professor, "is a difficult matter. But there are two things—perhaps more, but certainly two—on which I want light. The first is—nobody has succeeded in unearthing the man who went to the House of Commons to see Jacob on the night of the murder. In spite of everything, advertisements and all the rest of it, he's never come forward. If you remember, Halfpenny had a theory that the letter and the object which Mountain saw Jacob hand to that man were a note to the Safe Deposit people and the key of the safe. Now we know that's not so, because no one ever brought any letter to the Safe Deposit people and nobody's ever opened the safe. Halfpenny, too, believed, during the period of the police officials' masterly silence, that that man had put himself in communication with them. Now we know that the police have never heard anything whatever of him, have never traced him. I'm convinced that if we could unearth that man we should learn something. But how to do it, I don't know."

"And the other point?" asked Selwood, after a pause during which everybody seemed to be ruminating deeply. "You mentioned two."

"The other point," replied the Professor, "is one on which I am going to make a practical suggestion. It's this—I believe that Barthorpe told the truth in that statement of his which I've just read to you, but I should like to know if he told all the truth—all! He may have omitted some slight thing, some infinitesimal circumstance——"

"Do you mean about himself or—what?" asked Selwood.

"I mean some very—or seemingly very—slight thing, during his two visits to the estate office that night, which, however slight it may seem, would form a clue to the real murderer," answered the Professor. "He may have seen something, noticed something, and forgotten it, or not attached great importance to it. And, in short," he continued, with added emphasis, "in short, my friends, Barthorpe must be visited, interviewed, questioned—not merely by his legal advisers, but by some friend, and the very person to do it"—here he turned and laid his great hand on Peggie's shoulder—"is—you, my dear!"

"I!" exclaimed Peggie.

"You, certainly! Nobody better. He will tell you what he would tell no one else," said the Professor. "You're the person. Am I not right, Tertius?"

"I think you are right," assented Mr. Tertius. "Yes, I think so."

"But—he's in prison!" said Peggie. "Will they let me?"

"Oh, that's all right," answered the Professor. "Halfpenny will arrange that like winking. You must go at once—and Selwood there will go with you. Far better for you two young people to go than for either Halfpenny, or Tertius, or myself. Youth invites confidence."

Peggie turned and looked at Selwood.

"You'll go?" she asked.

Selwood felt his cheeks flush and rose to conceal his sudden show of feeling. "I'll go anywhere and do anything!" he answered quietly. "I don't know whether my opinion's worth having, but I think exactly as Professor Cox-Raythwaite does about this affair. But—who's the guilty man? Is it—can it be Burchill? If what Barthorpe Herapath says about that will affair is true, Burchill is cunning and subtle enough for——"

"Burchill, my dear lad, is at present out of our ken," interrupted Cox-Raythwaite. "Barthorpe, however, is very much within it, and Halfpenny must arrange for you two to see him without delay. And once closeted with him, you must talk to him for his soul's good—get him to search his memory, to think of every detail he can rake up—above everything, if there's anything he's keeping back, beg him, on your knees if necessary, to make a clean breast of it. Otherwise——"

Two days later Peggie, sick at heart, and Selwood, nervous and fidgety, sat in a room which gave both of them a feeling as of partial suffocation. It was not that it was not big enough for two people, or for six people, or for a dozen people to sit in—there was space for twenty. What oppressed them was the horrible sense of formality, the absence of life, colour, of anything but sure and solid security, the intrusive spick-and-spanness, the blatant cleanliness, the conscious odour of some sort of soap, used presumably for washing floors and walls, the whole crying atmosphere of incarceration. The barred window, the pictureless walls, the official look of the utterly plain chairs and tables, the grilles of iron bars which cut the place in half—these things oppressed the girl so profoundly that she felt as if a sharp scream was the only thing that would relieve her pent-up feelings. And as she sat there with thumping heart, dreading the appearance of her cousin behind those bars, yet wishing intensely that he would come, Peggie had a sudden fearful realization of what it really meant to fall into the hands of justice. There, somewhere close by, no doubt, Barthorpe was able to move hands and feet, legs and arms, body and head—but within limits. He could pace a cell, he could tramp round an exercise yard, he could eat and drink, he could use his tongue when allowed, he could do many things—but always within limits. He was held—held by an unseen power which could materialize, could make itself very much seen, at a second's notice. There he would stop until he was carried off to his trial; he would come and go during that trial, the unseen power always holding him. And one day he would either go out of the power's clutches—free, or he would be carried off, not to this remand prison but a certain cell in another place in which he would sit, or lounge, or lie, with nothing to do, until a bustling, businesslike man came in one morning with a little group of officials and in his hand a bundle of leather straps. Held!—by the strong, never-relaxing clutch of the law. That——

"Buck up!" whispered Selwood, in the blunt language of irreverent, yet good-natured, youth. "He's coming!"

Peggie looked up to see Barthorpe staring at her through the iron bars. He was not over good to look at. He had a two days' beard on his face; his linen was not fresh; his clothes were put on untidily; he stood with his hands in his pockets lumpishly—the change wrought by incarceration, even of that comparative sort, was great. He looked both sulky and sheepish; he gave Selwood no more than a curt nod; his first response to his cousin was of the nature of a growl.

"Hanged if I know what you've come for!" he said. "What's the good of it? You may mean well, but——"

"Oh, Barthorpe, how can you!" exclaimed Peggie. "Of course we've come! Do you think it possible we shouldn't come? You know very well we all believe you innocent."

"Who's all?" demanded Barthorpe, half-sneeringly. "Yourself, perhaps, and the parlour-maid!"

"All of us," said Selwood, thinking it was time a man spoke. "Cox-Raythwaite, Mr. Tertius, myself. That's a fact, anyhow, so you'd better grasp it."

Barthorpe straightened himself and looked keenly at Selwood. Then he spoke naturally and simply.

"I'm much obliged to you, Selwood," he said. "I'd shake hands with you if I could. I'm obliged to the others, too—especially to old Tertius—I've wronged him, no doubt. But"—here his face grew dark and savage—"if you only knew how I was tricked by that devil! Is he caught?—that's what I want to know."

"No!" answered Selwood. "But never mind him—we've come here to see what we can do for you. That's the important thing."

"What can anybody do?" said Barthorpe, with a mirthless laugh. "You know all the evidence. It's enough—they'll hang me on it!"

"Barthorpe, you mustn't!" expostulated Peggie. "That's not the way to treat things. Tell him," she went on, turning to Selwood, "tell him all that Professor Cox-Raythwaite said the other night."

Selwood repeated the gist of the Professor's arguments and suggestions, and Barthorpe began to show some interest. But at the end he shook his head.

"I don't know that there's anything more that I can tell," he said. "Whatever anybody may think, I told the entire truth about myself and this affair in that statement before the magistrate. Of course, you know they didn't want me to say a word—my legal advisers, I mean. They were dead against it. But you see, I was resolved on it—I wanted it to get in the papers. I told everything in that. I tried to put it as plainly as I could. No—I've told the main facts."

"But aren't there any little facts, Barthorpe?" asked Peggie. "Can't you think of any small thing—was there nothing that would give—I don't know how to put it."

"Anything that you can think of that would give a clue?" suggested Selwood. "Was there nothing you noticed—was there anything——"

Barthorpe appeared to be thinking; then to be hesitating—finally, he looked at Selwood a little shamefacedly.

"Well, there were one or two things that I didn't tell," he said. "I—the fact is, I didn't think they were of importance. One of them was about that key to the Safe Deposit. You know you and I couldn't find it when we searched the office that morning. Well, I had found it. Or rather, I took it off the bunch of keys. I wanted to search the safe at the Safe Deposit myself. But I never did. I don't know whether the detectives have found it or not—I threw it into a drawer at my office in which there are a lot of other keys. But, you know, there's nothing in that—nothing at all."

"You said one or two other things just now," remarked Selwood. "That's one—what's the other?"

Barthorpe hesitated. The three were not the only occupants of that gloomy room, and though the official ears might have been graven out of stone, he felt their presence.

"Don't keep anything back, Barthorpe," pleaded Peggie.

"Oh, well!" responded Barthorpe. "I'll tell you, though I don't know what good it will do. I didn't tell this, because—well, of course, it's not exactly a thing a man likes to tell. When I looked over Uncle Jacob's desk, just after I found him dead, you know, I found a hundred-pound note lying there. I put it in my pocket. Hundred-pound notes weren't plentiful, you know," he went on with a grim smile. "Of course, it was a shabby thing to do, sort of robbing the dead, you know, but——"

"Do you see any way in which that can help?" asked Selwood, whose mind was not disposed to dwell on nice questions of morality or conduct. "Does anything suggest itself?"

"Why, this," answered Barthorpe, rubbing his chin. "It was a brand-new note. That's puzzled me—that it should be lying there amongst papers. You might go to Uncle Jacob's bank and find out when he drew it—or rather, if he'd been drawing money that day. He used, as you and I know, to draw considerable amounts in notes. And—it's only a notion—if he'd drawn anything big that day, and he had it on him that night, why, there's a motive there. Somebody may have known he'd a considerable amount on him and have followed him in there. Don't forget that I found both doors open when I went there! That's a point that mustn't be overlooked."

"There's absolutely nothing else you can think of?" asked Selwood.

Barthorpe shook his head. No—there was nothing—he was sure of that. And then he turned eagerly to the question of finding Burchill. Burchill, he was certain, knew more than he had given him credit for, knew something, perhaps, about the actual murder. He was a deep, crafty dog, Burchill—only let the police find him!——

Time was up, then, and Peggie and Selwood had to go—their last impression that of Barthorpe thrusting his hands in his pockets and lounging away to his enforced idleness. It made the girl sick at heart, and it showed Selwood what deprivation of liberty means to a man who has hitherto been active and vigorous.

"Have we done any good?" asked Peggie, drawing a deep breath of free air as soon as they were outside the gates. "Any bit of good?"

"There's the affair of the bank-note," answered Selwood. "That may be of some moment. I'll go and report progress on that, anyway."

He put Peggie into her car to go home, and himself hailed a taxi-cab and drove straight to Mr. Halfpenny's office, where Professor Cox-Raythwaite and Mr. Tertius had arranged to meet him.

Table of Contents

CHAPTER XXVII

The three elderly gentlemen, seated in Mr. Halfpenny's private room, listened with intense, if silent, interest to Selwood's account of the interview with Barthorpe. It was a small bundle of news that he had brought back and two of his hearers showed by their faces that they attached little importance to it. But Professor Cox-Raythwaite caught eagerly at the mere scrap of suggestion.

"Tertius!—Halfpenny!" he exclaimed. "That must be followed up—we must follow it up at once. That bank-note may be a most valuable and effective clue."

Mr. Halfpenny showed a decided incredulity and dissent.

"I don't see it," he answered. "Don't see it at all, Cox-Raythwaite. What is there in it? What clue can there be in the fact that Barthorpe picked up a hundred pound bank-note from his uncle's writing-desk? Lord bless me!—why, every one of us four men knows very well that hundred pound notes were as common to Jacob Herapath as half-crowns are to any of us! He was a man who carried money in large amounts on him always—I've expostulated with him about it. Don't you know—no, I dare say you don't though, because you never had business dealings with him, and perhaps Tertius doesn't, either, because he, like you, only knew him as a friend—you don't know that Jacob had a peculiarity. Perhaps Mr. Selwood knows of it, though, as he was his secretary."

"What peculiarity?" asked the Professor. "I know he had several fads, which one might call peculiarities."

"He had a business peculiarity," replied Mr. Halfpenny, "and it was well known to people in his line of business. You know that Jacob Herapath had extensive, unusually extensive, dealings in real property—land and houses. Quite apart from the Herapath Flats, he dealt on wide lines with real estate; he was always buying and selling. And his peculiarity was that all his transactions in this way were done by cash—bank-notes or gold—instead of by cheque. It didn't matter if he was buying a hundred thousand pounds' worth of property, or selling two hundred thousand pounds' worth—the affairs had to be completed by payment in that fashion. I've scolded him about it scores of times; he only laughed at me; he said that had been the custom when he went into the business, and he'd stuck to it, and wasn't going to give it up. God bless me!" concluded Mr. Halfpenny, with emphasis. "I ought to know, for Jacob Herapath has concluded many an operation in this very room, and at this very table—I've seen him handle many a hundred thousand pounds' worth of notes in my time, paying or receiving! And, as I said, the mere picking up of a hundred pound note from his desk is—why, it's no more than if I picked up a few of those coppers that are lying there on my chimney-piece!"

"Just so, just so!" observed Mr. Tertius mildly. "Jacob was a very wealthy man—the money evidence was everywhere."

But Professor Cox-Raythwaite only laughed and smote the table with his big fist.

"My dear Halfpenny!" he exclaimed. "Why, you've just given us the very best proof of what I've been saying! You're not looking deeply enough into things. The very fact to which you bear testimony proves to me that a certain theory which is assuming shape in my mind may possibly have a great deal in it. That theory, briefly, is this—on the day of his death, Jacob Herapath may have had upon his person a large amount of money in bank-notes. He may have had them paid to him. He may have drawn them from his bank, to pay to somebody else. Some evil person may have been aware of his possession of those notes and have tracked him to the estate offices, or gained entrance, or—mark this!—have been lurking—lurking!—there, in order to rob him. Don't forget two points, my friend—one, that Barthorpe (if he's speaking the truth, and I, personally, believe he is) tells us that the doors of the offices and the private room were open when he called at twelve o'clock; and, too, that, according to Mountain, the coachman, Jacob Herapath had been in those offices since twenty-five minutes to twelve—plenty of time for murder and robbery to take place. I repeat—Jacob may have had a considerable sum of money on him that night, some one may have known it, and the motive of his murder may have been—probably was—sheer robbery. And we ought to go on that, if we want to save the family honour."

Mr. Tertius nodded and murmured assent, and Mr. Halfpenny stirred uneasily in his chair.

"Family honour!" he said. "Yes, yes, that's right, of course. It would be a dreadful thing to see a nephew hanged for the murder of his uncle—quite right!"

"A much more dreadful thing to stand by and see an innocent man hanged, without moving heaven and earth to clear him," commented the Professor. "Come now, I helped to establish the fact that Barthorpe visited Portman Square that night—Tertius there helped too, by his quickness in seeing that the half-eaten sandwich had been bitten into by a man who had lost two front teeth, which, of course, was Barthorpe's case—so the least we can do is to bestir ourselves now that we believe him to have told the truth in that statement."

"But how exactly are we to bestir ourselves?" asked Mr. Halfpenny.

"I suggest a visit to Jacob Herapath's bankers, first of all," answered the Professor. "I haven't heard that any particular inquiry has been made. Did you make any, Halfpenny?"

"Jacob's bankers are Bittleston, Stocks and Bittleston," replied the old lawyer. "I did make it in my way to drop in there and to see Mr. Playbourne, the manager of their West End branch, in Piccadilly. He assured me that there was nothing whatever out of the common in Jacob Herapath's transactions with them just before his death, and nothing at all in their particulars of his banking account which could throw any possible light on his murder."

"In his opinion," said the Professor, caustically, "in his opinion, Halfpenny! But—you don't know what our opinion might be. Now, I suggest that we all go at once to see this Mr. Playbourne; there's ample time before the bank closes for the day."

"Very well," assented Mr. Halfpenny. "All the same, I'm afraid Playbourne will only say just what he said before."

Mr. Playbourne, a good typical specimen of the somewhat old-fashioned bank manager, receiving this formidable deputation of four gentlemen in his private room, said precisely what he had said before, and seemed astonished to think that any light upon such an unpleasant thing as a murder could possibly be derived from so highly respectable a quarter as that in which he moved during the greater part of the day.

"I can't think of anything in our transactions with the late Mr. Herapath that gives any clue, any idea, anything at all," he said, somewhat querulously. "Mr. Herapath's transactions with us, right up to the day of his death, were just what they had been for years. Of course, I'm willing to tell you anything, show you anything. You're acting for Miss Wynne, aren't you, Mr. Halfpenny?"

"I have a power of attorney from Miss Wynne, for that matter," answered Mr. Halfpenny. "Everything of that sort's in my hands."

"I'll tell you what, then," said the bank manager, laying his hand on a bell at his side. "You'd better see Jacob Herapath's pass-book. I recently had it posted up to the day of his death, and of course we've retained it until you demanded it. You can't have a better index to his affairs with us than you'll find in it. Sellars," he went on, as a clerk appeared, "bring me the late Mr. Herapath's pass-book—Mr. Ravensdale has it."

The visitors presently gathered round the desk on which Mr. Playbourne laid the parchment-bound book—one of a corresponding thickness with the dead man's transactions. The manager turned to the pages last filled in.

"You're aware, of course, some of you at any rate," he said, "you, Mr. Halfpenny, and you, Mr. Selwood, that the late Jacob Herapath dealt in big sums. He always had a very large balance at this branch of our bank; he was continually paying in and drawing out amounts which, to men of less means, must needs seem tremendous. Now, you can see for yourselves what his transactions with us were during the last few days of his life; I, as I have said, see nothing out of the way in them—you, of course," he continued, with a sniff, "may see a good deal!"

Professor Cox-Raythwaite ran his eye over the neatly-written pages, passing rapidly on to the important date—November 12th. And he suddenly thrust out his arm and put the tip of a big yellow finger on one particular entry.

"There!" he exclaimed. "Look at that. 'Self, £5,000.' Paid out, you see, on November 12th. Do you see?"

Mr. Playbourne laughed cynically.

"My dear sir!" he said. "Do you mean to say that you attach any importance to an entry like that? Jacob Herapath constantly drew cheques to self for five, ten, twenty, thirty—aye, fifty thousand pounds! He dealt in tens of thousands—he was always buying or selling. Five thousand pounds!—a fleabite!"

"All the same, if you please," said the Professor quietly, "I should like to know if Jacob Herapath presented that self cheque himself, and if so, how he took the money it represents."

"Oh, very well!" said the manager resignedly. He touched his bell again, and looked wearily at the clerk who answered it. "Find out if the late Mr. Herapath himself presented a cheque for five thousand on November 12th, and if so, how he took it," he said. "Well," he continued, turning to his visitors. "Do you see anything with any further possible mystery attached to it?"

"There's an entry there—the last," observed Mr. Halfpenny. "That. 'Dimambro: three thousand guineas.' That's the same date."

Mr. Playbourne suddenly showed some interest and animation. His eyes brightened; he sat up erect.

"Ah!" he said. "Well, now, that is somewhat remarkable, that entry!—though of course there's nothing out of the common in it. But that cheque was most certainly the very last ever drawn by Jacob Herapath, and according to strict law, it never ought to have been paid out by us."

"Why?" asked Professor Cox-Raythwaite.

"Because Jacob Herapath, the drawer, was dead before it was presented," replied the manager. "But of course we didn't know that. The cheque, you see, was drawn on November 12th, and it was presented here as soon as ever the doors were opened next morning and before any of us knew of what had happened during the night, and it was accordingly honoured in the usual way."

"The payee, of course, was known?" observed Mr. Halfpenny.

"No, he was not known, but he endorsed the cheque with name and address, and there can be no reason whatever to doubt that it had come to him in the ordinary way of business," replied the manager. "Quite a usual transaction, but, as I say, noteworthy, because, as you know, a cheque is no good after its drawer's demise."

Professor Cox-Raythwaite, who appeared to have fallen into a brown study for a moment, suddenly looked up.

"Now I wonder if we might be permitted to see that cheque—as a curiosity?" he said. "Can we be favoured so far?"

"Oh, certainly, certainly," answered Mr. Playbourne. "No trouble. I'll—ah, here's your information about the other cheque—the self cheque for five thousand."

He took a slip of paper from the clerk who just then entered, and read it aloud.

"Here you are," he said. "'Mr. Herapath cashed cheque for £5,000 himself, at three o'clock; the money in fifty notes of £100 each, numbered as follows'—you can take this slip, if you like," he continued, handing the paper to Professor Cox-Raythwaite, as the obviously most interested man of his party. "There are the numbers of the notes. Of course, I can't see how all this throws any light on the mystery of Herapath's murder, but perhaps you can. Sellers," he continued, turning to the clerk, and beckoning him to look at the pass-book, "find me the cheque referred to there, and bring it here."

The clerk returned in a few minutes with the cheque, which Mr. Playbourne at once exhibited to his visitors.

"There you are, gentlemen," he said. "Quite a curiosity!—certainly the last cheque ever drawn by our poor friend. There, you see, is his well-known signature with his secret little mark which you wouldn't detect—secret between him and us, eh!—big, bold handwriting, wasn't it? Sad to think that that was—very likely—the last time he used a pen!"

Professor Cox-Raythwaite in his turn handled the cheque. Its face gave him small concern; what he was most interested in was the endorsement on the back. Without saying anything to his companions, he memorized that endorsement, and he was still murmuring it to himself when, a few minutes later, he walked out of the bank.

"Luigi Dimambro, Hotel Ravenna, Soho."

Table of Contents

CHAPTER XXVIII

the hotel ravenna

Once closeted together in the private room at Halfpenny and Farthing's office, Mr. Halfpenny, who had seemed somewhat mystified by the happenings at the bank, looked inquiringly at Professor Cox-Raythwaite and snapped out one suggestive monosyllable:

"Well?"

"Very well indeed," answered Cox-Raythwaite. "I consider we have done good work. We have found things out. That bank manager is a pompous ass; he's a man of asinine, or possible bovine, mind! Of course, he ought to have revealed these things at both the inquest and the magisterial proceedings!—they'll certainly have to be put in evidence at Barthorpe Herapath's trial."

"What things?" demanded the old lawyer, a little testily.

"Two things—facts," replied the Professor, composedly. "First, that Jacob Herapath drew five thousand pounds in hundred pound notes at three o'clock on the day of his death. Second, that at some hour of that day he drew a cheque in favour of one Luigi Dimambro, which cheque was cashed as soon as the bank opened next morning."

"Frankly," observed Mr. Halfpenny, "frankly, candidly, Cox-Raythwaite, I do not see what these things—facts—prove."

"Very likely," said the Professor, imperturbable as ever, "but they're remarkably suggestive to me. They establish for one thing the fact that, in all probability, Jacob Herapath had those notes on him when he was murdered."

"Don't see it," retorted Mr. Halfpenny. "He got the fifty one-hundred-pound notes from the bank at three o'clock in the afternoon. He's supposed to have been murdered at twelve—midnight. That's nine hours. Plenty of time in which to pay those notes away—as he most likely did."

"If you'll let your mind go back to what came out in evidence at the inquest," said the Professor, "you'll remember that Jacob Herapath went to the House of Commons at half-past three that day and never left it until his coachman fetched him at a quarter-past eleven. It's not very likely that he'd transact business at the House."

"Plenty of time between three and half-past three," objected Mr. Halfpenny.

"Quite so, but we haven't heard of any transaction being carried out during that time. Make inquiry, and see if he did engage in any such transaction," said the Professor. "If he didn't, then my theory that he had the notes on him is correct. Moreover, Barthorpe has told Selwood that he picked up one note from the desk in his uncle's private room."

"One note!" exclaimed Mr. Halfpenny.

"One note—quite so," agreed the Professor. "May it not have been—it's all theory, of course—that Jacob had all the notes on the desk when he was murdered, that the murderer grabbed them afterwards, and in his haste, left one? Come, now!"

"Theory—theory!" said Mr. Halfpenny. "Still, I'll make inquiries all around, to see if Jacob did pay five thousand away to anybody that afternoon. Well, and your other point?"

"I should like to know what the cheque for three thousand guineas was for," answered the Professor. "It was paid out to one Luigi Dimambro, whose address was written down by himself in endorsing the cheque as Hotel Ravenna, Soho. He, presumably, is a foreigner, an Italian, or a Corsican, or a Sicilian, and the probability is that Jacob Herapath bought something from him that day, and that the transaction took place after banking hours."

"How do you deduce that?" asked Mr. Halfpenny.

"Because Dimambro cashed his cheque as soon as the bank opened its doors next morning," answered the Professor. "If he'd been given the cheque before four o'clock on November 12th, he'd have cashed it then."

"The cheque may have been posted to him," said Mr. Halfpenny.

"May be; the point is that it was drawn by Jacob on November 12th and cashed at the earliest possible hour next day," replied the Professor. "Now, though it may have nothing to do with the case, I want to know what that cheque referred to. More than this, I have an idea. May not this man Dimambro be the man who called on Jacob Herapath at the House of Commons that night—the man whom Mountain saw, but did not recognize as one of his master's usual friends or acquaintances? Do you see that point?"

Mr. Tertius and Selwood muttered expressions of acquiescence, but Mr. Halfpenny shook his head.

"Can't see anything much in it," he said. "If this foreign fellow, Dimambro, was the man who called at the House, I don't see what that's got to do with the murder. Jacob Herapath, of course, had business affairs with all sorts of queer people—Italians, Spaniards, Chinese—many a Tom, Dick, and Harry of 'em; he bought curios of all descriptions, and often sold them again as soon as bought."

"Very good suggestion," said Professor Cox-Raythwaite. "He may have bought something extremely valuable from this Dimambro that day, or that night, and—he may have had it on him when he was murdered. Clearly, we must see this Luigi Dimambro!"

"If he's the man who called at the House, you forget that he's been advertised for no end," said Selwood.

"No, I don't," responded the Professor. "But he may be out of the country: may have come to it specially to see Jacob Herapath, and left it again. I repeat, we must see this man, if he's to be found. We must make inquiries—cautious, guarded inquiries—at this hotel in Soho, which is probably a foreigners' house of call, a mere restaurant. And the very person to make those inquiries," he concluded, turning to Selwood and favouring him with a smack of the shoulder, "is—you!"

Selwood flinched, physically and mentally. He had no great love of the proposed rôle—private detective work did not appeal to him. And he suggested that Professor Cox-Raythwaite had far better apply to Scotland Yard.

"By no means," answered the Professor calmly. "You are the man to do the work. We don't want any police interference. This Hotel Ravenna is probably some café, restaurant, or saloon in Soho, frequented by foreigners—a place where, perhaps, a man can get a room for a night or two. You must go quietly, unobtrusively, there; if it's a restaurant, as it's sure to be, or at any rate, a place to which a restaurant is attached, go in and get some sort of a meal, keep your eyes open, find out the proprietor, get into talk with him, see if he knows Luigi Dimambro. All you need is tact, caution, and readiness to adapt yourself to circumstances."

Then, when they left Mr. Halfpenny's office he took Selwood aside and gave him certain hints and instructions, and enlarged upon the advantages of finding Dimambro if he was to be found. The Professor himself was enthusiastic about these recent developments, and he succeeded in communicating some of his enthusiasm to Selwood. After all, thought Selwood, as he went to Portman Square to tell Peggie of the afternoon's doings, whatever he did was being done for Peggie; moreover, he was by that time certain that however mean and base Barthorpe Herapath's conduct had been about the will, he was certainly not the murderer of his uncle. If that murderer was to be tracked—why, there was a certain zest, an appealing excitement in the tracking of him that presented a sure fascination to youthful spirits.

That evening found Selwood, quietly and unassumingly attired, examining the purlieus of Soho. It was a district of which he knew little, and for half an hour he perambulated its streets, wondering at the distinctly foreign atmosphere. And suddenly he came across the Hotel Ravenna—there it was, confronting him, at the lower end of Dean Street. He drew back and looked it well over from the opposite pavement.

The Hotel Ravenna was rather more of a pretentious establishment than Selwood had expected it to be. It was typically Italian in outward aspect. There were the usual evergreen shrubs set in the usual green wood tubs at the entrance; the usual abundance of plate-glass and garish gilt; the usual glimpse, whenever the door opened, of the usual vista of white linen, red plush, and many mirrors; the waiter who occasionally showed himself at the door, napkin in hand, was of the type which Selwood had seen a thousand times under similar circumstances. But all this related to the restaurant—Selwood was more interested that the word "Hotel" appeared in gilt letters over a door at the side of the establishment and was repeated in the windows of the upper storeys. He was half-minded to enter the door at once, and to make a guarded inquiry for Mr. Luigi Dimambro; on reflection he walked across the street and boldly entered the restaurant.

It was half-past seven o'clock, and the place was full of customers. Selwood took most of them to be foreigners. He also concluded after a first glance around him that the majority had some connection, more or less close, with either the dramatic, or the musical, or the artistic professions. There was much laughter and long hair, marvellous neckties and wondrous costumes; everybody seemed to be talking without regard to question or answer; the artillery of the voices mingled with the rattling of plates and popping of corks. Clearly this was no easy place in which to seek for a man whom one had never seen!

Selwood allowed a waiter to conduct him to a vacant seat—a plush throne half-way along the restaurant. He ordered a modest dinner and a bottle of light wine, and following what seemed to be the custom, lighted a cigarette until his first course appeared. And while he waited he looked about him, noting everything that presented itself. Out of all the folk there, waiters and customers, the idle and the busy, he quickly decided that there was only one man who possessed particular interest for him. That man was the big, smiling, frock-coated, sleek-haired patron or proprietor, who strode up and down, beaming and nodding, sharp-eyed and courteous, and whom Selwood, from a glance at the emblazoned lettering of the bill-of-fare, took to rejoice in the name of Mr. Alessandro Bioni. This man, if he was landlord, or manager, of the Ravenna Hotel, was clearly the person to approach if one wanted information about the Luigi Dimambro who had given the place as his address as recently as November 12th.

While he ate and drank, Selwood wondered how to go about his business. It seemed to him that the best thing to do, now that he had seen the place and assured himself that it was a hotel evidently doing a proper and legitimate business, was to approach its management with a plain question—was Mr. Luigi Dimambro staying there, or was he known there? Since Dimambro, whoever he might be, had given that as his address, something must be known of him. And when the smiling patron presently came round, and, seeing a new customer, asked politely if he was being served to his satisfaction, Selwood determined to settle matters at once.

"The proprietor, I presume?" he asked.

"Manager, sir," answered the other. "The proprietor, he is an old gentleman—practically retired."

"Perhaps I can ask you a question," Selwood. "Have you got a Mr. Luigi Dimambro staying at your hotel? He is, I believe"—here Selwood made a bold shot at a possibility—"a seller of curios, or art objects. I know he stops here sometimes."

The manager rubbed his hands together and reflected.

"One moment, sir," he said. "I get the register. The hotel guests, they come in here for meals, but always I do not recollect their names, and sometimes not know them. But the register——"

He sped down the room, through a side door, vanished; to return in a moment with a book which he carried to Selwood's side.

"Dimambro?" he said. "Recently, then? We shall see."

"About the beginning or middle of November," answered Selwood.

The manager found the pages: suddenly he pointed to an entry.

"See, then!" he exclaimed dramatically. "You are right, sir. There—Luigi Dimambro—November 11th to—yes—13th. Two days only. Then he go—leave us, eh?"

"Oh, then, he's not here now," said Selwood, affecting disappointment. "That's a pity. I wanted to see him. I wonder if he left any address?"

The manager showed more politeness in returning to the hotel office and making inquiry. He came back full of disappointment that he could not oblige his customer. No—no address—merely there for two nights—then gone—nobody knew where. Perhaps he would return—some day.

"Oh, it's of no great consequence, thank you," remarked Selwood. "I'm much obliged to you."

He had found out, at any rate, that a man named Dimambro had certainly stayed at the Hotel Ravenna on the critical and important date. Presumably he was the man who had presented Jacob Herapath's cheque at Bittleston's Bank first thing on the morning after the murder. But whether this man had any connection with that murder, whether to discover his whereabouts would be to reveal something of use in establishing Barthorpe Herapath's innocence, were questions which he must leave to Professor Cox-Raythwaite, to whom he was presently going with his news.

He had just finished his coffee, and was about to pay his bill when, looking up to summon the waiter, he suddenly saw a face appear behind the glass panel of the street door—the face of a man who had evidently stolen quietly into the entry between the evergreen shrubs and wished to take a surreptitious peep into the interior of the little restaurant. It was there, clearly seen through the glass, but for one fraction of a second—then it was withdrawn as swiftly as it had come and the panel of glass was blank again. But in that flash of time Selwood had recognized it.

Burchill!

Table of Contents

CHAPTER XXIX

the note in the prayer-book

Selwood hurried out of that restaurant as soon as he had paid his bill, but it was with small hopes of finding the man whose face had appeared at the glass panel for the fraction of a second. As well look for one snowflake in a drift as for one man in those crowded streets!—all the same, he spent half an hour in wandering round the neighbourhood, looking eagerly at every tall figure he met or passed. And at the end of that time he went off to Endsleigh Gardens and reported progress to Professor Cox-Raythwaite.

The Professor heard both items of news without betraying any great surprise.

"You're sure it was Burchill?" he asked.

"As sure," answered Selwood, "as that you're you! His is not a face easy to mistake."

"He's a daring fellow," observed the Professor, musingly. "A very bold fellow! There's a very good portrait of him on those bills that the police have put out and posted so freely, and he must know that every constable and detective in London is on the look-out for him, to say nothing of folk who would be glad of the reward. If that was Burchill—and I've no doubt of it, since you're so certain—it suggests a good deal to me."

"What?" asked Selwood.

"That he's not afraid of being recaptured as you'd think he would be," replied the Professor. "It suggests that he's got some card up his sleeve—which is what I've always thought. He probably knows something—you may be certain, in any case, that he's playing a deep and bold game, for his own purpose, of course. Now, I wonder if Burchill went to that restaurant on the same errand as yourself?"

"What!—to look for Dimambro?" exclaimed Selwood.

"Why not? Remember that Burchill was Jacob Herapath's secretary before you were," answered the Professor. "He was with Jacob some time, wasn't he? Well, he knew a good deal about Jacob's doings. Jacob may have had dealings with this Dimambro person in Burchill's days. You don't remember that Jacob had any such dealings in your time?"

"Never!" replied Selwood. "Never heard the man's name until yesterday—never saw any letters from him, never heard Mr. Herapath mention him. But then, as Mr. Halfpenny said, yesterday, Mr. Herapath had all sorts of queer dealings with queer people. It's a fact that he used to buy and sell all sorts of things—curios, pictures, precious stones—he'd all sorts of irons in the fire. It's a fact, too, that he was accustomed to carrying not only considerable sums of money, but valuables on him."

"Ah!" exclaimed the Professor. He rose out of his chair, put his hands behind his broad back, and began to march up and down his study. "I'll tell you what, young man!" he said earnestly. "I'm more than ever convinced that Jacob Herapath was robbed as well as murdered, and that robbery and murder—or, rather, murder and robbery, for the murder would go first—took place just before Barthorpe entered the offices to keep that appointment. Selwood!—we must find this Dimambro man!"

"Who's most likely left the country," remarked Selwood.

"That's probable—it may be certain," said the Professor. "Nevertheless, he may be here. And Burchill may be looking for him, too. Now, if Dimambro stopped two days at that Hotel Ravenna, from November 11th to 13th, there must be somebody who knows something of him. We must—you must—make more inquiry—there at the hotel. Talk quietly to that manager or the servants. Get a description of him. Do that at once—first thing tomorrow morning."

"You don't want to tell the police all this?" asked Selwood.

"No! Not at present, at any rate," answered the Professor. "The police have their own methods, and they don't thank anybody for putting them off their beaten tracks. And—for the present—we won't tell them anything about your seeing Burchill. If we did, they'd be incredulous. Police-like, they'll have watched the various seaports much more closely than they'll have watched London streets for Burchill. And Burchill's a clever devil—he'll know that he's much safer under the very nose of the people who want him than he would be fifty miles away from their toes! No, it's my opinion that Master Burchill will reveal himself, when the time comes."

"Give himself up, do you mean?" exclaimed Selwood.

"Likely—but if he does, it'll be done with a purpose," answered the Professor. "Well—keep all quiet at present, and tomorrow morning, go and see if you can find out more about Dimambro at that hotel."

Selwood repaired to the polite manager again next day and found no difficulty in getting whatever information the hotel staff—represented by a manageress, a general man-servant, and a maid or two—could give. It was meagre, and not too exact in particulars. Mr. Dimambro, who had never been there before, had stopped two days. He had occupied Room 5—the gentleman could see it if he wished. Mr. Dimambro had been in and out most of the time. On the 13th he had gone out early in the morning; by ten o'clock he had returned, paid his bill, and gone away with his luggage—one suit-case. No—he had had no callers at the hotel. But a waiter in the restaurant was discovered who remembered him as Number 5, and that on the 12th he had entertained a gentleman to dinner at seven o'clock—a tall, thin, dark-faced gentleman, who looked like—yes, like an actor: a nicely dressed gentleman. That was all the waiter could remember of the guest; he remembered just about as much of Number 5, which was that Dimambro was a shortish, stoutish gentleman, with a slight black beard and moustache. There was a good reason why the waiter remembered this occurrence—the two gentlemen had a bottle of the best champagne, a rare occurrence at the Hotel Ravenna—a whole bottle, for which the surprising sum of twelve shillings and sixpence was charged! In proof of that startling episode in the restaurant routine, he produced the desk book for that day—behold it, the entry: Number 5—1 Moet & Chandon, 12*s*. 6*d*.

"It is of a rare thing our customers call for wine so expensive," said the polite manager. "Light wines, you understand, sir, we mostly sell. Champagne at twelve and six—an event!"

Selwood carried this further news to Professor Cox-Raythwaite, who roused himself from his microscope to consider it.

"Could that tall, dark, nicely-dressed gentleman have been Burchill?" he muttered. "Sounds like him. But you've got a description of Dimambro, at any rate. Now we know of one man who saw the caller at the House of Commons—Mountain, the coachman. Come along—I'll go with you to see Mountain."

Mountain, discovered at the mews wherein the Herapath stable was kept, said at once that he remembered the gentleman who had come out of the House of Commons with his late master. But when he came to be taxed with a requirement of details, Mountain's memory proved to be of no real value. The gentleman—well, he was a well-dressed gentleman, and he wore a top hat. But whether the gentleman was dark or fair, elderly or middle-aged, short or medium-heighted, he did not know—exactly. Nevertheless——

"I should know him again, sir, if I was to set eyes on him!" said Mountain, with such belief in his powers. "Pick him out of a thousand, I could!"

"Queer how deficient most of our people are in the faculty of observation!" remarked the Professor as he and Selwood left the mews. "It really is most extraordinary that a man like that, with plenty of intelligence, and is no doubt a good man in his own line, can look at another man for a full minute and yet be utterly unable to tell you anything definite about him a month later! No help there, Selwood."

It seemed to Selwood that they were face to face with an impossible situation, and he began to feel inclined to share Mr. Halfpenny's pessimistic opinions as to the usefulness of these researches. But Professor Cox-Raythwaite was not to be easily daunted, and he was no sooner baulked in one direction than he hastened to try another.

"Now, let's see where we are," he said, as they went round to Portman Square. "We do know for a certainty that Jacob Herapath had a transaction of some sort with one Luigi Dimambro, on November 12th, and that it resulted in his handing, or sending, the said Luigi a cheque for three thousand guineas. Let's see if we can't find some trace of it, or some mention of it, or of previous dealings with Dimambro, amongst Jacob's papers. I suppose we can get access to everything here at the house, and down at the office, too, can't we? The probability is that the transaction with Dimambro was not the first. There must be something, Selwood—memoranda, letters, receipts—must be!"

But Selwood shook his head and uttered a dismal groan.

"Another of my late employer's peculiarities," he answered, "was that he never gave or took receipts in what one may call word-of-mouth transactions! He had a rooted—almost savage—objection to anybody asking him for a receipt for cash; he absolutely refused to take one if he paid cash. I've seen him pay several thousand pounds for a purchase and fling the proffered receipt in the fire in the purchaser's presence. He used to ask—vehemently!—if you wanted receipts for a loaf of bread or a pound of beef-steak. I'm afraid we shan't find much of that sort. As to letters and memoranda, Mr. Herapath had a curious habit which gave me considerable trouble of mind when I first went to him, though I admit it was a simple one. He destroyed every letter he ever got as soon as he'd answered it. And as he insisted on everything being answered there and then, there's no great accumulation of paper in that way!"

"We'll see what there is, anyhow," said the Professor. "If we could find something, anything—a mere business card, a letter-heading—that would give us Dimambro's permanent address, it would be of use. For I'm more and more convinced that Dimambro was the man who called at the House of Commons that night, and if it was Burchill who dined with him that same evening, why, then—but come along, let's have a look at Jacob's desk in the house here, and after that we'll go down to the estate offices and see if we can find anything there."

This was a Saturday morning—during the whole of that afternoon and evening the Professor and Selwood examined every drawer and receptacle in which Jacob Herapath's papers lay, both at Portman Square and at Kensington. And, exactly as Selwood had said, there was next to nothing of a private nature. Papers relating to Parliamentary matters, to building schemes, to business affairs, there were in plenty, duly filed, docketed, and arranged, but there was nothing of the sort that Cox-Raythwaite hoped to find, and when they parted, late at night, they were no wiser than when they began their investigations.

"Go home to bed," counselled the Professor. "Put the whole thing out of your head until Monday morning. Don't even think about it. Come and see me on Monday, first thing, and we'll start again. For by the Lord Harry! I'll find out yet what the real nature of Jacob Herapath's transaction with Dimambro was, if I have to track Dimambro all through Italy!"

Selwood was glad enough to put everything out of his mind; it seemed to him a hopeless task to search for a man to whose identity they only had the very faintest clue. But before noon of the next day—Sunday—he was face to face with a new phase of the problem. Since her uncle's death, Peggie had begun to show a quiet reliance on Selwood. It had come to be tacitly understood between them that he was to be in constant attendance on her for the present, at any rate. He spent all his time at the house in Portman Square; he saved its young mistress all the trouble he could; he accompanied her in her goings and comings. And of late he had taken to attending her to a certain neighbouring church, whereto Peggie, like a well-regulated young lady, was constant in her Sunday visits. There in the Herapath family pew, he and Peggie sat together on this particular Sunday morning, neither with any thought that the Herapath mystery had penetrated to their sacred surroundings. Selwood had been glad to take Cox-Raythwaite's advice and to put the thing out of his mind for thirty-six hours: Peggie had nothing in her mind but what was proper to the occasion.

Jacob Herapath had been an old-fashioned man in many respects; one of his fads was an insistence upon having a family pew in the church which he attended, and in furnishing it with his own cushions, mats, and books. Consequently Peggie left her own prayer-book in that pew from Sunday to Sunday. She picked it up now, and opened it at the usual familiar place. And from that place immediately dropped a folded note.

Had this communication been a *billet-doux*, Peggie could hardly have betrayed more alarm and confusion. For a moment she let the thing rest in the palm of her hand, holding the hand out towards Selwood at her side; then with trembling fingers she unfolded it in such a fashion that she and Selwood read it together. With astonished eyes and beating hearts they found themselves looking at a half-sheet of thin, foreign-looking notepaper, on which were two or three lines of typewriting:

"If you wish to save your cousin Barthorpe's life, leave the church and speak to the lady whom you will find in a private automobile at the entrance to the churchyard."

Table of Contents

CHAPTER XXX

the white-haired lady

The two young people who bent over this mysterious message in the shelter of that old-fashioned pew were each conscious of a similar feeling—they were thankful that they were together. Peggie Wynne had never been so glad of anything in her life as for Selwood's immediate presence at that moment: Selwood felt a world of unspeakable gratitude that he was there, just when help and protection were wanted. For each recognized, with a sure instinct and intuition, that those innocent-looking lines of type-script signified much, heralded some event of dire importance. To save Barthorpe Herapath's life!—that could only mean that somebody—the sender of the note—knew that Barthorpe was innocent and some other person guilty.

For a moment the girl stared with startled eyes and flushed cheeks at the scrap of paper; then she turned with a quick, questioning look at her companion. And Selwood reached for his hat and his stick, and murmured one word:

"Come!"

Peggie saw nothing of the surprised and questioning looks which were turned on Selwood and herself as they left the pew and passed down the aisle of the crowded church. She had but one thought—whom was she going to meet outside, what revelation was going to be made to her? Unconsciously, she laid a hand on Selwood's arm as they passed through the porch, and Selwood, with a quick throb of pride, took it and held it. Then, arm in arm, they walked out, and a verger who opened the outer door for them, smiled as they passed him; he foresaw another passing-out, whereat Peggie would wear orange blossoms.

The yard of this particular church was not a place of green sward, ancient trees, and tumble-down tombs; instead it was an expanse of bare flagstones, shut in by high walls which terminated at a pair of iron gates. Outside those gates an automobile was drawn up; its driver stood attentively at its door. Selwood narrowly inspected both, as he and Peggie approached. The car was evidently a private one: a quiet, yet smart affair; its driver was equally smart in his dark green livery. And that he had received his orders was evident from the fact that as the two young people approached he touched his cap and laid a hand on the door of the car.

"Be watchful and careful," whispered Selwood, as he and Peggie crossed the pavement. "Leave all to me!"

He himself was keenly alert to whatever might be going to happen. It seemed to him, from the chauffeur's action, that they were to be invited, or Peggie was to be invited, to enter the car. Very good—but he was going to know who was in that car before any communications of any sort were entered upon. Also, Peggie was not going to exchange one word with anybody, go one step with anybody, unless he remained in close attendance upon her. The phraseology of the mysterious note; the clandestine fashion in which it had been brought under Peggie's notice; the extraordinary method adopted of procuring an interview with her—all these things had aroused Selwood's suspicions, and his natural sense of caution was at its full stretch as he walked across to the car, wondering what he and Peggie were about to confront.

What they did confront was a pleasant-faced, white-haired, elderly lady, evidently a woman of fashion and of culture, who bent forward from her seat with a kindly, half-apologetic smile.

"Miss Wynne?" she said inquiringly. "How do you do? And this gentleman is, no doubt, Mr. Selwood, of whom I have heard? You must forgive this strange conduct, this extraordinary manner of getting speech with you—I am not a free agent. Now, as I have something to say—will you both come into the car and hear it?"

Peggie, who was greatly surprised at this reception, turned diffidently to her companion. And Selwood, who had been gazing earnestly at the elderly lady's face, and had seen nothing but good intention in it, felt himself considerably embarrassed.

"I—well, really, this is such a very strange affair altogether that I don't know what we ought to do," he said. "May I suggest that if you wish to talk to Miss Wynne, we should go to her house? It's only just round the corner, and——"

"But that's just what I am not to do," replied the lady, with an amused laugh. "I repeat—I am not exactly a free agent. It's all very strange, and very unpleasant, and sounds, no doubt, very mysterious, but I am acting—practically—under orders. Let me suggest something—will you and Miss Wynne come into the car, and I will tell the man to drive gently about until you have heard what I have to say? Come now!—I am not going to kidnap you, and you can't come to much harm by driving round about Portman Square for a few minutes, in the company of an old woman! Dickerson," she went on, as Selwood motioned Peggie to enter the car, "drive us very slowly round about here until I tell you to stop—go round the square—anywhere."

The car moved gently up Baker Street, and Selwood glanced inquiringly at their captor.

"May we have the pleasure of——"

The elderly lady brought out a card-case and some papers.

"I am Mrs. Engledew," she said. "I live in the Herapath Flats. I don't suppose you ever heard of me, Miss Wynne, but I knew your uncle very well—we had been acquaintances, nay, friends, for years. I thought it might be necessary to prove my *bona fides*," she continued, with a laugh, "so I brought some letters of Jacob Herapath's with me—letters written to me—you recognize his big, bold hand, of course."

There was no mistaking Jacob Herapath's writing, and the two young people, after one glance at it, exchanged glances with each other.

"Now you want to know why I am here," said Mrs. Engledew. "The answer is plain—if astonishing. I have managed to get mixed up in this matter of Jacob Herapath's murder! That sounds odd, doesn't it?—nevertheless, it's true. But we can't go into that now. And I cannot do more than tell you that I simply bring a message and want an answer. My dear!" she continued, laying a hand on Peggie's arm, "you do not wish to see Barthorpe Herapath hanged?"

"We believe him innocent," replied Peggie.

"Quite so—he is innocent—of murder, anyway," said Mrs. Engledew. "Now—I speak in absolute confidence, remember!—there are two men who know who the real murderer is. They are in touch with me—that is, one of them is, on behalf of both. I am really here as their emissary. They are prepared to give you and the police full particulars about the murder—for a price."

Selwood felt himself grow more suspicious than ever. This lady was of charming address, pleasant smile, and apparently candid manners, but—price!—price for telling the truth in a case like this!

"What price?" he asked.

"Their price is ten thousand pounds—cash," answered Mrs. Engledew, with a little shrug of her shoulders. "Seems a great deal, doesn't it? But that is their price. They will not be moved from it. If Miss Wynne will agree to pay that sum, they will at once not only give their evidence as to the real murderer of Jacob Herapath, but they will point him out."

"When?" demanded Selwood.

"Tonight!" replied Mrs. Engledew. "Tonight—at an hour to be fixed after your agreement to their terms."

Selwood felt himself in a difficult position. Mr. Tertius was out of town for the day, gone to visit an antiquarian friend in Berkshire: Mr. Halfpenny lived away down amongst the Surrey hills. Still, there was Cox-Raythwaite to turn to. But it seemed as if the lady desired an immediate answer.

"You know these men?" he asked.

"One only, who represents both," answered Mrs. Engledew.

"Why not point him out to the police, and let them deal with them?" suggested Selwood. "They would get his evidence out of him without any question of price!"

"I have given my word," said Mrs. Engledew. "I—the fact is, I am mixed up in this, quite innocently, of course. And I am sure that no living person knows the truth except these men, and just as sure that they will not tell what they know unless they are paid. The police could not make them speak if they didn't want to speak. They know very well that they have got the whip-hand of all of us in that respect!"

"Of you, too?" asked Selwood.

"Of me, too!" she answered. "Nobody in the world, I'm sure, knows the secret but these men. And it's important to me personally that they should reveal it. In fact, though I'm not rich, I'll join Miss Wynne in paying their price, so far as a thousand pounds is concerned. I would pay more, but I really haven't got the money—I daren't go beyond a thousand."

Selwood felt himself impressed by this candid offer.

"Precisely what do they ask—what do they propose?" he asked.

"This. If you agree to pay them ten thousand pounds, you and Professor Cox-Raythwaite are to meet them tonight. They will then tell the true story, and they will further take you and the police to the man, the real murderer," answered Mrs. Engledew. "It is important that all this should be done tonight."

"Where is this meeting to take place?" demanded Selwood.

"It can take place at my flat: in fact, it must, because, as I say, I am unfortunately mixed up," said Mrs. Engledew. "If you agree to the terms, you are to telephone to me—I have written my number on the card—at two o'clock this afternoon. Then I shall telephone the time of meeting tonight, and you must bring the money with you."

"Ten thousand pounds in cash—on Sunday!" exclaimed Selwood. "That, of course, is utterly impossible."

"Not cash in that sense," replied Mrs. Engledew. "An open cheque will do. And, don't you see, that, I think, proves the *bona fides* of the men. If they fail to do what they say they can and will do, you can stop payment of that cheque first thing tomorrow morning."

"Yes, that's so," agreed Selwood. He glanced at Peggie, who was silently listening with deep interest. "I don't know how things stand," he went on. "Mr. Halfpenny, Miss Wynne's solicitor, lives a long way out of town. Miss Wynne would doubtless cheerfully sacrifice ten thousand pounds to save her cousin——"

"Oh, twenty thousand—anything!" exclaimed Peggie. "Don't let us hesitate about money, please."

"But I don't know whether she can draw a cheque," continued Selwood. "At least, for such an amount as that. Perhaps Professor Cox-Raythwaite can tell us. Let me ask you a question or two, if you please, Mrs. Engledew," he went on. "You say you only know one of these men. Do you know his name?"

"No—I don't," confessed Mrs. Engledew. "Everything is secret and mysterious."

"Are you convinced—has he done anything to convince you—of his good faith?"

"Yes—absolutely!"

"You don't doubt his—their—ability to clear all this up?"

"I'm quite sure they can clear it up."

"Have you any idea as to the identity of the real murderer?"

"Not the least!"

"One more question, then," concluded Selwood. "Are the police to be there when Cox-Raythwaite and I come tonight?"

"That I don't know," replied Mrs. Engledew. "All I know is—just what I am ordered to say. Pay them the money—they will tell the truth and take you and the police to the real criminal. One more thing—it is understood that you will not approach the police between now and this evening. That part—the police part—is to be left to them."

"I understand," said Selwood. "Very well—we will get out, if you please, and we will go straight to Professor Cox-Raythwaite. At two o'clock I shall ring you up and give you our answer."

He hurried Peggie into a taxi-cab as soon as Mrs. Engledew's car had gone away, and they went hastily to Endsleigh Gardens, where Professor Cox-Raythwaite listened to the strange story in dead silence.

"Mrs. Engledew—lady living in Herapath Flats—old friend of Jacob's—possessed letters of his—instrument for two men in possession of secret—willing to fork out a thousand of her own," he muttered. "Gad!—I take that to be genuine, Selwood! The only question is for Peggie here—does she wish to throw away nine thousand to save Barthorpe's neck?"

"The only question, Professor," said Peggie, reprovingly, "is—can I do it? Can I draw a cheque for that amount?"

"Why not?" replied the Professor. "Everything's in order. Barthorpe withdrew that wretched caveat—the will's been proved—every penny that Jacob possessed is yours. Draw a cheque for fifty thousand, if you like!"

"And you will go with Mr. Selwood?" asked Peggie, with a touch of anxiety which was not lost on the Professor.

"Go with him—and take care of him, too," answered the Professor, digging his big fingers into Selwood's ribs. "Very good. Now stop here and lunch with me, and at two o'clock we'll telephone."

He and Peggie stood breathlessly waiting in the hall that afternoon while Selwood was busy at the telephone in an adjacent lobby. Selwood came back to them nodding his head.

"All right!" he said. "You and I, Professor, at her flat—tonight, at nine o'clock."

Table of Contents

CHAPTER XXXI

the interrupted dinner-party

Triffitt's recent inquiries in connection with the Herapath affair had been all very well from a strictly professional point of view, but not so well from another. For nearly twelve months he had been engaged to a sweet girl, of whom he was very fond, and who thoroughly reciprocated his affection; up to the time of the Herapath murder he had contrived to spend a certain portion of each day with her, and to her he had invariably devoted the whole of his Sundays. In this love affair he was joined by his friend, to whom Triffitt's young lady had introduced her great friend, with whom Carver had promptly become infatuated. These ladies, both very young and undeniably charming, spent the greater part of the working week at the School of Needlework, in South Kensington, where they fashioned various beautiful objects with busy needles; Sundays they gave up to their swains, and every Sunday ended with a little dinner of four at some cheap restaurant whereat you could get quite a number of courses at the fixed price of half a crown or so and drink light wine which was very little dearer than pale ale. All parties concerned looked forward throughout the week to these joyful occasions; the girls wore their best frocks, and the young men came out bravely in the matter of neckties; there was laughter and gaiety and a general escape from the prosaic matters which obtained from Monday to Saturday—consequently, Triffitt felt it a serious thing that attention to this Herapath business had come to interfere with his love-making and his Sunday feast of mirth and gladness. More than once he had been obliged to let Carver go alone to the usual rendezvous; he himself had been running hither and thither after chances of news which never materialized, while his sweetheart played gooseberry to the more favoured people. And as he was very much in love, Triffitt had often been tempted to throw his clues and his theories to the winds, and to vow himself to the service of Venus rather than to that of Mercury.

But on that Sunday which saw the white-haired lady interviewing Peggie Wynne and Selwood, Triffitt, to his great delight, found that newspaper requirements were not going to interfere with him. The hue-and-cry after the missing Burchill was dying down—the police (so Davidge told Triffitt in strict confidence) were of the firm opinion that Burchill had escaped to the continent—probably within a few hours of the moment wherein he made his unceremonious exit from Mr. Halfpenny's office. Even Markledew was not so keen about the Herapath affair as he had been. His policy was—a new day, a new affair. The Herapath mystery was becoming a little stale—it would get staler unless a fresh and startling development took place. As it was, nothing was likely to arise which would titillate the public until Barthorpe Herapath, now safely lodged in the remand prison, was brought to trial, or unless Burchill was arrested. Consequently, Triffitt was not expected to make up a half or a whole column of recent and sensational Herapath news every morning. And so he gladly took this Sunday for a return to the primrose paths. He and Carver met their sweethearts; they took them to the Albert Hall Sunday afternoon concert—nothing better offering in the middle of winter—they went to tea at the sweethearts' lodgings; later in the evening they carried them off to the accustomed Sunday dinner.

Triffitt and Carver had become thoroughly seasoned men of the world in the matter of finding out good places whereat to dine well and cheaply. They knew all the Soho restaurants. They had sampled several in Oxford Street and in Tottenham Court Road. But by sheer luck they had found one—an Italian restaurant—in South Kensington which was, in their opinion, superior to all of their acquaintance. This establishment had many advantages for lovers. To begin with, it bore a poetical name—the Café Venezia—Triffitt, who frequently read Byron and Shelley to his adored one, said it made one think of moonlight and gondolas, and similar adjuncts to what he called *parfaite amour*. Then it was divided off into little cabinets, just holding four people—that was an advantage when you were sure of your company. And for the *prix fixe* of two shillings they gave you quite a good dinner; also their Chianti was of exceptional quality, and according to the proprietor, it came straight from Siena.

On this Sunday evening, then, Triffitt on one side of a table with his lady-love, Carver on the other with his, made merry, with no thought of anything but the joys of the moment. They had arrived at the last stages of the feast; the heroes puffed cigarettes and sipped Benedictine; the heroines daintily drank their sweetened coffee. They all chattered gaily, out of the fulness of their youthful hearts; not one of them had any idea that anything was going to happen. And in the midst of their lightsomeness, Triffitt, who faced a mirror, started, dropped his cigarette, upset his liqueur glass and turned pale. For an instant he clutched the tablecloth, staring straight in front of him; then with a great effort he controlled his emotion and with a cautious hissing of his breath, gazed warningly at Carver.

"'Sh!" whispered Triffitt. "Not a word! And don't move—don't show a sign, any of you. Carver—turn your head very slowly and look behind you. At the bar!"

At the entrance to that restaurant there was a bar, whereat it was possible to get a drink. There were two or three men, so occupied, standing at this bar at that moment—Carver, leisurely turning to inspect them, suddenly started as violently as Triffitt had started a moment before.

"Good heavens!" he muttered. "Burchill!"

"Quiet!" commanded Triffitt. "Quiet, all of you. By Gad!—this is——"

He ended in an eloquent silence and with a glare at his companions which would have imposed silence on an unruly class-room. He was already at work—the quick, sure journalistic instinct had come up on top and was rapidly realizing the situation. That the man standing there, openly, calmly, taking a drink of some sort, was Frank Burchill he had no more doubt than of his own identity. The thing was—what was to be done?

Triffitt was as quick of action as of thought—in two seconds he had made up his mind. With another warning glance at the startled girls, he bent across the table to Carver.

"Carver!" he whispered. "Do exactly what I tell you. When Burchill goes out, Trixie and I'll follow him. You pay the bill—then you and Lettie jump into the first taxi you can get and go to Scotland Yard. Find Davidge! If Davidge isn't there, get somebody else. Wait there until I ring you up! What I'll do will be this—we'll follow Burchill, and if I see that he's going to take to train or cab I'll call help and stop him. You follow me? As soon as I've taken action, or run him to earth, I'll ring up Scotland Yard, and then——"

"He's going," announced Carver, who had taken advantage of the many mirrors to keep his eye on Burchill. "He's off! I understand——"

Triffitt was already leading his sweetheart quietly out. In the gloom of the street he saw Burchill's tall figure striding away towards Cromwell Road. Triffitt's companion was an athletically inclined young woman—long walks in the country on summer Sundays had toughened her powers of locomotion and she strode out manfully in response to Triffitt's command to hurry up.

"Lucky that you were with me, Trixie!" exclaimed Triffitt. "You make a splendid blind. Supposing he does look round and sees that he's being followed? Why, he'd never think that we were after him. Slip your hand in my arm—he'll think we're just a couple of sweethearts, going his way. Gad!—what a surprise! And what a cheek he has—with all those bills out against him!"

"You don't think he'll shoot you if he catches sight of you?" asked Trixie, anxiously. "He'd be sure to recognize you, wouldn't he?"

"We'll not come within shooting distance," replied Triffitt grimly. "All I want to do is to track him. Of course, if he gets into any vehicle, I'll have to act. Let's draw a bit nearer."

Burchill showed no sign of hailing any vehicle; indeed, he showed no sign of anything but cool confidence. It was certainly nearly nine o'clock of a dark winter evening, but there was plenty of artificial light in the streets, and Burchill made no attempt to escape its glare. He walked on, smoking a cigar, jauntily swinging an umbrella, he passed and was passed by innumerable people; more than one policeman glanced at his tall figure and took no notice. And Triffitt chuckled cynically.

"There you are, Trixie!" he said. "There's a fellow who's wanted about as badly as can be, whose picture's posted up outside every police-station in London, and at every port in England, and he walks about, and stares at people, and passes policemen as unconcernedly as I do. The fact of the case is that if I went to that bobby and pointed Burchill out, and told the bobby who he is, all that bobby would say would be, 'Who are you a-kiddin' of?'—or words to that equivalent. And so—still ahead he goes, and we after him! And—where?"

Burchill evidently knew very well where he was going. He crossed Cromwell Road, went up Queen's Road, turned into Queen's Gate Terrace, and leisurely pursuing his way, proceeded to cut through various streets and thoroughfares towards Kensington High Street. Always he looked forward; never once did he turn nor seem to have any suspicion that he was being followed. There was nothing here of the furtive slink, the frightened slouch of the criminal escaped from justice; the man's entire bearing was that of fearlessness; he strode across Kensington High Street in the full glare of light before the Town Hall and under the noses of several policemen.

Five minutes later Triffitt pulled himself and Trixie up with a gasp. The chase had come to an end—for that moment, at any rate. Boldly, openly, with absolute nonchalance, Burchill walked into a brilliantly-lighted entrance of the Herapath Flats!

Table of Contents

CHAPTER XXXII

the yorkshire proverb

In the course of Triffitt's brief and fairly glorious journalistic career, he had enjoyed and suffered a few startling experiences. He had been fastened up in the darker regions of a London sewer in flood, wondering if he would ever breathe the fine air of Fleet Street again or go down with the rats that scurried by him. He had been down a coal-mine in the bad hour which follows an explosion. He had several times risked his neck; his limbs had often been in danger; he had known what it was to feel thumpings of the heart and catchings of the breath from sheer fright. He had come face to face with surprise, with astonishment, with audacious turnings of Fortune's glass. But never in all his life had he been so surprised as he now was, and after one long, low whistle he relieved his feelings by quoting verse:

"Is things what they seem? Or is visions about?"

"Trixie!" he went on in a low, concentrated voice. "This licks all! This bangs Banagher! This—but words fail me, Trixie!"

"What is it, Herbert?" demanded Trixie anxiously. "What does it all mean?"

"Ah!" responded Triffitt, wildly smiting the crown of his deerstalker. "That's just it! What does it all mean, my dear! Gad!—this is—to use the common language of the common man, a fair licker! That that chap Burchill should march as bold as brass into those Herapath Flats, is—well, I couldn't be more surprised, Trixie, than if you were to tell me that you are the Queen of Sheba's grand-daughter! Not so much so, in fact. You see——"

But at that moment a taxi-cab came speeding round the corner, and from it presently emerged Carver and Davidge. The detective, phlegmatic, quiet as ever, nodded familiarly to Triffitt and lifted his hat to Trixie.

"Evening, Mr. Triffitt," he said quietly.

"He's in there!" exclaimed Triffitt, grabbing Davidge's arm and pointing wildly to the brilliantly lighted entrance, wherein two or three uniformed servants lounged about to open doors and attend to elevators. "Walked in as if the whole place belonged to him! You know—Burchill!"

"Ah, just so!" responded Davidge unconcernedly. "Quite so—I wouldn't name no names in the street if I were you, Mr. Triffitt. Ah!—to be sure, now. Well, of course, he would have to go in somewhere, wouldn't he?—as well here as anywhere, perhaps. Yes. Now, if this young lady would join the other young lady in the cab, Mr. Carver'll escort 'em home, and then he can come back here if he likes—we might have a bit of a job for him. And when the ladies retire, you and me can do our bit of business, d'ye see, Mr. Triffitt. What?"

Trixie, urged towards the cab, showed signs of uneasiness.

"Promise me you won't get shot, or poisoned, or anything, Herbert!" she entreated. "If you do——"

"We aren't going in for any shooting tonight, miss," said Davidge gravely. "Some other night, perhaps. All quiet and serene tonight—just a little family gathering, as it were—all pleasant!"

"But that dreadful man!" exclaimed Trixie, pointing to the door of the flats. "Supposing——"

"Ah, but we won't suppose," answered Davidge. "He's all right, he is. Mild as milk we shall find him—my word on it, miss. Now," he continued, when he had gently but firmly assisted Trixie into the cab, said a word or two to Carver, taken Triffitt's arm, and led him across the street, "now we'll talk a bit, quietly. So he's gone in there, has he, Mr. Triffitt? Just so. Alone, now?"

"Quite alone," replied Triffitt. "What's it all about—what does it mean? You seem remarkably cool about it!"

"I shouldn't be much use in my trade if I didn't keep cool, Mr. Triffitt," answered Davidge. "You see, I know a bit—perhaps a good deal—of what's going on—or what's going to go on, presently. So will you. I'll take you in there."

"There? Where?" demanded Triffitt.

"Where he's gone," said Davidge. "Where—if I'm not mistaken—that chap's going."

He pointed to a man who had come quickly round the corner from the direction of the High Street, a middle-sized, apparently well-dressed man, who hurried up the broad steps and disappeared within the glass-panelled doors.

"That's another of 'em," observed Davidge. "And I'm a Dutchman if this taxi-cab doesn't hold t'other two. You'll recognize them, easy."

Triffitt gaped with astonishment as he saw Professor Cox-Raythwaite and Selwood descend from the taxi-cab, pass up the steps, and disappear.

"Talk of mysteries!" he said. "This——"

Davidge pulled out an old-fashioned watch.

"Nine o'clock," he remarked. "Come on—we'll go in. Now, then, Mr. Triffitt," he continued, pressing his companion's arm, "let me give you a tip. You mayn't know that I'm a Yorkshireman—I am! We've a good old proverb—it's often cast up against us: 'Hear all—say naught!' You'll see me act on it tonight—act on it yourself. And—a word in your ear!—you're going to have the biggest surprise you ever had in your life—and so's a certain somebody else that we shall see in five minutes! Come on!"

He took Triffitt's arm firmly in his, led him up the stairs, in at the doors. The hall-porter came forward.

"Take me up," said Davidge, "to Mrs. Engledew's flat."

Table of Contents

CHAPTER XXXIII

It seemed to Triffitt, who possessed, and sedulously cultivated, a sense of the dramatic, that the scene to which he and Davidge were presently conducted by a trim and somewhat surprised-looking parlour-maid, was one which might have been bodily lifted from the stage of any theatre devoted to work of the melodramatic order. The detective and the reporter found themselves on the threshold of a handsomely furnished dining-room, vividly lighted by lamps which threw a warm pink glow over the old oak furniture and luxurious fittings. On one side of the big table sat Professor Cox-Raythwaite and Selwood both looking a little mystified; at the further end sat a shortish, rather fat man, obviously a foreigner, who betrayed anxiety in every line of his rather oily countenance. And posed in an elegant attitude on the hearthrug, one elbow resting on the black marble of the mantelpiece, one hand toying with a cigarette, stood Burchill, scrupulously attired as usual, and conveying, or endeavouring to convey to whoever looked upon him, that he, of all people present, was master of himself and all of the scene.

Triffitt took all this in at a glance; his next glance was at the elegant, white-haired lady who came forward to meet him and his companion. Davidge gave him a nudge as he executed a duck-like bow.

"Servant, ma'am," said Davidge in his quietest and coolest manner. "I took the liberty of bringing a friend with me. You see, ma'am, as these proceedings are in what we may call the public way, Mrs. Engledew, no objection I'm sure to having a press gentleman at them. Mr. Triffitt, ma'am, of the *Argus* newspaper. Known to these gentlemen—all of 'em—unless it's the gentleman at the far end, there. Known, at any rate, to Mr. Selwood and the Professor," continued Davidge, nodding with much familiarity to the person he named. "And likewise to Mr. Burchill there. How do you do, sir, this evening? You and me, I think, has met before, and shall no doubt meet again. Well, ma'am, and now that I've come, perhaps I might ask a question. What have I come for?"

Davidge had kept up this flow of talk while he took stock of his surroundings, and now, with another nudge of his companion's elbow, he took a chair between the door and the table, planted himself firmly in it, put his hands on top of his stout stick, and propped his chin on his hands. He looked at Mrs. Engledew once more, and then let his eyes make another inspection of her guests.

"What have I come for, ma'am?" he repeated. "To hear those revelations you spoke of when you called on me this afternoon? Just so. Well, ma'am, the only question now is—who's going to make 'em? For," he added, sitting up again after his further inspection, and bestowing a general smile all round, "revelations, ma'am, is what I chiefly hanker after, and I shall be glad—delighted!—to hear any specimens from—anybody as chooses to make 'em!"

Mrs. Engledew looked at Burchill as she resumed her seat.

"I think Mr. Burchill is the most likely person to tell you what there is to tell," she said. "His friend——"

"Ah!—the gentleman at the other end of the table, no doubt," observed Davidge. "How do you do, sir? And what might that gentleman's name be, now?"

Burchill, who had been watching the detective carefully, threw away his cigarette and showed an inclination to speak.

"Look here, Davidge!" he said. "You know very well why you're here—you're here to hear the real truth about the Herapath murder! Mrs. Engledew told you that this afternoon, when she called on you at Scotland Yard. Now the only two people who know the real truth are myself and my friend there—Mr. Dimambro."

Selwood and Cox-Raythwaite, who until then had remained in ignorance of the little foreigner's identity, started and looked at him with interest. So this was the missing witness! But Davidge remained cool and unimpressed.

"Ah, just so!" he said. "Foreign gentleman, no doubt. And you and Mr. Dimambro are the only persons who know the real truth about that little affair, eh, Mr. Burchill. Very good, so as——"

"As Mr. Dimambro doesn't speak English very well——" began Burchill.

"I speak it—you understand—enough to say a good many words—but not so good as him," observed Mr. Dimambro, waving a fat hand. "He say it for me—for both of us, eh?"

"To be sure, sir, to be sure," said Davidge. "Mr. Burchill is gifted that way, of course. Well, Mr. Burchill, and what might this story be, now? Deeply interesting, I'll be bound."

Burchill pulled a chair to the table, opposite Selwood and the Professor. He put the tips of his fingers together and assumed an explanatory manner.

"I shall have to begin at the beginning," he said. "You'll all please to follow me closely. Now, to commence—Mrs. Engledew permits me to speak for her as well as for Mr. Dimambro. The fact is, I can put the circumstances of the whole affair into a consecutive manner. And I will preface what I have to say by making a statement respecting a fact in the life of the late Mr. Herapath which will, I believe, be substantiated by Mr. Selwood, my successor as secretary to the deceased gentleman. Mr. Herapath, in addition to being an authority on the building of up-to-date flats, was also more or less of an expert in precious stones. He not only bought and sold in these things, but he gave advice to his friends in matters relating to them. Mr. Selwood has, I am sure, had experience of that fact?"

"To a certain extent—yes," agreed Selwood. "But I had not been long enough in Mr. Herapath's employ to know how much he went in for that sort of thing."

"That is immaterial," continued Burchill. "We establish the fact that he did. Now we come to the first chapter of our story. This lady, Mrs. Engledew, a tenant of this flat since the Herapath Estate was built, is an old acquaintance—I am permitted to say, friend—of the late Jacob Herapath. She occasionally consulted him on matters of business. On November 12th last she consulted him on another affair—though it had, of course, a business complexion. Mrs. Engledew, by the death of a relative, had just come into possession of some old family jewels—chiefly diamonds. These diamonds, which, Mrs. Engledew tells me, had been valued by Spinks at about seven thousand pounds, were in very old, considerably worn settings. Mrs. Engledew wished to have them reset. Knowing that Jacob Herapath had great taste and knowledge in that direction, she saw him at his office on the noon of November 12th, showed him the diamonds, and asked his advice. Jacob Herapath—I am giving you Mrs. Engledew's account—told her to leave the diamonds with him, as he was going to see, that very day, an expert in that line, to whom he would show the stones with the idea of his giving him his opinion on what ought to be done with them. Mrs. Engledew handed him the diamonds in a small case, which he put in his pocket. I hope," added Burchill, turning to Mrs. Engledew, "that I have given all this quite correctly?"

"Quite," assented Mrs. Engledew. "It is perfectly correct."

"Then," continued Burchill, "we pass on to Mr. Dimambro. Mr. Luigi Dimambro is a dealer in precious stones, who resides in Genoa, but travels widely about Europe in pursuance of his business. Mr. Dimambro had had several dealings with Jacob Herapath during past years, but previous to November 12th last they had not met for something like twelve months. On their last previous meeting Jacob Herapath told Mr. Dimambro that he was collecting pearls of a certain sort and size—specimens of which he showed him—with a view to presenting his niece, Miss Wynne, with a necklace which was to be formed of them. He gave Dimambro a commission to collect such pearls for him. On November 11th last Dimambro arrived in London from the Continent, and wrote to Mr. Herapath to tell him of his arrival, and to notify him that he had brought with him some pearls of the sort he wanted. Mr. Herapath thereupon made an appointment with Dimambro at the House of Commons on the evening of November 12th at half-past ten o'clock. Dimambro kept that appointment, showed Mr. Herapath the pearls which he had brought, sold them to him, and received from him, in payment for them, a cheque for three thousand guineas. This transaction being conducted, Mr. Herapath drew from his pocket (the same pocket in which he had already placed the pearls, which I understand, were wrapped up in a small bag or case of wash-leather) the diamonds which Mrs. Engledew had entrusted to him, showed them to Dimambro, and asked his opinion as to how they could best be reset. It is not material to this explanation to repeat what Dimambro said on that matter—suffice it to say that Dimambro gave an expert opinion, that Mr. Herapath once more pocketed the diamonds, and soon afterwards left the House of Commons for his estate offices with both lots of valuable stones in his possession—some ten thousand pounds' worth in all. As for Dimambro, he went home to the hotel at which he was stopping—a little place called the Ravenna, in Soho, an Italian house—next morning, first thing, he cashed his cheque, and before noon he left for the Continent. He had not heard of the murder of Jacob Herapath when he left London, and he did not hear of it until next day. I think I have given Mr. Dimambro's account accurately—his account so far," concluded Burchill, turning to the Italian. "If not, he will correct me."

"Quite right, quite right!" said Dimambro, who had listened eagerly. "I do not hear of the murder, eh, until I am in Berlin—it is, yes, next day—day after I leave London—that I hear of it, you understand? I then see it in the newspaper—English news, eh?"

"Why did you not come back at once?" asked Cox-Raythwaite.

Dimambro spread out his hands.

"Oh, I have my business—very particular," he said. "Besides, it has nothing to do with me, eh? I don't see no—no connection between me and that—no! But in time, I do come back, and then—he tell you," he broke off, pointing to Burchill. "He tell you better, see?"

"I am taking everything in order," said Burchill. "And for the present I have done with Mr. Dimambro. Now I come to myself. I shall have to go into details about myself which I should not give if it were not for these exceptional circumstances. Mr. Davidge, I am sure, will understand me. Well, about myself—you will all remember that at both the coroner's inquest and at the proceedings before the magistrate at which Barthorpe Herapath was present and I—for reasons well known!—was not, there was mention made of a letter which I had written to Jacob Herapath and was subsequently found in Barthorpe's possession, on his arrest. That letter was taken to be a blackmailing letter—I don't know whether any of you will believe me, and I don't care whether you do or not, but I declare that it was not meant to be a letter of that sort, though its wording might set up that opinion. However, Jacob Herapath resented that letter, and on its receipt he wrote to me showing that it had greatly displeased him. Now, I did not want to displease Jacob Herapath, and on receipt of his letter, I determined to see him personally at once. Being, of course, thoroughly familiar with his habits, I knew that he generally left the House of Commons about a quarter past eleven, every night when the House was sitting. I accordingly walked down to Palace Yard, intending to accost him. I arrived at the entrance to the Hall soon after eleven. A few minutes later Mountain, the coachman, drove up with the coupé brougham. I remained within the shadow of the porch—there were other people about—several Members, and men who were with them. At a quarter past eleven Jacob Herapath came down the Hall, accompanied by Dimambro. I knew Dimambro, though I had not seen him for some time—I used to see him, very occasionally, during my secretaryship to Mr. Herapath. When I saw these two in conversation, I drew back, and neither of them saw me. I did not want to accost Mr. Herapath in the presence of a second party. I watched him part from Dimambro, and I heard him tell Mountain to drive to the estate office. When both he and Dimambro had gone, I walked out into Parliament Square, and after thinking things over, I hailed a passing taxi-cab, and told the driver to go to Kensington High Street, and to pull up by the Metropolitan Station."

Burchill here paused—to give Davidge a peculiarly knowing look.

"Now I want you all—and particularly Mr. Davidge—to follow closely what I'm going to tell you," he continued. "I got out of the cab at the station in the High Street, dismissed it, walked a little way along the street, and then crossed over and made for the Herapath Flats—for the estate office entrance. I think you are all very well acquainted with that entrance. You know that it lies in a covered carriage way which leads from the side-street into the big quadrangle round which the flats are built. As I went up the side-street, on the opposite side, mind, to the entrance, I saw a man come out of the covered carriage way. That man I knew!"

Burchill made a dramatic pause, looking impressively around him amidst a dead silence.

"Knew!" he repeated, shaking his finger at the expectant faces. "Knew well! But—I am not going to tell you his name at this moment. For the present we will call him Mr. X."

Table of Contents

CHAPTER XXXIV

davidge's trump card

Burchill paused for a moment, to give full effect to this dramatic announcement, which, to tell truth, certainly impressed every member of his audience but one. That one skilfully concealed his real feelings under a show of feigned interest.

"You never say!" exclaimed Davidge, dropping into a favourite colloquialism of his native county. "Dear me, today! A man that you knew, Mr. Burchill, and that for the present you'll call Mr. X. You knew him well, then?"

"Better than I know you," replied Burchill. He was beginning to be suspicious of Davidge's tone, and his resentment of it showed in his answer. "Well enough to know him and not to mistake him, anyhow! And mind you, there was nothing surprising in his being there at that time of night—that's a point that you should bear in mind, Davidge—it's in your line, that. I knew so much of Jacob Herapath's methods and doings that it was quite a reasonable thing for this man to be coming out of the estate offices just before midnight."

"Exactly, sir—I follow you," said Davidge. "Ah!—and what might this Mr. X. do then, Mr. Burchill?"

Burchill, who had addressed his remarks chiefly to the listeners on the other side of the table, and notably to Cox-Raythwaite, turned away from the detective and went on.

"This man—Mr. X," he said, "came quickly out of the door, turned down the side-street a little, then turned back, passed the carriage-entrance, and went away up the street in the opposite direction. He turned on his own tracks so quickly that I was certain he had seen somebody coming whom he did not wish to meet. He——"

"Excuse me a moment," broke in Cox-Raythwaite. "How was it X. didn't see you?"

"Because I was on the opposite side of the street, in deep shadow," replied Burchill. "Besides that, the instant I caught sight of him I quietly slipped back into a doorway. I remained there while he turned and hurried up the street, for I was sure he had seen somebody coming, and I wanted to find out who it was. And in another minute Barthorpe Herapath came along, walking quickly. Then I understood—X. had seen him in the distance, and didn't want to meet him."

"Just so, just so," murmured Davidge. "To be sure."

"Barthorpe Herapath turned into the carriageway and went into the office," continued Burchill. "Now, as I've already said, I knew Jacob Herapath's methods; I hadn't served him for nothing. He was the sort of man who makes no distinction between day and night—it was quite a common thing for him to fix up business appointments with people at midnight. I've been present at such appointments many a time. So, I dare say, has Mr. Selwood; any one who acted as secretary to Jacob Herapath knows well that he'd think nothing of transacting business at three o'clock in the morning. So I knew, of course, that Barthorpe had gone there to keep some such appointment. I also knew that it would probably last some time. Now I wanted to see Jacob Herapath alone. And as there didn't seem to be any chance of it just then, I went home to my flat in Maida Vale."

"Walked in?" asked Davidge.

"If you're particular as to the means, I took a taxi-cab at the Gardens end of the High Street," replied Burchill, half-contemptuously. He turned his attention to Selwood and the Professor again. "Now, I'm going to tell you the plain truth about what happened afterwards," he continued. "This part of the story is for the particular benefit of you two gentlemen, though it has its proper connection with all the rest of the narrative. I sat up rather late when I got home that night, and I lay in bed next day until afternoon—in fact, I'd only just risen when Barthorpe Herapath called on me at three o'clock. Now, as I don't have papers delivered, but go out to buy what I want, it's the fact that I never heard of Jacob Herapath's murder until Barthorpe told me of it, then! That's the truth. And I'll at once anticipate the question that you'll naturally want to ask. Why didn't I at once tell Barthorpe of what I'd seen the night before?—of the presence of the man whom we're calling Mr. X.?"

"Just so!" murmured Davidge. "Ah, yes, why not?"

"I'll tell you," continued Burchill. "Because Barthorpe immediately sprang upon me the matter of the will. And I just as immediately recognized—I think I may count myself as a quick thinker—that the really important matter just then was not the murder of Jacob Herapath, but the ultimate disposal of Jacob Herapath's immense wealth."

"Clever!" sighed Davidge. "Uncommonly clever!"

"Now, Professor Cox-Raythwaite, and you, Mr. Selwood," Burchill went on, adding new earnestness to his tone. "I want you to fully understand that I'm giving you the exact truth. I firmly believed at that moment, and I continued to believe until the eventful conference at Mr. Halfpenny's office, that the gentleman whom I had known as Mr. Tertius was in reality Arthur John Wynne, forger and ex-convict. I say I firmly believed it, and I'll tell you why. During my secretaryship to Jacob Herapath, he one day asked me to clear out a box full of old papers and documents. In doing so I came across an old North-country newspaper which contained a full account of the trial at Lancaster Assizes of Arthur John Wynne on various charges of forgery. Jacob Herapath's name, of course, cropped up in it, as a relative. The similarity of the names of Jacob Herapath's ward, Miss Wynne, and that of the forger, roused my suspicions, and I not only put two and two together, but I made some inquiries privately, and I formed the definite conclusion that Tertius and Wynne were identical, and that the semi-mystery of Tertius's residence in Jacob Herapath's house was then fully accounted for. So when Barthorpe told me what he did, and explained his anxiety about the will, I saw my way to upsetting that will, for his benefit and for my own. If I swore that I'd never signed that will, and could prove that Tertius was Wynne, the forger, why then, of course, the will would be upset, for it seemed to me that any jury would believe that Tertius, or Wynne, had forged the will for his daughter's benefit. And so Barthorpe and I fixed that up. Reprehensible, no doubt, gentlemen, but we all have to live, and besides, Barthorpe promised me that he'd treat Miss Wynne most handsomely. Well, that procedure was settled—with the result that we're all aware of. And now I'd like to ask Mr. Davidge there a question—as I'm about to tell him who the real murderer of Jacob Herapath was, perhaps he'll answer it. I take it, Davidge, that the only evidence you had against me in regard to the murder was the document which you found at my flat, by which Barthorpe Herapath promised to pay me ten per cent. on the value of the Herapath estate? That and the fact that Barthorpe and I were in league about the will? Come now—as all's being cleared up, isn't that so?"

Davidge rubbed his chin with affected indifference.

"Oh, well, you can put it down at something like that, if you like, Mr. Burchill," he answered. "You're a very clever young fellow, and I dare say you're as well aware of what the law about accessories is as I am. 'Tisn't necessary for a party to a murder to be actually present at the execution of the crime, sir—no! And there's such a thing as being accessory after the crime—of course. Leave it at that, Mr. Burchill, leave it at that!"

Cox-Raythwaite, who had been eyeing Burchill with ill-concealed disgust, spoke sharply.

"And—the rest?" he asked.

"I'm going along in order," answered Burchill coolly. "Well, I come to the time when Davidge there arrested Barthorpe and myself at Halfpenny and Farthing's, and when I escaped. There's no need to tell you what I did with myself," he went on, with an obvious sneer in the detective's direction. "But I can tell you that I didn't particularly restrict my movements. And eventually—a few days ago—I come into touch with Dimambro, who had returned to England. As I said before, we had met during the time I was secretary to Jacob Herapath. Dimambro, when I met him—accidentally—was on his way to the police, to tell them what he knew. I stopped him—he told his story to me instead. I told him mine. And the result of our deliberations was that we got an interview—at least I did—with Mrs. Engledew here, with respect to the diamonds which she had entrusted to Jacob Herapath. And——"

"I should like to ask you a question, Mrs. Engledew," said Cox-Raythwaite, interrupting Burchill without ceremony. "Why did you not inform the police about your diamonds as soon as you heard of the murder?"

Mrs. Engledew betrayed slight signs of confusion, and Davidge gave the questioner a look.

"I think if I were you, I shouldn't go into that matter just now, Professor," he said apologetically. "Ladies, you know, have their reasons for these little—what shall we call 'em?—peculiarities. No, I wouldn't press that point, sir. We're having a nice, straight story—quite like a printed one!—from Mr. Burchill there, and I think we'd better let him come to what we may term the last chapter in his own way—what?"

"I'm at the last chapter," said Burchill. "And it's a short one. I saw Mrs. Engledew and made certain arrangements with her. And just after they were made—yesterday in fact—Dimambro and I got a new piece of evidence. When Dimambro was collecting those pearls for

Jacob Herapath he bought some from a well-known dealer in Amsterdam, a specialist in pearls. Yesterday, Dimambro got a letter from this man telling him that a small parcel of those very pearls had been sent to him from London, for sale. He gave Dimambro the name and address of the sender, who, of course, was the Mr. X. of whom I have spoken. So then Dimambro and I resolved to act, through Mrs. Engledew——"

"For a slight consideration, I think," suggested Davidge dryly. "A matter of a little cheque, I believe, Mr. Burchill."

"We've quite as much right to be paid for our detective services, amateur though they are, as you have for yours, Davidge," retorted Burchill. "However, I've come to an end, and it only remains for me to tell you who Mr. X. really is. He hasn't the slightest notion that he's suspected, and if you and your men, Davidge, go round to his house, which isn't half a mile away, you'll probably find him eating his Sunday evening supper in peace and quietness. The man is——"

Davidge suddenly rose from his chair, nudging Triffitt as he moved. He laughed—and the laugh made Burchill start to his feet.

"You needn't trouble yourself, Mr. Burchill!" said Davidge. "Much obliged to you for your talk, there's nothing like letting some folks wag their tongues till they're tired. I know who murdered Jacob Herapath as well as you do, and who your Mr. X. is. Jacob Herapath, gentlemen," he added, turning to his astonished listeners, "was shot dead and robbed by his office manager, James Frankton, and if James Frankton's eating his Sunday supper in peace and quietness, it's in one of our cells, for I arrested him at seven o'clock this very evening—and with no help from you, Mr. Burchill! I'm not quite such a fool as I may look, my lad, and if I made one mistake when I let you slip I didn't make another when I got on the track of the real man. And now, ma'am," he concluded, with an old-fashioned bow to Mrs. Engledew, "there's no more to be said—by me, at all events, and I've the honour to wish you a good night. Mr. Triffitt—we'll depart."

Outside, Davidge took the reporter's arm in a firm grip, and chuckled as he led him towards the elevator.

"That's surprise one!" he whispered. "Wait till we get downstairs and into the street, and you'll have another, and it'll be of a bit livelier nature!"

Table of Contents

CHAPTER XXXV

the second warrant

Davidge preserved a strict silence as he and Triffitt went down in the elevator, but when they had reached the ground floor he took the reporter's arm again, and as they crossed the entrance hall gave it a significant squeeze.

"You'll see two or three rather heavy swells, some of 'em in evening dress, hanging about the door," he murmured. "Look like residents, coming in or going out, puffing their cigars and their cigarettes, eh? They're my men—all of 'em! Take no notice—there'll be your friend Carver outside—I gave him a hint. Join him, and hang about—you'll have something to do a bit of newspaper copy about presently."

Triffitt, greatly mystified, joined Carver at the edge of the pavement outside the wide entrance door. Glancing around him he saw several men lounging about—two, of eminently military appearance, with evening dress under their overcoats, stood chatting on the lower steps; two or three others, all very prosperous looking, were talking close by. There was nothing in their outward show to arouse suspicion—at any other time, and under any other circumstances Triffitt would certainly have taken them for residents of the Herapath Flats. Carver, however, winked at him.

"Detectives," he said. "They've gathered here while you were upstairs. What's up now, Triffitt? Heard anything?"

"Piles!" answered Triffitt. "Heaps! But I don't know what this is all about. Some new departure. Hullo!—here's the secretary and the Professor."

Cox-Raythwaite and Selwood just then appeared at the entrance door and began to descend the steps. Davidge, who had stopped on the steps to speak to a man, hailed and drew them aside.

"What has gone on up there?" asked Carver. "Anything really——"

Triffitt suddenly grasped his companion's shoulder, twisting him round towards the door. His lips emitted a warning to silence; his eyes signalled Carver to look.

Burchill came out of the doors, closely followed by Dimambro. Jauntily swinging his walking-cane he began to descend, affecting utter unconsciousness of the presence of Cox-Raythwaite, Selwood, and Davidge. He passed close by the men in evening dress, brushing the sleeve of one. And the man thus brushed turned quickly, and his companion turned too—and then something happened that made the two reporters exclaim joyfully and run up the steps.

"Gad!—that was quick—quick!" exclaimed Triffitt, with the delight of a schoolboy. "Never saw the bracelets put on more neatly. Bully for you, Davidge, old man!—got him this time, anyhow!"

Burchill, taken aback by the sudden onslaught of Davidge's satellites, drew himself up indignantly and looked down at his bands, around the wrists of which his captors had snapped a pair of handcuffs. He lifted a face white with rage and passion and glanced at Cox-Raythwaite and Selwood.

"Liars!" he hissed between his teeth. "You gave me safe conduct! It was understood that I was to come and go without interference, you hounds!"

"Not with me, nor I should think with anybody, my lad," exclaimed Davidge, bustling forward. "Not likely! You forget that you're under arrest for the old charge yet, and though you'll get off for that, you won't go scot-free, my friend! I've got a second warrant for you, and the charge'll be read to you when you get to the station. You'll clear yourself of the charge of murder, but not of t'other charge, I'm thinking!"

"Second warrant! Another charge!" growled Burchill. "What charge?"

"I should think you know as well as I do," replied Davidge quietly. "You're a bigger fool than I take you for if you don't. Conspiracy, of course! It's a good thing to have two strings to one's bow, Mr. Frank Burchill, in dealing with birds like you. This is my second string. Take him off," he added, motioning to his men, "and get him searched, and put everything carefully aside for me—especially a cheque for ten thousand pounds which you'll find in one of his pockets."

When the detectives had hurried Burchill into a taxi-cab which suddenly sprang into useful proximity to the excited group, Davidge spat on the ground and made a face. He motioned Cox-Raythwaite, Selwood, and the two reporters to go down the street; he himself turned to Dimambro. What he said to that highly-excited gentleman they did not hear, but the Italian presently walked off looking very crestfallen, while Davidge, joining them, looked highly pleased with himself.

"Of course, you'll stop payment of that cheque at the bank first thing tomorrow, gentlemen," he said. "Though that'll only be for form's sake, because I shall take charge of it when I go round to the police-station presently—they'll have got Burchill searched when I get there. Of course, I wasn't going to say anything up there, but Mrs. Engledew has been in with us at this, and she took Burchill and Dimambro in as beautifully as ever I saw it done in my life! Clever woman, that! We knew about her diamonds, gentlemen, within a few hours of the discovery of the murder, and of course, I thought Barthorpe had got them; I did, mistaken though I was! I didn't want anybody to know about those diamonds, though, and I kept it all dark until these fellows came on the scene. And, anyway, we didn't get the real culprit through the diamonds, either!"

"That's what we want to know," said Selwood. "Have you got the real culprit? Are you certain? And how on earth did you get him—a man that none of us ever suspected!"

"Just so!" answered Davidge with a grim laugh. "As nice and quiet-mannered a man as ever I entered as a candidate for the gallows! It's very often the case, gentlemen. Oh, yes—it's true enough! He's confessed—crumpled up like a bit of tissue paper when we took him—confessed everything to me just before I came along here. Of course we didn't get him through anything we've heard tonight; quite different line altogether, and a simple one."

"We should like to know about it," said Cox-Raythwaite. "Can't you give us a mere outline?"

"I was going to," answered Davidge. "No secret about it. I may as well tell you that after hearing what Barthorpe Herapath insisted on saying before the magistrate, I began to feel that he was very likely telling the truth, and that somebody'd murdered and robbed his uncle just before he got to the offices. But, of course, there was nothing to connect the murder and robbery with any person that I knew of. Well, now then, this is how we got on the track. Only two or three days ago a little, quiet man, who turned out to be a bit of a property-owner down at Fulham, came to me and said that ever since Mr. Jacob Herapath's murder he'd been what he called studying over it, and he thought he ought to tell me something. He said he was a very slow thinker, and it had taken him a long time to think all this out. Then he told me his tale. He said that for some time Jacob Herapath had been waiting to buy a certain bit of land which he had to sell. On November 12th last he called to see Jacob at these offices, and they agreed on the matter, price to be £5,000. Jacob told him to come in at ten o'clock next morning, and in accordance with his usual way of doing business, he'd hand him the money in cash—notes, of course. Well, the chap d next morning, only to hear of what had happened, and so his business had fallen through. d it wasn't until some time later—he's a bit of a slow-witted fellow, dullish of brain, you understand," continued Davidge indulgently, "that he remembered a certain conversation, or rather a remark which Jacob Herapath made during that deal. This man, James Frankton, the manager, was present when the deal was being effected, and when they'd concluded terms, Jacob said, turning to Frankton. 'I'll get the money in notes from the bank this afternoon, Frankton, and if I don't give it to you in the meantime, you'll find the notes in the top left-hand drawer of my desk tomorrow morning.' Well, that was what the man told me; said he'd been bothering his brains in wondering if Jacob did draw that money, and so on—Frankton, of course, had told him that he knew nothing about it, and that as Jacob was dead, no more could be done in the matter. Now on that, I at once began some inquiries. I found out a thing or two—never mind what—one was to trace a hundred pound note which Frankton had cashed recently. I found, only yesterday morning, that that note was one of fifty similar notes paid to Jacob Herapath by his bankers in exchange for his own cheque on the afternoon of November 12th. And, on that, I had Frankton watched all yesterday, last night, and today, and as I said, I arrested him tonight—and, in all my experience I never saw a man more surprised, and never knew one who so lost his nerve."

"And his confession?" asked Selwood.

"Oh! ordinary," answered Davidge. "Jacob had made an appointment with him for half-past eleven or so. Got there a bit late, found his master sitting at his desk with a wad of bank notes on the blotting-pad, a paper of pearls on one side of him, a lot of diamond ornaments at the other—big temptation to a chap, who, as it turns out, was hard up, and had got into the hands of money-lenders. And, oh, just the ordinary thing in such cases, happened to have on him a revolver that he'd bought abroad, yielded to temptation, shot his man, took money and valuables, went home, and turned up at the office next day to lift his hands in horror at the dreadful news. You see what truth is, gentlemen, when you get at it—just a common, vulgar murder, for the sake of robbery. And he'll swing!"

"'Just a common, vulgar murder, and he'll swing!'" softly repeated Cox-Raythwaite, as he and Selwood walked up the steps of the house in Portman Square half an hour later. "Well, that's solved, anyway. As for the other two——"

"I suppose there's no doubt of their guilt with respect to their conspiring to upset the will?" said Selwood. "And that's a serious offence, isn't it?"

"In this eminently commercial country, very," answered Cox-Raythwaite, sententiously. "Barthorpe and Burchill will inevitably retire to the shelter of a convict establishment for awhile. Um! Well, my boy, good night!"

"Not coming in?" asked Selwood, as he put a key in the latch.

The Professor gave his companion's shoulder a pressure of his big hand.

"I think," he said, turning down the steps with a shy laugh, "I think Peggie will prefer to receive you—alone."

the end

called next morning, only to hear of what had happened, and so his business had fallen through. And it wasn't until some time later—he's a bit of a slow-witted fellow, dullish of brain, you understand," continued Davidge indulgently, "that he remembered a certain conversation, or rather a remark which Jacob Herapath made during that deal. This man, James Frankton, the manager, was present when the deal was being effected, and when they'd concluded terms, Jacob said, turning to Frankton. 'I'll get the money in notes from the bank this afternoon, Frankton, and if I don't give it to you in the meantime, you'll find the notes in the top left-hand drawer of my desk tomorrow morning.' Well, that was what the man told me; said he'd been bothering his brains in wondering if Jacob did draw that money, and so on—Frankton, of course, had told him that he knew nothing about it, and that as Jacob was dead, no more could be done in the matter. Now on that, I at once began some inquiries. I found out a thing or two—never mind what—one was to trace a hundred pound note which Frankton had cashed recently. I found, only yesterday morning, that that note was one of fifty similar notes paid to Jacob Herapath by his bankers in exchange for his own cheque on the afternoon of November 12th. And, on that, I had Frankton watched all yesterday, last night, and today, and as I said, I arrested him tonight—and, in all my experience I never saw a man more surprised, and never knew one who so lost his nerve."

"And his confession?" asked Selwood.

"Oh! ordinary," answered Davidge. "Jacob had made an appointment with him for half-past eleven or so. Got there a bit late, found his master sitting at his desk with a wad of bank notes on the blotting-pad, a paper of pearls on one side of him, a lot of diamond ornaments at the other—big temptation to a chap, who, as it turns out, was hard up, and had got into the hands of money-lenders. And, oh, just the ordinary thing in such cases, happened to have on him a revolver that he'd bought abroad, yielded to temptation, shot his man, took money and valuables, went home, and turned up at the office next day to lift his hands in horror at the dreadful news. You see what truth is, gentlemen, when you get at it—just a common, vulgar murder, for the sake of robbery. And he'll swing!"

"'Just a common, vulgar murder, and he'll swing!'" softly repeated Cox-Raythwaite, as he and Selwood walked up the steps of the house in Portman Square half an hour later. "Well, that's solved, anyway. As for the other two——"

"I suppose there's no doubt of their guilt with respect to their conspiring to upset the will?" said Selwood. "And that's a serious offence, isn't it?"

"In this eminently commercial country, very," answered Cox-Raythwaite, sententiously. "Barthorpe and Burchill will inevitably retire to the shelter of a convict establishment for awhile. Um! Well, my boy, good night!"

"Not coming in?" asked Selwood, as he put a key in the latch.

The Professor gave his companion's shoulder a pressure of his big hand.

"I think," he said, turning down the steps with a shy laugh, "I think Peggie will prefer to receive you—alone."

the end